FOR SHOSHANNA KOSTANT, JEFFREY GREELEY,
MADELEINE KOSTANT-GREELEY,
SYLVIE KOSTANT-GREELEY

Skerries and 1460 Days

MICHAEL GREELEY

By the author of Kodiak

authorHOUSE®

AuthorHouse™
1663 Liberty Drive
Bloomington, IN 47403
www.authorhouse.com
Phone: 833-262-8899

Published by AuthorHouse 10/10/2024

ISBN: 979-8-8230-3355-8 (sc)
ISBN: 979-8-8230-3354-1 (e)

Library of Congress Control Number: 2024919032

Print information available on the last page.

Any people depicted in stock imagery provided by Getty Images are models, and such images are being used for illustrative purposes only.
Certain stock imagery © Getty Images.

This book is printed on acid-free paper.

Because of the dynamic nature of the Internet, any web addresses or links contained in this book may have changed since publication and may no longer be valid. The views expressed in this work are solely those of the author and do not necessarily reflect the views of the publisher, and the publisher hereby disclaims any responsibility for them.

Contents

1460 Days

Skerries

Chapter 1

H.P. is in trouble. He is on his way to meet a delectable married woman on Stephen's Green but he is late and what makes it worse is that he is being escorted by the voluble Pat O'Flaherty who insists on telling him of his mis-adventures the previous night on Lesson Street. H.P. isn't sure but it is reasonable that Pat knows Liz Kennedy or her husband or both. H.P. must shake Pat and quickly. He proposes a pint at the Bailey and without waiting for Pat's assent – sure to come as it is – escorts him into the pub.

They sit at the bar and order Guiness.

Now H.P., says Pat, while I was trying to sort out the tangle last night who do you think came walking along as bold as brass?

H.P. checks his watch: He is already twenty minutes late.

Pat, I don't have a clue.

Well, I'll tell your honor: It was Jimmy Costello himself. Yes, I'm telling the truth. He looked like he had just been sprung from the lockup. You know: His face was all dark; he'd lost weight and he wouldn't look me in the eye.

H.P. fiddles with his pint. He checks his watch again.

Well, says Pat, Jimmy was squiring this fantastic blonde. She looked to be six-foot tall and thin as a ruler. I was dying to meet her but Jimmy kept on walking with her leaning on his arm. He made out that he hadn't seen me. Just then this bloke came out of a pub on the corner. He looked to be twenty stones and as wide as one of those medieval broad axes.

So get on with it. I'm late for an important conference.

Em, anyone I know?

H.P. shrugs. He rotates the pint letting his fingers slide along the cool glass.

Well, the blonde saw the bloke before he saw her. She let out a shriek right there on Lesson Street. She lunged at the broad-axe with her nails flashing.

Ah, one minute Pat I'm dying to hear the rest but I'm called out.

H.P. makes for the loo but veers off to an exit around the corner. Unfortunately, he has to leave a half pint on the bar. A price that had to be paid.

It is one of those glorious but oh so rare Dublin days when the sun slants down out of a cloudless September sky. Grafton Street is crowded with shoppers causing H.P. to weave through the mothers pushing prams and minding their little heathens. He cuts too close to one mother and her quartet of children brushing against the mother and causing a shopping bag to fall to the ground spilling toasties over the sidewalk. The mother hurls every invective at the sprinting H.P. whose fear of missing Liz overrides his fear of being publicly branded.

He turns the corner escaping into the park slowing as he nears that fine blade of Henry Moore commemorating Yeats.

Liz stands there her arms folded across her chest a shoe tapping the sidewalk like a blind beggar negotiating the way forward.

Where have you been? she says. I've been waiting nearly an hour.

Now Liz, there, there. You know it hasn't been an hour. Now look let's just go over to our bench. I see that it's empty.

H.P. takes Liz's arm by the elbow and steers her toward a secluded bench just by the memorial.

H.P. is flustered by the consternation evident on Liz's face. He makes little pushing motions against the air with his hands as if to soothe her. Now, now, he says, let's just sit here.

Liz dearest let's not waste any more time. You know I would have been here on the dot if it had been humanly possible.

H.P.'s hand moves inside Liz's coat where it rests on the sweet, uphill run of her stomach. The kiss which follows this gambit turns, in a matter of seconds, from the lightest brush of the lips into the most acceptable form of tongue-lashing.

Without warning and in the middle of that delicious exercise Liz pushes H.P. violently away. This causes him to lose his balance and fall with a thud on the brickwork.

H.P. understands the advantage he has just been given. He closes his eyes as if he has been dealt a mortal blow and – the move that puts him over the top – jerks his leg spasmodically. This brings Liz down to her knees along with a fresh clap of thunder from the storm which had been interrupted on the bench.

H.P. pleads with Liz to accompany him to his flat while Liz, as tempted as a temptress can be, decides that she can not since she is late to tea at her mother-in-law's. After a final kiss and frenzied grope, Liz breaks free and passes determinedly through the trees and out of the park.

Just then a round of applause breaks out from two stock-broker types who, unbeknownst to our frenzied pair, have been eating their lunch sitting at a bench partly obscured by the memorial. Right you are calls one of the pair, a fellow with bright red hair and, as far as H.P. is concerned, a jack-ass laugh.

H.P. moves away to a bench alongside a scruffy looking fellow with a monstrous red nose. A lush gaggle of teenage girls in their school uniforms gets his attention as they skip past on their way home from school

Oh my, thinks H.P., now don't they look fine. The school girls, aware of the attention paid to them by H.P., giggle as one of them, a pale-skinned one with black hair and a small, delicately rounded butt, turns it toward H.P. and then marches away - as she imagines - like a Hollywood star. H.P., never one to deny talent, applauds which brings howls of laughter from the gaggle.

He rises from the bench, stretches in the sunshine and then ambles back toward Trinity College and his office. There is still an appointment with a student at three and then it will be time for a pint at the Bailey.

If anything the crowds are now thicker on Grafton Street. There is a constantly changing kaleidoscope of faces which emerge from behind the stream of people walking toward him. From out of that brace of Irish faces emerges the face of Colleen McCormack with her bright red hair like frozen fire. The fellow squiring Colleen is her husband.

H.P. had heard that their immaculate union had produced five identical copies of the husband except for the bright, red hair.

Colleen looks sharply to the right signaling a desire to avoid contact with H.P.. She brushes her hair back and smiles at the big fellow.

3

Never mind, thinks H.P.. I'm not going to break in on that happy little scene. Their ships pass without a ripple.

Good luck to you Colleen. Five kids and that husband who should own shares in Guiness the way he guzzles the stout.

And then there's Liz, thinks H.P.. Her husband treats her like dirt or, more accurately, like bath water. It seems incredible that a woman who has seven kids and a moron for a husband could still like sex although "like" is clearly too weak to convey the craziness which pours out of her. No wonder she's calling me every chance she gets.

This reminds him of that last time at his flat in Churchtown.

Come in Liz. Good god, it's been far too long. Liz looks furtively around before she slips past H.P. and, without waiting for his lead, climbs the stairs meanwhile dropping her coat and scarf mid-way up and then her shoes just before the top step. By the time H.P. collects her coat and hat and shuts the door behind, Liz is down to her underwear which, as if in a fit, she pulls off in all her freckled glory. Now Liz, says H.P., more defensively than for politeness, wouldn't you like a cup of tea? Liz grabs hold of H.P. as if he is a fire-pole down which she is going to slide and H.P responds as any well-made fire-pole would.

Later, H.P. observes Liz from the safety of his bed as she re-dresses both her body and her demeanor exiting like a freak storm which had erupted on an otherwise cloudless day but leaving behind a battered countryside.

Ah me, what a lovely woman. Smooth, smooth as a baby's arse and just as wholesome. He wonders what she will do next. Will she make love with her husband? Could she? Of course she could and would no doubt as she herself had told him once in response to the question. Are you the be-all and end-all, is that what you think? she said. You're good honey but that's it.

Ah, you've mortally wounded me, said H.P., clutching at his throat.

Chapter 2

All of H.P.'s writing – as he is acutely aware - is in some fashion about Clara. He has tried many times to break free of her power but, syllable-by- syllable, Clara is there, as it were, in the interstices. At times, H.P. has despaired of ever writing a satisfactory story which doesn't, somehow, look backward toward her and his childhood in Skerries.

Clara's preoccupation, as far as H.P. is concerned, is with the fact that not only is he not married (and, hence, she believes, childless) but for the fact that he has no desire to marry. Is he, she wonders, queer? After all, she has never met nor even heard him talk about women friends despite several invitations to do so. There is the matter of that one story of his – she doesn't, it is true, like his stories but she feels duty–bound to read them – the story in which she thinks she caught, retrospectively, a reference to homosexuality in (...And so dangled desperately his line...). Her neighbor and good friend Molly Atkins, had shown this line to the priest who said it was undoubtedly a reference to maleness which when combined with the fact that the story is about boyhood friends nailed the coffin shut.

For Clara this is the worst possibility she can imagine. Better his death, she avers. H. P. represents for her a continuation, a prolongation into the unknowable future of her family; without him there is no future. Her brother Clancy had long ago abdicated his responsibilities by deserting his wife (apparently barren) after ten years of marriage. No, H. P. is the last chance for what she views as the only guaranteed immortality (she views Catholicism at best as a mere insurance policy). She wants grandchildren and great-grandchildren to visit her grave on the anniversary of her death to lovingly tend the site just as she has tended the graves of her own mother and father. Such veneration is for her the key to survival. It implies that no matter how poorly or well life is lived it can be redeemed in the minds of future generations.

But, there is H.P. himself, apparently happy in his singularity playing – or so she interprets it – at writing and never holding a sensible job for long. Clara has tried many approaches to get him to change. She has argued, pleaded and even bribed (she has, after all, her own house and a tidy nest egg in the All–Ireland fund left to her by her husband Michael), but nothing has succeeded. His answer – if one wants to call it an answer – is that he needs to be free to explore his muse.

They sit at the kitchen table in Skerries. They drink gin and tonic (her and Michael's favorite). The Irish Sea is just beyond the strand in back of the house.

Now look, says Clara, you've finished college. You haven't a permanent job unless you count the tutoring. Can't you ease your old Mam's worries? What's to become of you?

H.P. sips the gin and tonic. Amazing the way it seems to bear-hug his forehead. It's the ice.

Look Ma, I know you're anxious about me. But, I've got plans. I think I'm onto something that will carry the day.

Your stories, you mean?

That's it. I think they're good; there are others who think so too. Why shouldn't I give it a go. Just two nights ago I read some of my stories in Trinity at this big-time gathering. A fellow from the states introduced himself. He says I should consider zooming over to Harvard. He says he could get me a small stipend to do some reading.

What should I do? Give up just as I'm getting started? And here's another thing. It's not sure but I think I might have a job at Trinity. Nothing definite but I'm holding me breath. Would that satisfy you – your only son a Fellow at Trinity? A scholar. I'd be charged with liberating those young minds. Wouldn't that prove I'm on the right track? Now, wouldn't it?

Clara refills the glasses. Now, right down there, she says pointing to a spot about fifteen feet along the strand. Right about there was where you used to play. You spent hours there. I watched you from the window. Maybe you're still playing in the sand? My Lord, I wish you were more like your da. Now, he was a man to reckon with. He had a job and it was an honorable one. He bought this house which God only knows is our only security. It wasn't easy raising a child on my own. There were times – oh yes there were times – when I don't know how I did it.

Ay, says H.P., and here we are. But look Mam, you did fine. You've got a son who loves his Mam and who might become famous. Don't laugh, I said "might". Anyway, to my reckoning it's worth the gamble. Look, I'll make a deal. Give me five years. If I haven't gotten anywhere I'll give it up and become a bank clerk or a newspaper sod. And – I know, I know – I'll find some pretty lass, marry, and have those kids you are picturing in your head. What do you say; do we have a deal?

Clara lifts her glass. Well I hope you live up to your promise.

That calls for another g-and-t, says H.P.

It's such a grand day, says Clara. Look at the sea. I don't remember it ever being so flat. It lays like a tablecloth.

Now I know where I get me words. The sea a tablecloth? And close to dinner is it?

Now Mam I've always wondered. How is it that you and Da got together. You went to college but Da was a laborer from the start. What did you talk about?

Well it's true what you say. At first I had me doubts. My da was dead against it. He as much as told me that it would never work; that I'd rue the day. The only day I ever rued was when Michael died. Up until then it was glorious. Before you came along we used to do everything together. You probably don't know this but your Da was something of a naturalist. I see that skeptical look. Some of his books are still in the garage. The ones he used to study. If he had had the chance he would've gone to college. So don't think we weren't right for each other. My word, I don't know of any other pair that were as right for each other as we were.

There isn't much light left in the day. A man wearing a toque walks along the strand just above the tide. A Jack Russell runs circles around him.

Well, said Clara, that roast smells like it's done.

They eat dinner in silence.

Chapter 3

Clara follows Molly's suggestion that she investigate the perpetual care services at the Rectory. They do such a good job tending flowers for the grave on anniversaries, she says. They could take care of both you and Michael.

Clara belongs to a branch of the Dublin Theosophical society. Molly is a member and the two attend meetings at the Hibernian Hall in Skerries. Clara tries to get H.P. to go along citing the example of W.B. Yeats.

Mam, I don't go in for that. And as far as Yeats goes it was a youthful dalliance of his. He got over that soon enough.

Yes, but don't you believe in ghosts? Surely, people still exist after they die.

H.P. bows his head. Don't let the priest hear you talk like that. You'll be up for a bagful of demerits.

Why he told me he couldn't say anything against it, said Clara. That's as good as saying it's true.

I'll think on it, I will.

On the day of the Theosophical meeting H.P. takes the 33 bus from Dublin to Skerries. Molly Atkins is there with Clara and the pair are imbibing, they say, a little something to chase the damp away.

They walk down Rush Road into town. The Hibernian Hall is a grey, stone structure squat in shape like some crouched beast. Inside a group of six people sit in a circle around a spirit board, at least that's what H.P. assumes it is. Molly coolly greets the participants. There are two places set aside for Clara and Molly.

She must be a regular, thinks H.P. who sits in a chair on the outside of the circle.

Clara introduces H.P. to the group. H.P. is my son, she says. His father Michael died when he was just seven. Sure to God it would be grand if he could get something from his da.

The medium (Clara later identifies him as Sean) says that Clara has requested a special channel to her Michael. There is a general sign of assent to the request.

All right then, says Sean, let's start. And please everyone, I must have silence if we are to get across.

Except for H.P. and Sean the congregants are all women. Nearly all of them wear shawls, plain black or brown. H.P. thinks they look as if they are at a wake which, he realizes, is close to the truth. Clara sits with her knees together, her hands clasped in her lap.

It is an eerie scene, thinks H.P. He will have to find a way to get it into one of his stories. There is only the light from a single candle which reaches a little way into the sepulchral darkness. The remainder of the cavern is as black as a cave. There are shadowy lumps here and there backlit by what moonlight is coming in through the windows.

Sean asks again for silence. The cold in the Hall reinforces the silence adding weight to the shadows.

Michael, says Sean in a voice right from the tomb. Michael, Clara is here. She seeks you for her son. Michael, if you hear me speak through me. Sean sits tensely on his chair, his eyes closed. Suddenly Sean yells as if he has touched a hot poker. He mumbles unintelligibly. Then a few words emerge: The … granite … no…Laddie … stay …married …Clara …

And just as suddenly Sean snaps back, his eyes open. He blinks around. Did … did we get through, he says. The circle murmurs assent.

It is Michael, says Clara. He calls our son "Laddie". Only Michael knows that. Only Michael. Oh my god I've heard nothing for … twenty years.

Michael said that he hopes H.P. will get married. He seemed anxious about that, says Sean.

On the walk back home H.P. does his best to go along with Clara and Molly's enthusiasm. They are refreshed and eager for the next encounter.

H.P. thinks better of questioning the exchange of Pounds with Sean at the end of the meeting. It's no use, he thinks. And what of it? Mother of God it's harmless. But how in God's name did he know I was called Laddie? The devil take it.

9

Chapter 4

On a late, gray Dublin afternoon H.P. leaves his office in an appropriately melancholy mood; the skies threaten a downpour. He is on his way for a bit of liquid sunshine at the Stag's Head. His ruminations on this glum day take their usual grim path: Jaysus, I'm getting on and what do I have to show for it. A few measly stories, a list of satisfied lassies, a vanishingly small share of the world's assets, and now the damn rain is coming in buckets.

Pushed by the wind the rain slants in driving into H.P.'s face. His umbrella is ineffective against this onslaught. In short order his pants below the knee are soaked. As he turns the corner at the soccer pitch David steps out of the Maths building.

Ah, there you are. What a coincidence. Is your gauge hitting on empty then?

I don't know what you mean, says David. I'm just out for a rainy-day stroll. Are you saying you're on your way for a pint?

And you're joining me?

Just as they approach Trinity Gate, Gerard angles in from the right. Whoa, and look what I've found.

No one comments on the fact that the three meet nearly every day at the same time and place and with the same mission.

Unfortunately, Gerard is Dublin and David is Belfast, two substances which are volatile in contact.

All right, says H.P.. I'm dying but the two of you have to swear on a stack of Catholic and Protestant Bibles that you will not come to blows. We must behave like saints or whatever it is that the Protestants have.

What do they have anyway? Never mind, let's take ourselves off for some well-deserved black refreshment. Stag's Head anyone?

The Stag's Head on Dame Street is packed; in one snook sits a lady wearing a shawl. She is talking – more like declaiming – to a nattily dressed bloke by her side. These young kippers don't show proper respect and, she says, she doesn't know what in the hell the world is coming to. The nattily dressed one nods his head his attention alternating between the Guinness and a cigarette.

The ceiling at Stag's Head is stucco, there are ornate mirrors on the wall behind the bar and green tile on the floor. The room is filled with talk: Gem-a-sons please; two pints, if you please; lively now.

Now then, says H.P., let us give praise to the one who makes all of this possible.

And who would that be, says David.

Why the Provost himself. He's the very one who set us down in the middle of Trinity College with but one admonition: Go forth and multiply. Or is that the speech he gave to the Maths Department?

This little witticism draws only smirks from Gerard and David, possibly one of the few agreements ever achieved between them.

Now then says Gerard, how was that trip you took to London last week? My God what are the highlights?

See that fellow over there, the one with the shaggy mane, the one smoking up a blue streak? He's a dead ringer for a bloke on the train. Mind you I'm in a no-smoking compartment on the Liverpool to London line. The world is whizzing by pleasantly enough when the bloke across from me lights up! Now you know how I abhor violence. In my school days I went out of my way to avoid any nastiness. The one time I couldn't avoid it I was popped in the jaw so hard that I fell down on me back and never got up. Well, there was something about that bloke lighting up in a non-smoker. With my stomach churning I says to him: My good man, this is a non-smoker. And what do you think he does? That's right: Nothing. He continues to spew his vile smoke into our little world. I couldn't think what to do. What happened next still makes me quake in me boots. I reached across and pulled the cigarette out of his mouth. His lip must have caught on a bit of the paper because there was a little ripping noise. I stepped on the cigarette and awaited my fate. Believe me there was dead-on silence in that compartment. The whole lot of them sitting on the edge of their seats. H.P. takes a long pull from the pint. The Guiness is as smooth as a baby's cheek, he says – not that he has any particular experience with babies' cheeks.

Well, says David, what happened. There aren't any visible bruises and neither of your two eyes is any blacker than usual.

Well, we sat there in that silence for what seemed an age and then he got up and left never to be seen again. Unless that's him at that table over there.

Gerard stubs out his cigarette in the ashtray.

And what else, says David. Is that the whole of the expedition?

David is a mathematician from Belfast who studied Cosmology at Oxford with one of the world's best cosmologists. H.P. thinks it ironic that a cosmologist – as grand as that sounds - could be shriveled up like an old prune. Gerard is a Dublin native who studied semiotics at T.C.D..

I met a charming lady at the hotel after the checking in rigmarole, says H.P.. Now, please, don't bother yourself with who "she" is because I'm not at liberty to say. Let's just say that meeting her was not an accident.

No doubt, says Gerard, you're not at liberty because there's a mate somewhere in the picture.

Well, mighty prescient of you. Let's just say that she is a marvelous figure of a woman old enough to have been around the block a few times.

So, go on, what next. Did you spend the whole weekend in bed?

No, no, of course not. We spent a pleasant and profitable couple of hours at the Tate perusing the masterpieces. But we did run into a bit of a conundrum. Do you know the painting by Lord Leighton called "The Bath of Psyche"? It's a dead-ringer for my companion: Delicately marbled skin, promiscuous mouth. Do you know it: A nude trailing diaphanous silk and posing against some phallic columns? Ah me, miraculously both of us are thinking the same thing at the same time so we high-tailed it out of there for the hotel and that was the Tate for that day.

"High-tailed"? did you, says David. You've been too many times to the States H.P..

Well, maybe you're right. So what do you say lads. Who are we drinking to?

I'd say your friend Psyche, says David. It would be worth a trip to the Tate just to see it.

Of course my interest in the picture was the small, ochre vase just to the side of Psyche. That was worth the trip itself.

You've always been interested in vessels.

Look at that will ye, says a Dubliner at the next table. They're at it again.

He holds up a copy of the Irish Times with a picture of a Belfast Street littered with bodies. Those bastard Orangemen. When will it stop?

The Stag's Head responds with a collective groan; threats circulate.

Jaysus, says Gerard. Bloody bastards all right.

Bloody bastards, is it, says David in a low voice. What do you say about the bloody I. R. A. then? What, nothing? Blowing up women and children. That's your lot.

Now hold on. Who started this? The bloody Orange. Bastards think they own this bloody country.

H.P. is used to this. Gerard and David can become so incensed with each other and so self-righteous that they have come near to blows. Once, on Trinity Green, they got to shoving each other so hard that they fell on a bed of lilies to the detriment of the lilies. It's a mystery as to why they continue to hang out together.

H.P. orders another round. He feels a pleasant edginess; his earlier melancholy has vanished. Now lads, he says, before you get going again I propose that we find a calmer venue in which to continue our perorations. What say you to Mulligan's on Poolberg Street.

Gerard and David follow H.P. to the door. When they come alongside the table with the dead ringer, H.P. stops. Now sir, he says, you wouldn't have been on the London to Liverpool train last week would you?

Yes, you little bastard. I've been eyeing you meself. If you know what's good for you you'll keep on your way before I decide to mop up this establishment with what remains of you. With that he blows a blast of cigarette smoke in H.P.'s face.

H.P. turns as quickly as the Guinness will allow and heads for the door. Whatever got into me. I must have lost me mind.

The rain is still coming down.

Jaysus, in buckets, is it? Mind that puddle the size of a lake.

The walk to Mulligan's takes only five minutes just long enough to drench the three from head-to-toe.

The amiable barman Cormack McGreevey presides at Mulligan's.

Well, well, look at what the cat dragged in. Let me guess: The College has been evacuated because of the prediction of a Biblical blizzard? Or, more likely, your students have rebelled and chased you gents out.

Ah yes, says Gerard, but the question is, just how do ye know these things? Is there some know-all genie crouching down behind the bar whispering to ye?

There might be but I'm not at liberty to divulge such important data to the likes of you.

Right as rain, says H.P. Now without further blather from you and your genie may we have the goods? Namely, three pints of that miracle brew.

And what were you telling me the last time you graced this establishment? says Cormack. An explanation, wasn't it, as to why we see these little waves in the pint of Guiness head to the bottom? And look at that will ya? There's a fair storm going on in there.

David clears his throat. Well, as I hope you remember from my last lecture there's at least two things going on apart from my desperate thirst. See the little bubbles moving up as the waves are moving down? David picks up a bar napkin. Now,

$$\frac{\partial a}{\partial t} + \frac{\partial Q}{\partial z} = 0$$

tells the whole story. He pushes the napkin over to Cormack who glances at it before pushing it back.

So this is what you bright fellows do for a living? I wonder we're getting our money's worth.

You don't understand it, says H.P.? My God man it's as plain as day. At last we have an explanation for the gushing.

You take the explanation; I'll take the black stuff.

So what is it David, says H.P..You seem troubled. Your jaw is hanging slack around your neck.

Well, my good man, you want me to drag it out of you?

I'll tell you what it is. The bloody IRA is at it again. This time it's a baby. A baby! fifteen months old sleeping in his pram. Sleeping peacefully and it gets blown to bits. What kind of monsters are they?

Both H.P. and David look to Gerard who appears not to have heard.

Well, says David what do you have to say to that?

Gerard minds the cascading waves inside the jar of Guinness as if trying to confirm the mathematical model.

Gerard, let's not get caught up in these border wars, says H.P.. This is a table of peacemakers.

Gerard looks up from his study of the Guinness undertow. So you think, he says, that they're about deliberately blowing up babies? You know – speaking now directly to David – what they're about is setting right what you Orange blokes and your bloody English masters have been up to for centuries. Nobody wanted that baby to get blown up. We both know who's guilty here.

I wonder what you're talking about, says David. I really wonder. One side of you keeps bleating about injustice while the other side cheers it on. You want injustice. Look at what the Republicans have done. Jaysus, they're now into setting off bombs in London.

Right, says Gerard. I don't condone it but I understand it. The English need to take their lumps just like the rest of us.

Like the rest of us? How would it be if the paramilitaries set off bombs in Dublin. What would you say to that? You'd scream bloody murder you would?

Sure I would. The Irish Republic doesn't send soldiers into the North to harass the Unionists, now does it?

Look boys, H.P. says. Are we going to come to blows here or are we going to get along? What do you say David, can we let it rest?

You're as bad as he is, says David. Catholics stick together like bloody tar babies.

H.P. points to his chest. I'm a poet. I don't give a damn who wins out as long as I get my stout and a few spuds.

Now then let us consider the endgame today. But there must be no more talk of war and such.

H.P. gets to his feet. David staggers against the table knocking an empty pint to the floor. I'll get it, he says, reaching over toward the pint. His balance – what there is left of it – gives way sending him to the floor.

Somebody go to the poor lad's aide, says an inmate. Loud as he is, says another, he deserves the floor.

H.P. attempts to lift him upright. Give us a hand will you Gerard? We can't let him lie here.

Who can't. Look at him. He's bonkers anyway.

As he says this Gerard attempts to step over David on his way to the door but a miscalculation (no doubt caused by a slight but significant bend in the local gravitational field) causes his foot to wedge under David's inert leg. This forces Gerard to stagger into the next table which is manned by an elderly couple in the neighborhood of eighty years, plus or minus.

Oh, pardon me, mumbles Gerard. So sorry. So sorry.

All right then, says Cormack. That's it.

Cormack rolls David onto his back picking him off the floor as if he is no more than an empty suit. Out the door then. Off you go.

David's Mini is parked at the car park a short walk back toward Trinity. David pushes Gerard into the back seat and the three drive off in the direction of David's flat in Raneleigh.

Inexplicably, David has near perfect control of the Mini. Effortlessly he maintains spacing with the cars ahead and signaling his intentions well in advance. Within fifteen minutes – traffic being unusually and providentially light – they park at Gerard's flat in Henley Court. The flat, in fact, is rented from the Provost who lives across the courtyard.

Look, I need to use the loo before we go on, H.P. says.

Gerard unlocks the front door; H.P. and David follow.

Gerard's flat is on the second floor. There are pots of petunias drawn up on the steps to take advantage of the south facing windows.

David appears to take offence at the petunias. He picks up a pot and with no apparent calculation drops it to the ground where it shatters spewing dirt and petunia casualties.

Jaysus, what are you doing. Those flowers belong to the flat below.

David shrugs.

All right lads, says H.P., we'll take care of it but I got to get to the loo. They trundle in.

The flat has floor-to-ceiling plate glass windows which look out onto a tennis court. Without a by-your-leave, David opens the door to the balcony, steps outside, and with an expression on his face that reminds H.P. of Lewis Carroll's Cheshire cat, stares back at Gerard. Gerard responds by locking the balcony door. A sharp "click" accompanies the move.

David turns back to the window and in one stupendous blow kicks the floor-to-ceiling plate glass window. Amazingly, the window shatters sending shards of glass crashing to the floor inside the flat.

For a few seconds our three actors are motionless: It seems to take minutes before the broken glass settles. Luckily, no one has been cut. Suddenly in a burst of energy, Gerard shouts "you eejet", grabs David by the shirt and pulls him back through the now open window. A push sends him tumbling down the stairs narrowly missing the surviving petunias.

The next morning Gerard finds his neighbor surveying the damage to the flowerpots. Good God, he says, I thought we were under attack from the tennis court.

Gerard reports the disaster to the Provost who is incredulous that anyone could bring down that window. Are you sure, he says, that that's all of the story: That that slight lad could bring down that monster window?

Gerard, head down, nods.

Drink involved? says the Provost.

Again, the nod.

The next day the Provost calls David to his office and hands him a bill for a hundred pounds from the glazers. David looks as if someone has dropped a brick on his head. A hundred pounds on an assistant professor's salary is a fortune. It is, in short, another catastrophe.

Chapter 5

It'll be easy, Colleen says. Triple-easy.

Lee repeats this triple-easy incantation without a shred of conviction. He wonders, in fact, what he is doing riding his bicycle up a totally deserted Beacon Street at two in the morning on his way, as he sees it, to his doom at the hands of Colleen's father, Man-Mountain McCullough, the king of real estate developers.

The plan was devised by Colleen earlier that night in the Tasty over cokes. It'll be easy. You ride your bike to my house. Around back, by the side of the garage is a ladder. My light will be on so all you have to do is set the ladder up and I'll climb down. Tomorrow is Sunday so my parents won't be up before ten. All I have to do is be back before then. It'll be triple-easy.

Maybe, thinks Lee. But what if something goes wrong. Suppose Man-Mountain hears them and thinks I am a burglar. Suppose he shoots first and asks questions later.

Ah, but the prize is too delectable to turn down. Colleen sits in front of Lee in last period English class. Over the course of the school year he has minutely studied the curls of her hair billowing out from the back of her head forming thickets above the collar of her blouse. Her shoulders are sloped like gentle ridges connecting an enchanted, but unreachable region on the far side of the moon. What he wouldn't give to travel to that country. And now, after that miraculous day when Colleen had turned to him and said, you've got the sexiest eyes, and followed that up by asking him - oh wonder of wonders - to the Spring dance, now, after two months of going steady he is on his way up those final steps into that far country.

But, Man-Mountain is there and Ruth, Lee's mother, like two dangerous border guards.

Lee leans his bike against the fence. The ladder is beside the garage just as Colleen had predicted. Her window is illumined by what looks like candle- light. Luckily, there is no moon and a mere dribble of stars. Just as the ladder, which is hard to control, bangs against the house, Colleen appears. She starts down looking more like a cat burglar than a sensible, Smith College-bound graduate of Cambridge Rindge and Latin High School. Hand-in-hand, they jog to Lee's bike. Colleen leaps up depositing her delightful, girlish rear-end on the handle bars. After ten minutes of hard, breathless, speechless peddling, they reach number 47 Calvin Street and, removing their shoes, creep quietly past Ruth's bedroom door and safely into Lee's own.

But then, just when everything not only seems but is possible, a curious thing happens: Lee, leaving Colleen stranded beside the bed, picks up his baseball glove and begins worrying the pocket. More than anything else, baseball has defined Lee's life. He knows the path of a sharply hit ball, its pits and peaks and turnings as easily as if the path had been mapped out before leaving the bat. He is not a power hitter but in high school his bat initiated many rallies. Lee's fame has extended so far that one afternoon a scout for the Red Sox watched him make two clutch fielding plays and deliver the winning hit - a rifle-shot down the third base line.

Lee, what are you doing pray tell? The "pray tell" is one of Colleen's theatrical flourishes: She aims to be an actress. At home her waking moments are calibrated in front of the full-length mirror in her bedroom. Once, at 14, she walked Revere beach with pebbles in her mouth practicing lines from the up-coming school play, Arsenic and Old Lace. The director of the play noticed the difference immediately commenting on her "vastly improved" oratory. This was enough to persuade her to continue these self-improvements and, in fact, she was nearly thirty years old before she gave up the effort concluding that her future lay in teaching and not theater.

Lee continues his intense study of the glove. It might, he thinks, need more Neat's Foot Oil.

Oh, good grief. Do you want me to send you an invitation?

Actually, the invitation comes in the form of a hot, slippery kiss which causes Lee to stagger backward onto the bed pulling Colleen after him.

Once there, despite the fact that his mitt is still on his hand, Lee begins a thorough examination of Colleen's infield.

Well, what happened, happened and afterward they fell asleep tucked together like two adjacent pieces from the same puzzle. It seems, really, only minutes later when they are jolted awake by what sounds like the bellow of an outraged elephant but it is only Ruth who has opened Lee's bedroom door expecting to find his tousled blond hair and cherubic face lying sweetly and singly on the pillow, but finds instead, Colleen's coppery-colored hair spread across the pillow like the fiery coils of an electric heater. Ruth's bellow causes the pair to pop up like targets in a shooting gallery. What a disaster! shouts Ruth, as she slams the door behind her.

Colleen leaps from the bed and begins rounding up her clothes. Oh my God, she says her foot catching in her underpants causing her to hop about like one of those strange birds which tuck a leg under its belly: My Dad is gonna kill us.

Us?

Oh my God, Colleen pleads, come on. You've got to get me out of here.

Lee understands this; the problem, of course, is how. He hears Ruth on the other side of the door. The window is the only option. Of course, the window is stuck. Lee bends his knees trying to lever the sill open.

Oh, come on, come on, says Colleen.

At last the window gives way.

Lee? says Ruth.

Lee climbs through the window; Colleen follows. Reaching the ground, they sprint around to the front of the house and retrieve the bicycle which is locked to the porch railing.

Oh my God, says Lee, the key is on my desk. I can't unlock it.

Oh, says Colleen, you make me so mad.

Lee retraces his steps to the bedroom window. Ruth is not in sight. He pulls himself up the side of the house and in through the window. He snatches the key from the desk, climbs back through the window and races around the corner. Ruth's rose bush exacts its tribute by pricking Lee's leg just below the knee.

Boy, I hope my Dad's not up, says Colleen.

Triple-boy for me, thinks Lee who pedals as if his life depends on it.

Before they have come to a full stop, Colleen leaps from the handlebars and sprints to the front porch. Lee, without losing a beat, turns and accelerates back down the drive.

Colleen's mother Monica emerges from the bathroom just as her daughter tip-toes up the stairs. The confrontation is immense but due to Monica's good sense sufficiently quiet that Man-Mountain sleeps peacefully through.

Lee dreads the confrontation with Ruth almost as much as the one with Man-Mountain. She is particularly unyielding when addressing issues arising from sexual sources. Their second floor tenant, a comely young woman from the Berkshires, was seen escorting an equally young man into her apartment around supper time. Ruth monitored the situation by positioning herself at the front window in order to see when the young man would vacate the apartment. In her moral calculation, ten o'clock was the latest that this could occur without a serious moral stain. Ten o'clock came and went, as did eleven, and then twelve. In fact, Ruth fell asleep her head propped on the back of a chair against the window. In effect, she did not learn the departure time but from then on the upstairs tenant was under close supervision in loco parentis.

Lee walks up the front steps as if he is on his way to his own execution. For a brief moment he thinks that Ruth has gone out and that he can get safely into his own room where he can think of a plausible, mitigating story.

But Ruth, however, is sitting on Lee's bed. At first she says nothing, but when Lee starts to speak she raises her hand. Her shame is Titanic.

For a small woman, Ruth's voice is capable of reaching impressive volumes. Lee braces himself. Son, she says in a whisper, what are we going to do? What, oh what, are we going to do?

Lee is not sure if she really intends him to answer this and, besides, he is too alarmed by her quiet, reflective tone to risk an answer.

And so, he waits.

On the bed in from of Ruth are some pictures taken when Lee was in kindergarten. She looks at them as if they might suddenly turn to ashes. She shakes her head slowly from side to side. I guess, she says, we'll have to leave it up to God. Reverend Jackson will guide us.

Reverend Jackson is Ruth's full-time minister and Lee's part-time headache. Reverend Jackson sees a challenge in Lee. He seems to believe that the poor, fatherless Lee requires special attention.

In fact, of course, this is Sunday morning and the service would already be half-over and yet here is Ruth calmly fingering those old pictures. Very disturbing. To Lee's recollection, Ruth has never missed a Sunday even that one time when she had just gotten home from the hospital with her leg in a cast.

Mom, you're late for church, Lee ventures. Ruth merely shakes her head and then, a small eternity later says: I don't know where I went wrong. I just don't know.

Lee is mystified. Their roles seem to have been reversed like the poles of a magnet in the presence of an electric field. Lee puts a consoling hand on her shoulder. You didn't do anything Mom; it was me.

The next day Colleen's mother calls. Monica is originally from Hospitality, Texas and, according to Ruth, she says that he (Lee) had better not show his face around Colleen anymore or Man-Mountain will smash his face in toot sweet.

Now alongside Ruth's moral code is an equally strong code which requires circling the wagons whenever there is a threat to the family.

Ruth counter-attacks, saying that Colleen is just as much to blame as Lee. She's your daughter and it's your moral laxity that's to blame.

There is a glimmer of hope for Lee in these words. He adopts a suitably penitent pose, head down, lips closed. There are several seconds of silence. He wants to reach for his baseball glove but he hesitates.

Ruth turns on the water in the kitchen. Several minutes later he hears the whistle of the tea kettle. Son, do you want tea?

Yeah sure. Thanks.

They sit opposite each other at the kitchen table. Lee puts three sugars into his cup. They sip the tea in silence. The only sound is from the still sputtering tea kettle.

Mom, I'm sorry.

Ruth peremptorily waives the apology away. What's done is done. I don't have a right to get on you for that. What's done is done. I should know that better than anybody.

Lee is mystified. Mom, don't blame yourself. You're not to blame. You're the best.

Again, Ruth swats this objection away.

Someday you'll know what I'm talking about. I just pray you won't be too hard on me.

Lee can make no sense out of this.

Never mind, says Ruth. Let's think about what to do. From what Monica says you'd better stay clear of Colleen. At least for a while. Do you love her?

Love?

Love?

Lee shakes his head. Look mom, I...

Does he love Colleen? He isn't too sure what that would be like.

Look son we've never talked about this before. Oh, I know, it is my responsibility and I shirked it. I guess that somehow you figured it out without my saying anything. But you do know – don't you? – that she could... get pregnant?

Pregnant? No, that is impossible. No way.

Oh yes, it can happen. And then what. At eighteen are you ready to be a father?

A father? The idea is preposterous.

I thought not. Let's hope she isn't pregnant. It only takes one time. One time, that's all.

Lee is still stuck with the idea that he could become a father. Oddly enough, once the word is out in the air it doesn't sound so bad.

Son, for my sake - for both our sakes - stay clear of her before you get in too deep. I pray you aren't in too deep already.

Lee sees Colleen in the Hall at school but she changes course so abruptly that her book bag drops to the floor.

Two days later Colleen's friend Geraldine stops him in the hall. She wants to see you. But not here. Her parents might find out. She isn't allowed.

Geraldine is as dramatic as Colleen. She likes to turn even routine events into productions. They can meet, she says, beside the Mary Baker Eddy Monument in Mount Auburn Cemetery. Geraldine says that that way there will be no chance of being seen by anyone who might know her.

The monument is beside a reflecting pool bordered by Lilies. Lee is sure he sticks out like a brick in plaster. After an uneasy ten minutes, Colleen arrives looking equally out of place. She says that it is spooky to be walking around on top of a lot of dead people. Lee agrees. They walk along a path over a small hill past hundreds of gravestones and monuments until they reach a stone bench alongside the grave of one Hosea Williams which, according to the inscription chiseled into the edge of the bench, has been left there by Mr. Williams so that he might, occasionally, have company on his journey.

What are we going to do? says Colleen. My mother's still livid.

Lee shrugs.

She does look very pretty there on Hosea Williams' bench. And, no one else is around. So why shouldn't he put his arm around her and kiss her on the lips and why shouldn't he let his hand slide down until it touches, ever so slightly, ever so cautiously, like a leaf which has slipped from its branch, her breast and then her thigh - oh, heavens! Soon, a kind of frenzy breaks out on Hosea Williams knuckle-hard bench but just when the frenzied pair are about to sink down on the grass beside Mr. Hosea Williams himself, a funeral mounts the hill not fifty feet away. The cavalcade continues slowly past on Calvary Lane until it is out of sight behind a hill.

Unexpectedly, Colleen begins to cry. Before Lee can say or do anything, she is up and running back over Calvary Hill toward Mt. Auburn Street and the main gate.

And that is the last time Lee will ever see Colleen.

Chapter 6

It was early in the summer of 1939 that Ruth's mother began to have stomach problems. The small hospital in Plainfield was unable to match her symptoms with any known ailment so it was decided to transport her to the Mass General Hospital in Boston. Ruth's father could not leave his business – a small hardware store – and so it was that Ruth, who had just graduated from high school, will go with her mother to Boston. Ruth's Aunt Betsy who lives in Cambridge agrees to let Ruth use a small room upstairs that doubles as a library. The trip by ambulance went well; Ruth's mother was admitted to the hospital and placed in a room with one other patient.

After seeing her mother safely in place, Ruth drove with Aunt Betsy over the Longfellow Bridge to Harvard Square and her house on Brattle Street.

Aunt Betsy is tall with an angular face reminding Ruth of a red-tailed hawk she used to see on her walks on the conservation land outside Plainfield.

After unpacking her suitcase and hanging up her clothes Ruth sits down on the edge of the narrow bed. Ruth, calls Aunt Betsy from the bottom of the stairs, will you come down? There's tea waiting in the kitchen.

Ruth stands and smoothes her blouse which has developed wrinkles on the long ride from Plainfield. Coming, she says, I'm coming.

There are two treads on the stairs which emit a loud shriek when she steps on them.

They sit at the kitchen table; Aunt Betsy pours hot water from a kettle into a ceramic pot. Lemon? says Aunt Betsy. Ruth shakes her head no. But, she says, I would like a little sugar if it isn't too much trouble.

Now Ruth dear, I just know we'll get along but there are a few rules that I have so there won't be any problems. I hope you understand?

Ruth nods. The tea is hot and tastes as if it is made of smoke. What kind is it Aunt? The tea I mean?

Ah, Lapsang-Souchang. From China. Betsy laughs: Somebody told me they drink this in the opium dens.

Now, I go to sleep early and wake early. Here's a key to the front door but I would like it if you don't stay out late. I would worry.

Oh no Aunt, I'm an early riser too.

I listen to the radio only if there's news of some calamity or other like that hurricane. I don't allow visitors unless there's an urgent need. That probably won't trouble you since I don't believe you know anyone here but, if you don't mind my sayings so, you're an attractive young woman so I'm sure I'll have to enforce this rule eventually. (This remark causes a flash of red to land on both of Ruth's chalk-like cheeks.)

Well, that's all for now. I don't want to scare you off so I'll save the others for when you're settled in. And so, my dear, welcome to Cambridge. I think we'll do well together.

Chapter 7

The next morning Ruth is out early for a walk. She stops at the kiosk in Harvard Square. The racks are filled with newspapers from around the world. Across the street are the buildings of Harvard College. Students – from their looks about the same age as Ruth – stream in both directions through the gates; cars pulse by on Mass Ave.. It is exciting and a little unnerving this purposeful bustle. A woman carrying a large bag squeezes past; the bag bumps against Ruth.

Ruth would like to go in to one of the small cafes for tea but she isn't confident on how that would work. She might not know what to order nor how much to pay. She has never been in a café or restaurant on her own. Her family did not go out much.

She counts her money: She has twelve dollars and seventy-six cents. Surely that is more than enough.

She opens the door to a small restaurant. She stands just inside unsure of what to do. Waitresses bustle past carrying trays of hot coffee and buns.

Excuse me miss. A waitress pushes past.

Un, excuse … but the waitress is already on the other side of the room.

Smoke from the many cigarette smokers hangs like a storm cloud over the patrons.

Yes, do you need something?

That waitress is back standing in front of Ruth.

Um, …

Well?

Um, no thank you. Ruth turns back to the entrance her face ablaze. She pushes open the door and retraces her steps to Aunt Betsy's.

The following day goes better. She perseveres at the restaurant eventually getting a table near a window. She drinks hot tea with milk and sugar. A Boston Daily Globe newspaper has been left at the table by a previous customer. The headline is about a ship sinking in the Atlantic. All of that business in Europe. Ruth doesn't know what to think about it. She sips the Earl Grey tea holding the warm cup in both hands.

Last night when she was in the bathroom brushing her teeth she heard what sounded like a window closing. This was odd because Aunt Betsy had gone to bed promptly at nine o'clock. Ruth stood still listening intently. After all she had been warned about break-ins.

When there was no further sound she walked carefully downstairs stepping across the squeaky treads. At the foot of the stairs directly across from Aunt Betsy's bedroom door she listened. There was a sound which Ruth can only compare to a child bouncing up and down on a bed.

Ruth wasn't sure what to do. She thought she should knock on the door to be sure her aunt was all right but that seemed extreme. If there was nothing wrong what would Betsy think? That her niece is a flighty piece of work prone to gross leaps of imagination?

When nothing further happened Ruth retraced her steps to her bedroom. Nevertheless, she lay awake listening for several minutes; but all was calm.

Chapter 8

Two days after the "bed bouncing" incident – Ruth laughs each time she thinks of it – she walks to a bookstore on Mass Ave.. She isn't looking for anything in particular just a pleasant book to read. On a table where several paperbacks are laid out, she picks up the closest one - "My Antonia" - and reads the first few pages.

Jim Burden is on a train back to his home in Nebraska. Ruth is fascinated by farm life on the Plains since her grandfather showed her pictures of his family and their life in Iowa before he immigrated to Massachusetts.

She pays the clerk for the book and thinks that a cup of tea is in order.

The café is full of students most of them are reading or writing in notebooks. Ruth sits at an empty table and orders Earl Grey tea. The young man looks from the book into a notebook. He wears horn-rimmed glasses which makes him look like a college professor.

A young woman sits at the table to her right. Her blond hair is cut shockingly short – Ruth believes that she has never seen a woman's hair cut so short. Still, the young woman with her heart-shaped face and blond hair is appealing.

Hello, the woman says. "My Antonia". What a good book.

Yes, I believe it is but I'm only getting started.

The young woman smiles in return and then returns to her own book.

May I ask what you're reading? Ruth feels that this isn't too intrusive since she spoke first.

Here it is, she says.

Oh, I don't know this one, says Ruth.

Well, it's a bit of a slog but I'm getting it. It's about a man in Dublin, Ireland. It all happens in one day.

My goodness: One day. And such a long book.

Umm. It is long. Look, my name is Elizabeth Cardozo.

Ruth Blake. Please to meet you.

Are you in college? I'm at Radcliff.

Oh no. I'm here because my mother is sick. She's in hospital in Boston. I only finished high school in June.

Then we're the same age. Where do you live?

Well, I'm staying with my aunt on Brattle Street but I live in Plainfield, Massachusetts.

Oh, where is that? Sorry I don't know much about Massachusetts. I'm from New York City.

Well, there's no reason you should know Plainfield. It's a small town in the Western part of the state. In the Berkshires, if you know where they are.

Gee, I think I'd like living in a small town. New York City is too big. Everybody is in a hurry.

What about Boston? Do you like it here? Well, Cambridge I mean.

Well, I've only been here for two weeks but so far it's good. I'm taking classes in literature at Harvard. I do like the professors and the students seem good although there are a few stuck-ups. Gosh, she says. I've got a class in ten minutes. Maybe we can get together again? I'm here about the same time tomorrow.

I'd like to. It was nice to meet you.

Ruth turns back to her book but the words have little impact. She sips the tea which is no longer hot.

During the next two weeks Ruth and Elizabeth meet over tea or for walks along the Charles River. Ruth gathers that Elizabeth's family is rich. They live in Manhattan but they also have property in the Poconos. Her father is a lawyer and her mother is a psychiatrist.

Well, my parents do have a lot of money but I'm on the side of working people. I told my father that I wanted to help people. He didn't want to hear it. But I do. Somehow. What about you?

Well, my father owns a hardware store. It's not very big. It does ok. Ruth laughs: Just ok, I should say.

Oh, isn't that interesting. You know Ruth I envy you. I think your family gave you the right lessons. I mean, about the world. I never met anyone except people like me. It was so isolating.

Ruth wonders about this. Elizabeth seems to have had so many advantages: Growing up in New York City, plenty of money, good schools. Ruth is a little jealous. Well, she says, I don't know. We seem to be two people on opposite sides of some barrier.

Yes, that's it. A barrier. A barrier of money.

But, still, says Ruth, we can be friends, can't we?

We sure can.

Chapter 9

Once again the morning is brilliant: A blue, October sky devoid of clouds, temperature in the fifties. Ruth is headed to the Red Line Subway on her way to visit her mother. The platform underground is not well-lighted. Ruth worries about her aunt's admonition to not speak to anyone unless it is absolutely necessary. There are, she said, murderers and rapists everywhere. It is comforting that there are other passengers waiting for an inbound train including a distinguished looking gentleman who seems, disconcertingly, to be paying attention to her.

By the time the train arrives there are many passengers waiting to board. Ruth is swept along by the crowd eventually being deposited alongside a post which she holds onto for support. When she looks up she sees that she is standing next to that distinguished looking gentleman who, she observes, is looking directly at her.

It's a lovely day, he says, which forces her despite Aunt's injunction, to agree. But he does look respectable possibly a business man or even a minister so that when he next asks if she is from Boston she feels it is quite acceptable to say that she is not that she is visiting.

Ah, he says, so am I, so am I.

He has an accent although Ruth can't say from where.

The train emerges from the tunnel and crosses the river on the Longfellow Bridge. The State House with its gold cap glitters in the light.

Ah, quite a sight wouldn't you agree?

Ruth does agree.

At the Mass General Stop she is chagrined to find that the gentleman is also disembarking.

Excuse me, he says, are you going to the hospital? When Ruth says that she is he asks if he can accompany her. Not wishing to appear rude Ruth nods her assent.

I hope I'm not bothering you but I'm here because of a friend who's in a bad way in the hospital. I'm quite worried about him.

Oh, says Ruth, I'm sure he'll be all right.

The gentleman responds by saying that her encouragement is like a beam of light flashing into a grave.

H.P. is my name and you are?

Ruth, she says, shaking H.P.'s hand which has been thrust toward her.

Would you mind dear Ruth if I were to telephone you tomorrow. I believe I can handle bad news if I know I can see you again.

Ruth doesn't know how she could refuse such a request and, in any case, it is clear that he is a gentleman. Ruth agrees and writes Aunt Betsy's telephone number on a small, writing pad that H.P. provides.

Ruth does not tell her mother – whose prognosis is still guarded and difficult – nor Aunt Betsy about meeting H.P. although she does take the precaution of telling her aunt that a friend from home might call.

And call he did to say that his friend had passed away during the night and he wonders if he might see her in order, he says, to bask once more in her ministering, sympathetic gaze.

Ruth can hardly refuse and agrees to meet him at the kiosk in Harvard Square at ten in the morning.

The next morning it is still warm but at night the temperature had dropped hinting at cooler Autumn weather. Ruth wears her warmest coat and a scarf that Jimmy Taylor gave her for Christmas.

As she waits in front of the kiosk she sees H.P. coming toward her along Brattle Street. She is surprised to see that he is smiling. She guesses it must be like that time that her grandfather died and her mother kept her pain in check by going about her business as if nothing had happened. Her mother said that was the best way to get on in life: Just keep going straight ahead no matter what. Ruth could not take the advice. She was too close to Grandfather to be able to do that.

Ah, there you are, H.P. says. And how are you on this glorious day?

Ruth is impressed by his ability to mask his grief at his friend's passing. She does not want to remind him of this but she thinks it would be discourteous not to say something.

I'm sorry, she says, about your friend.

H.P. takes her hand in his without speaking. Because of the look which suddenly closes on his face like a dark cloud passing in front of the sun, Ruth fears that he might cry. But, instead, H.P. thanks her for her concern and proposes that they repair to the Tasty across the street for, he says, he hasn't been able to eat all morning but his appetite is returning little-by-little.

Ruth concurs thinking this would be good for him. They cross Mass Ave at the light and enter the small eatery on the corner. The waitress seems to know H.P. who responds to her greeting with enthusiasm. He then tells Ruth that he is merely being polite. Jaysus, he says, if they knew they'd fall all over themselves with the sympathy.

Ruth orders tea; H.P., whose appetite appears to have rebounded, orders two poached eggs, ham, rashers and toast. Tea as well, he says.

Now then Ruth, let's talk about you. Are you from here? Where do they grow such sweet young plants?

Ruth fights against that maddening blush which so predictably wants to embrace her.

No, I'm from Plainfield. It's in the western part of the state. Not far from Pittsfield, if you know it.

Ah no, unfortunately. I've not been west of Boston. And are you employed?

No, I just graduated from high school in June. I would have looked for a job in Plainfield but my mother got sick and so we came here to Boston. Well, Cambridge, except she's in the hospital in Boston.

I'm sorry about your Mam but as Sir Walter Scott concluded: It's an ill wind that blows nobody good. It blew you to me, you see.

(Again that terrible blush.)

Ruth studies H.P. while he is busy with his breakfast. He has dark, wavy hair which is combed straight back like the streamlines of a fast moving river. His eyes are an uncanny blue like the sky in October when the temperature is in the forties and the wind is fresh from Canada. And he is distinguished looking even if he is a little down-at- the-heels. The collar of his white shirt is splintered and his tie has a brown spot down near the tongue.

H.P. finishes breakfast and pulls out a cigarette from a packet. He offers one to Ruth who does not smoke. The one time she tried to smoke at the urging of her boyfriend when they were hidden outside the high school was unpleasant. It took fully ten minutes to recover from a fit of coughing. Nevertheless, she accepts the offer from H.P. inhaling carefully. The bluish smoke smells like old, rolled-up rugs.

She begins to feel a little dizzy but not unpleasantly so. She likes sitting beside H.P. and blowing blue smoke into the air.

Ruth points to the book which protrudes from H.P.'s jacket pocket. Is that connected with what you do?

Oh that. Well, yes and no. Since the cat's out of the bag I may as well own up: I'm visiting Harvard earning my keep by leading those young Harvard toffs right up to the edge of the pool and giving them a shove or two.

Ah, from the look on that sweet face of yours you don't understand. Well, the full account is that I'm spoon-feeding them English-Irish lit except that the spoon is more like a fire hose. But I'm probably boring you with me complaints.

Ruth tries to object. No, no, I see that. I'll shut me mouth on that score. Now, you strike me as someone who's sensitive to the world what with those big, brown eyes and that nice smile which is always about your face. Would you mind very much if I just touched your hand there just to see how that soft looking skin actually feels? Ah, just as I thought: As soft as a baby's rear. (Not that H.P. has any experience with a baby's rear.)

I tell you what. It happens that I'm giving a reading at College tonight. Emerson Hall at eight. There's a small party on afterwards. Will you come?

I'd love to.

Ruth arrives early. She is worried that she might not find Emerson Hall but she does. She waits by the steps until ten minutes to eight and then follows two students up the steps. Just inside on a bulletin board is an announcement of the reading. "H.P.", it says, "Reads".

The room is a library with bound volumes shelved on all the walls. The floor is wood and the ceiling is embossed tin. There is a large fireplace at one end.

Ruth takes a seat at the back of the room. By eight o'clock most of the chairs are occupied. The audience seems to be mainly students but there are some older women.

H.P. arrives at eight-fifteen. A young woman with striking red hair comes to the podium – one of his students Ruth imagines. It is my honor, she says, to introduce you to the Irish short story writer and poet, H.P.. He has been here at Harvard wowing students with his lectures. There couldn't be a better way to end the week then by listening to H.P.'s mellifluous voice reading from his short story collection, "Skerries".

Well now, thanks Jen. But, my, my, mellifluous is it now? And me being a little tight in the throat without any lubrication the past twenty-four.

H.P. reads three stories all of which Ruth likes but the title story, "Skerries", for her is the best. The main character is Seamus a lad of ten. He lives with his mother Shauna in Skerries. The reader does not know where the father is until the very end of the story. Ruth is nearly brought to tears by the story.

In a question period after the reading someone asks H.P. if the boy is modeled on a real person. He responds by saying that he can't say he is and he can't say he isn't. What I can say is that I have a few copies autographed in my very own hand at the highly discounted price of four dollars a pop. Now, no stampede please. This isn't Montana.

And, indeed, a small crowd assembles at the podium. There are more would- be purchasers then books.

Ruth stays at the rim of the crowd until it drifts away.

And now, Ruth, was it to your liking?

Oh yes, I loved each story but I especially liked, "Skerries".

H.P. nods. Glad to hear it. What do you say that we amble over to the party?

I'd like a copy of "Skerries" but you don't have any left.

Ah no, I've reserved one for you. It's autographed but promise not to read the inscription until later – preferably after you're curled up in bed.

Ruth opens her pocketbook.

Oh no, it's a gift.

Oh no, I couldn't think of it.

Then you'd be taking away my pleasure in giving it to you. You wouldn't do that, would you now?

Now then, shall we high-tail it out of here?

They exit the Yard near the kiosk and proceed along Mt. Auburn

Street. H.P. offers his arm. Ruth thinks they look like an old married couple out for a stroll. She likes the thought.

They turn into an unlighted alley emerging at the rear of 17A Mt. Auburn Street. H.P. knocks but there is no answer. They hear loud music and voices coming from inside. H.P. pushes on the door which opens obligingly.

The room is crowded with people who are standing in knots of three or more like an archipelago of small islands. Everyone – or nearly everyone – has a bottle of beer or a glass of what looks like wine in hand. Low overhead is a bank of thick smoke. Ruth doesn't recognize the smell – a sort of sweet, smoky smell.

As they enter the main room several denizens turn to H.P.. Applause breaks out. H.P. bows to the left and right.

Now, now, he says. Let's get on with the party. None of that flattery, if you please.

A short blond woman comes over: She appears not to see Ruth.

Ah, so the great man did show. Lucky us, she says.

Now Mary Beth, none of that. Can we just be friends?

Mary Beth frowns. "Friends", she says, now that's rich.

Luckily Mary Beth pivots and walks toward the kitchen.

Pay her no mind, says H.P.. I don't know what got into her.

Someone hands H.P. a cigarette, or what looks like a hand-rolled cigarette the kind that Grandpa smoked. H.P. inhales deeply holding the smoke in before exhaling in one large burst. He offers the cigarette to Ruth who is unsure if she should try it.

Finally, she does inhale a small burst holding it in in the same way. It is rough in her throat. She is just able to avoid coughing. H.P. takes the cigarette and inhales for a second time. He passes the cigarette to someone on the next island who repeats the procedure.

Stay here a minute, says H.P.: I'll get us some refreshment.

H.P.'s journey through the crowd is interrupted several times by someone with something to say.

While H.P. is away a man disengages from his group and walks over to Ruth. Another hit? he says, and hands her another cigarette. Not bad is it, he says, as Ruth exhales.

I'm Cory, he says.

Cory is tall with blond hair and blue eyes.

What are you studying? he says.

Oh, I'm not a student. Well, I mean, I just graduated high school.

I see. And how do you know H.P.? I thought you might be one of his students.

Ruth chokes back a laugh.

I see you're getting high. Welcome.

"High"? Suddenly Ruth realizes that she has been smoking ... what ... marijuana. My god, she thinks, what would ... But it isn't bad. In fact it feels to her downright good. It feels as if she isn't connected to Cory or the room. It's as if she is floating but, as she can see, her feet are still on the ground.

I'm sorry, what did you say?

Just then H.P. appears holding two bottles of beer.

Ah no, Cory, he says, poaching on me territory are ye?

Cory laughs. No way. Encroach on the territory of the great H.P.? I'll move to that territory over there. The new world I think it's called.

Cory touches his index finger to his temple in salute.

The beer startles Ruth's tongue and the inside of her mouth. It's as if there are thousands of tiny bubbles bumping up against one another. On the whole it is very pleasant.

Well now Ruth dear. I hope you weren't bothered by that jackrabbit?

A permanent, half smile is embossed on Ruth's face. She shakes her head no.

Ah, the proverbial cat has your tongue, does it? Would you like another drag? H.P. offers another one of those rolled up cylinders.

Oh, I can't, says Ruth. No, please.

Feeling a little light-headed are ye now? Why don't we step outside for a breath of fresh air? This is a surly crowd, surely. That eejit Cory has put me on edge.

It is mild outside and surprisingly the Milky Way with its sheaf of stars is visible.

It's a grand evening, says H.P.. Shall we amble down to the river?

Ruth thinks that's a good idea and says so.

As they cross Memorial Drive, H.P. takes her hand. They continue holding hands even after they are safely on the other side.

H.P. says that the blackness of the night and the river suit his mood. If you weren't here Ruth I might leap off that bridge.

Ruth suppresses a giggle because it is no more than twenty feet from the bridge down to the river.

I'm only partly joking, says H.P..

Ruth turns to face him. His head – that aquiline head – is tilted forward onto his chest. What is it? she says.

H.P.'s deep voice is now no more than a hoarse whisper. I don't know Ruth. I hardly know you but I feel I can talk to you. I just don't know if I should burden you with my problems. You see, I get these moods, black, hellish moods which come on without warning. When one of them is on me life isn't worth living. And then there's Roger, my friend who passed out of this life yesterday. I can't stop thinking about suicide.

This disclosure horrifies Ruth. The influence of the marijuana instantly evaporates. It was rumored that the high school principal in Plainfield committed suicide. It was early on a Sunday morning. They said he got up before his wife and children were awake and went down to the basement where his hunting rifles were stored. The sound of the shot woke his little boy.

H.P. turns to look into her face. Those large, round eyes and full lips which are half-parted in an encouraging but tentative smile.

As inevitable as gravity H.P.'s head descends until their lips touch and then their tongues. Soon they are locked in a stimulating conversation although at first it is the conversation of two strangers speaking slightly different accents, different tongues. But they do communicate and after several exhilarating minutes they are close to agreement on several important points. In fact they find it essential to seek a less public place in which to continue their deliberations. Thankfully H.P.'s studio is nearby. There they continue their dialogue in earnest.

That conversation was so stimulating that Ruth shuts herself in her room for the next twenty-four hours emerging only with Aunt Betsy's insistence.

When H.P. has not called three days later – he had promised to call on the day following their conversation – Ruth goes by the studio but there is no answer to her knock. Through the window the room appears to be empty. Alarmed now Ruth goes to 17A Mt. Auburn Street. Her knock on the door is answered by Cory who says that H.P. left town the day after the party.

Chapter 10

I t is six weeks later that Ruth's pregnancy is confirmed by a doctor. Strangely, this news does not disconcert her. She had already guessed the truth and thus partly discounted the confirmation. Without a doubt she understands that she cannot return to Plainfield even though her mother is well enough to return. She dreads informing her family but, surprisingly, they are not as upset as she had imagined. They concur with her that returning to Plainfield would not be in her best interest and, she suspects, not in their best interest either. Her family pledges to support her during her pregnancy and beyond until Ruth finds, as her mother puts it, a proper, new path on which to walk.

Equally surprising is that no one asks about the father. Perhaps it is the result of Ruth's tactical move to disarm them by declaring that there is no chance of marriage (although she has not ruled it out completely).

And so Lee is born on July 10, 1940 at the Cambridge Lying-In Hospital after twenty hours of labor. Mother and son leave the hospital by taxi on a scorching hot day and drive to Aunt Betsy's house on Kirkland Street where they will stay until more permanent accommodations can be found.

Unfortunately, it will take nearly five years before Ruth's real estate business – Ruth studied for and successfully passed the broker's license in two years – generated enough income to allow her to buy a triple-decker on Calvin Street just over the line in Somerville. The capital to buy the brokerage was supplied by Grandfather Hiram whose loan was paid back in full within four years

Chapter 11

The morning after his romp with Ruth, H.P. wakes to sunshine streaming in his studio apartment windows. It takes several minutes to collect the shards of his memory into a meaningful whole.

Now what in the devil was her name? Something Biblical. Nice taut little body but — Jaysus — what was her name? Ah well, it's no matter. What was it after she left. Ah right, The Plough and The Stars. Cory and that bunch. Tossed us out at closing. That mincing little fellow from M.I.T.. claimed he was an expert in something or other. Some useless bit of garbage. So useless I can't even think what it was.

H.P. turns the bath on full hot. He lathers and soaks for fifteen minutes. The alcoholic shivers induced by the previous night's debacle loosening by the minute. He exits the water pink in body and spirit.

Ah me, none of that tonight. I've got to get going. Ship leaves at 1700. Cabin number two thousand something.

I'll send her a postcard today. Let her know I'm on my way back. Poor old Mam. Wastrel for a son. I'm about as low on her ladder as one can go. Just above the rubbish-man. That way no one has to go far to get rid of me. Into the dust bin.

H.P. dresses. He collects his copy of "At Swim Two Birds" and steps out to brilliant sunshine. A pastry and a read, he thinks. The alcohol from the previous night has left no trace. The Tasty. Maybe Dorie is on. His step feels unnaturally light, buoyant even. Nothing better, he thinks, nothing better.

A young female — student probably — with long blond hair approaches along the sidewalk. H.P. nods to her as she passes but there is no response.

41

Dorie is on at the Tasty. Good morning professor, she says. You're up early.

Ah, don't tell me. It is an ungodly hour.

H.P. sits at the counter. Now be a good lass and fetch me scrambled eggs, a rasher of bacon and hot tea.

A gent to his right is reading the Boston Morning Globe. The panes of his glasses look to be a quarter-inch thick. His eyes appear double-sized through the lenses.

How'd the Sox do then, says H.P..

The gent appears not to have heard. H.P. is going to repeat the question when Dorie returns with his order. He's deaf, she says, but they won 6-3. Great pitching by Lefty Grove. Struck out the side in the 9th. Jimmy Fox got the winning hit.

Ah Dorie now, don't bother with the play-by-play. It sails right over me head. But, you're mighty spruce this morning.

Now, none of your blather professor. I've got work to do.

Dorie has a two-year old son with no father in evidence. H.P. thinks he must have been a bastard to leave her like this. But, he assures himself, it's not my affair. The little pun prompts an inward smile.

Now Dorie, H.P. says as he leaves money for the bill, when did you say you would be free? We could take in a movie or grab a pint. What do you say?

You know I have little Michael.

H.P. shrugs. Mind you, this offer doesn't come around every day.

No it doesn't, says Dorie. More like every other day.

All right my lass. I'll leave you. It's been a pleasure.

H.P. returns to the apartment. He packs his clothes into a satchel, checks around the apartment once more and then locks the door. He leaves the key under the mat for the owner.

The Red Line subway deposits him at South Station at 10:30. He pays for a one-way ticket to New York City. The waiting room is moderately crowded but nothing to draw his attention. He takes "At Swim Two Birds" from a pocket of the satchel and opens it to the bookmark: "Dermot is examining three different openings while chewing bread for the full three minutes". My god, the man's bonkers. Still, quite good.

The all-aboard announcement for track fifteen cuts short the perusal of Flann O'Brien's creation. H.P. boards the train, deposits the satchel in the overhead bin and takes the window seat.

The train pulls away from the station with a lurch and slowly makes its way through the rail yards. Within twenty minutes the train is moving moderately fast. H.P. watches the Boston suburbs flow by.

Ah, I don't know when I'll be back. It will be good to get back to the auld sod.

Travel always seems to produce a state of melancholy in H.P.. Something about the motion and changing landscapes. He thinks it's because he has nothing, really, to hold to.

He opens the side pocket of the satchel to retrieve the O'Brien. He reads, inattentively, a page then two. Concentration disappears in this state. The words merge into long, incomprehensible strings. He closes the book and looks out the window. Time dilation, he thinks: No use fighting it.

The train stops in Providence where a young, dark-haired woman wearing a pleated skirt points to the empty aisle seat. Do you mind? she says.

Ah, it would be a pleasure, says H.P.. Here, let me help you with that.

No, no, thanks. I've got it, as she lifts her suitcase into the overhead.

H.P.'s my name. I'm on to New York.

Laura, me too.

Laura notices the O'Brien lying on the seat. Oh, I've read that. It's exceptional.

Aye, Flann O'Brien is an exception. Mind you I've some problems with him but he is a good read. Are you from New York?

No, I'm just down for the weekend. My boyfriend is at Columbia.

Now that's a pity, says H.P. signaling at the same time by a smile that he wasn't to be taken too seriously.

Laura takes a copy of "Dubliners" from her handbag. Do you know this? she says. The stories I've read so far have been super.

Are you steeped in Irish literature?

Well, I am studying European lit at B.U..

And Ulysses?

Not yet. We're supposed to read it next semester.

Laura opens the book and H.P. retreats to the window. The Connecticut shoreline is in view along with salt marshes on either side of the tracks.

The melancholy has lifted like a gauze curtain but it descends again without warning.

Jaysus, we're all Micks thinks H.P.. We've all read that bastard Joyce. There's no way to get at him as high up as they've pushed him. And what have I got: One little book; a few poems.

Rain pelts the window. Rain has a calming effect on H.P.. He reckons that it began with the rain off the Irish Sea lashing the windows in Skerries. The rain deepens the melancholy while simultaneously interweaving a nostalgia which is not at all unpleasant.

Laura and H.P. part amicably at Penn Station. Her boyfriend is there to meet her on the platform. A tall, sandy-haired lad of twenty. They clutch each other and laugh. The last H.P. sees of her they are walking briskly down the passage hand-in-hand.

The travel documents say that H.P. is to be at the Passenger Ship Terminal by five. He stores his satchel in a rental locker and heads out of the station. The rain has stopped; light blue skies appear between the towers. The taxi horns are New York's music.

Times Square is seedy: Strip joints and bars. H.P. ducks into a small restaurant and orders corned beef. Not bad, he thinks, when it arrives.

A short taxi ride deposits him at the pier. He walks up the gangway to the ship. The Purser welcomes him on board.

Ah now, is there anything to worry about?

No, no says the Purser. That trouble last week was a mistake. The Germans already apologized for it.

Apology is it? A lot of good that does for the poor souls at the bottom.

The Purser nods in agreement.

H.P. unpacks his satchel in the cabin. His cabin-mate (lower bunk) is a Brit from Liverpool.

What do you think? says H.P.. Will the German bastards try to get us?

Bloody well they might.

H.P. nods in agreement.

The ship is tugged away from the pier. On deck, the sky is cleansed to a powdery blue.

H.P. stands on the deck watching New York slide by. Lady Liberty holds up her green greeting. The wind has a small bite as it blows into H.P.'s face. He closes his eyes. The rumble of the engines and the blowing of the wind are the only sounds.

A young couple appear on deck. From the look H.P. surmises that they've just been married. Probably on their honeymoon. They hold hands and look out to sea as the ship passes through the Narrows.

Ah, here we are. Take notice all you U-Boats out there.

Chapter 12

R uth works hard to establish her business. It is commonly accepted in Plainfield that her hard work is a reaction to what she and the rest of the family consider her unfortunate circumstances. For the inquisitive outside-world she responds to indelicate questions about Lee's paternity by saying that her husband was killed in the War. Sad, they would say, and that poor little Lee without a father. Let us know if we can do anything to help. Well yes, Ruth would say, there is one thing. Her interlocutor would lean in to hear what he or she might do: If you are going to buy or sell in Cambridge, Ruth practically whispers, let me know. I've got sellers and buyers ready to move. She closes this tender, little message with a brilliant smile and a "may Jesus be with you". The last is a favorite saying – according to her Grandmother – of her deceased Grandfather. She likes the implication that she is a Christian woman with all that it implies, particularly honesty and piety. And, indeed, Ruth is a good Christian as well as a good capitalist. She joins the Methodist Church on High Street, becomes friends with the Reverend Jackson and his family and when the church has to find a place for the Reverend to live she finds just the place a scant two blocks from the church – producing surplus value in both ledgers: God's and Ruth's own balance sheet.

Lee is a bright child. He learns to read – mostly on his own – at three. When he is five he asks Ruth about his father. It was at a Halloween party that Lee's best friend asked Lee that question. It had not occurred to Lee before his friend's query to ask the question. Everyone has a father, said Lee's friend.

At dinner that night Lee asks Ruth to solve the conundrum: Momma, do I have a daddy?

Ruth is not prepared for this question although she knew it was going to come. Yes dear, you have a daddy but he was killed in the War. He was a hero. He flew an airplane that carried soldiers from England to the fighting but his airplane was shot down. It was shot down by the Germans in France. Everybody on the airplane was killed. He was a hero.

In retrospect Ruth wishes that she hadn't volunteered so much. She would have to keep track of the lies so as not to contradict herself.

What's a hero? Lee wants to know. And why did Daddy have to be in the war. Why couldn't he stay home with us?

Alarmingly, this brings tears to Ruth's eyes. It does make me sad, she says. He couldn't stay with us even though he wanted to. Our country needed him. He had to go.

What is a "country"?

Well, it's something like Cambridge only much bigger. Look, here's a map in this book. Right there is where we live. That's Cambridge. But all of the rest of this is our country. A hero is someone who does brave things in a war. Your daddy was a hero. You can be proud of him.

And so he is. He tells his inquisitive friend that his father is a hero who was killed in the war. This explanation suffices until Memorial Day five years later. Lee's teacher in the fifth grade speaks to the class about Memorial Day and how the graves of the soldiers are decorated with small American flags. Momma, says Lee, we need to get a flag for Daddy's grave.

Oh son, that's such a good idea but – and this makes me so, so sad – we don't have a grave for your daddy. You see, his body was never found.

Why?

Well, I'm not sure but the body may have fallen into the sea between England and France. They flew from England to France carrying paratroopers so he might have crashed in the sea. Do you want to see it on a map?

Lee makes a large copy of that map. It lies flat on his desk. His finger traces what Ruth said was the flight of his Daddy's airplane. Even later – much later – when he wants a tangible reminder of his father the map is there.

From that day to his twelfth birthday Lee never asks another question about his father. Without even a picture let alone a name to guide him he appropriates a picture from a book of an American pilot standing beside his airplane. A pilot with dark hair, white teeth and with - although the picture is in black-and-white - what Lee interpolates as blue eyes; exactly like his own. He buys a balsa-wood airplane kit at a toy store in Harvard Square.

The wood floor between two of the rugs in his room becomes the Channel between England and France. The airplane is a C47 just like – so Lee was told – the kind that flew paratroopers to France. Lee lifts the plane high over his head to escape the German fire. Lee turns the airplane re-crossing the Channel before landing safely at High Wycombe.

On some days the C47 is hit by enemy fire but his father parachutes to safety.

Lee is in high school at Cambridge Rindge and Latin. His best subject is Mathematics but his favorite subject is Mrs. Frank's photography class. She lets Lee borrow a Cannon 35mm Range Finder camera and initiates him into the intricacies of the darkroom. One of his prints taken near Fresh Pond on a late, November day is shown at the Boston Evening Globe's photography show. Ruth takes this as a sign that Lee will one day become famous. Not necessarily, she says, as a photographer but in something. After the show the print is hung in the living room at 47 Calvin Street until after Ruth's death.

There is, of course, a plan for Lee to go to college after high school. He applies to several Ivy League schools but is not accepted. He settles on Boston College following the recommendation of Mrs. Frank who had graduated from B.C..

Lee is well into his senior year in high school when Ruth is hit by a car as she is crossing Beacon street. It is just after dark; the driver speeds through a red light. Ruth is declared dead at the hospital.

Just like that.

Chapter 13

Ruth's burial is in Mt. Auburn Cemetery not far, in fact, from Hoseia Spaulding's knuckle-hard bench. At first Grandma Blake wanted Ruth to be buried in the family plot in Plainfield but Lee insisted that she be buried in Cambridge. That way, he said, he can be with her whenever he wishes. This reasoning prevailed.

Lee wears a dark suit and tie which he bought the day before at the Coop in Harvard Square. Ruth's family is there similarly dressed in black: Grandma Blake, Aunt Betsy and several Plainfield neighbors whom Lee does not know.

Before the internment there is a eulogy in the Methodist Church presided over by Reverend Jackson. Ruth's friends and business associates fill the small annex of the church. Before the Service Reverend Jackson asks Lee if he would like to speak. And Lee does want to speak but he can't think of a thing to say. He quietly declines.

She was a gentlewoman, says Reverend Jackson, but of a special type. I'm sure you all know that she raised and nurtured this fine young man alone while building, through grit and determination, a business which is one of the finest in this city. Please consider how difficult all of that was. Firstly, the demands of a young, fatherless child and then the inescapable demands of an always-on business. I know that there was one thing which helped to ameliorate these twin burdens: And that is the loving God of Christianity. Without fail she would be here on Sundays for service and during the week she could be found following Christ's teaching with good works. I know that I couldn't have done what I have done without Ruth's faithful assistance.

Jesus, thinks Lee, who is this about anyway?

Lee wants to believe the stuff about Christ and an afterlife. It was Mr. Stevens in tenth grade that fired the first shots. It was in Philosophy Club.

And how can you reconcile - Mr. Stevens said during a discussion of the scientific method - this method with the wild, improbable leap into the arms of a loving god and life in the hereafter?

Mr. Stevens said this with a knowing sneer. There were four in the club including Lee who met every other week. Students were required to choose a club each semester. Lee learned chess in the chess club and fly-tying in Mr. Evans club although it didn't look as if he would ever put those brightly colored flies to use catching trout because he had never been fishing.

Lee decided on the Philosophy Club after reading the essays of R.W. Emerson: "Whoso would be a man would be a non -conformist"; "nothing is at last sacred but the integrity of your own heart".

Lee never told Ruth about the Philosophy Club. He reckoned that she would be sorely hurt if she knew. Toward the end of the term Mr. Stevens seemed to back away from his hard position: Well, he said, there might be merit in Christianity and if you find it so you're welcome to it. But – and this is the important point – don't confuse religion with science.

The Reverend Jackson continues on for several minutes. There are some kind words about Ruth from the congregants. One lady – with tears in her eyes – says that Ruth had helped her after her twelve-year old son had died. I'll never forget her, she says, never.

Lee feels increasingly guilty about not speaking up but he is terrified of speaking in front of an audience. But when the Reverend looks once more at him before ending the eulogy, Lee feels he has no choice.

He stands and turns part way around toward the listeners. The lady who had just spoken pitches a wide smile his way. Lee feels his face color.

I, I want to … say something about my mother. All those eyes are on him. Why hadn't he worked out what to say when he had the chance?

She … She was my mom. I loved her. I don't know what I'll do now.

Unexpectedly – at least to Lee – tears spill from his eyes. He chokes. He tries to say how much she meant to him but no words emerge. In confusion he sits back down.

At the cemetery the hole in the ground is an open wound. Ruth's white casket is held by straps over the hole attended to by the grounds' keepers who slowly lower the casket into the ground.

Chapter 14

The first few days after the burial are hard. Ruth seems to be in every room of 47 Calvin Street. Lee thinks he saw her as he turned the corner from the dining room into the kitchen. She appeared to smile at him. He nearly said "Mom" before checking himself. Reverend Jackson, he thinks, wouldn't get it.

Aunt Betsy tries to get him to focus on the future. Ruth wanted you to go to college. It would have meant a lot to her.

Lee couldn't answer that but he had little ambition. Maybe next year, he says. Betsy leaves college brochures on the end table. Lee desultorily leafs through them. The pictures of nineteen and twenty year olds studying in the library or strolling around the beautiful campus leave him cold.

He had promised Ruth that he would go to college. That did feel like an obligation but one that he could fulfill at any time.

One afternoon Lee sits on Ruth's bed idly looking around. Her clothes are still in the closet – what am I going to do with them? – the sheets on the bed haven't been changed. Her shoes are neatly stacked on shelves. His eye rests on a box that he had never noticed. The box is partly hidden by a pair of shoes.

Lee takes the box down. Except for a gold-colored hasp and lock the box is undistinguished. It is letter-sized and about a foot deep.

It's probably more pictures, thinks Lee. Ruth had a penchant for taking pictures. There were pictures of Lee as a toddler, sitting on Santa's knee or on his first bicycle and, as odd as it seems, a picture of the two-year old sitting naked on the toilet.

Probably more of the same.

Nevertheless, he continues to balance the box on his knee. There is some force, some magnetism which draws him irresistibly to the box. There are keys in the desk but none of them fit.

Lee takes down a screw driver from the box of tools in the pantry. He wedges the driver between the lock and the box lid. When the lock pops it opens with a sigh.

As he had thought, there are pictures inside. He picks up several. A picture of he and Ruth when he must have been three or four; a picture a couple of years later of the two of them standing in front of the rose bush outside.

Lee starts to put the pictures back but then he sees a book hidden under the pictures. It is a book of short stories by someone named H.P.. On the back jacket is a picture of a lean, lanky man with hair combed back over his head standing by a gate. The caption says it is the main gate of Trinity College, Dublin.

Lee opens the book. On the fly leaf is a dedication:

To Sweet Ruth
H.P., Cambridge, August 19, 1939

He turns the pages to the title story "Skerries":

The wind off the Irish Sea rattles the glass of the bungalow. He hears
Mam poking at the fire. A smell of burning peat mixes with the smell
Of cooking coming from the kitchen …

Chapter 15

It is two days later before it strikes Lee: August, 1939 – that's nine months before I was born! He could be my father!

She kept that book all this time in that box. "Sweet Ruth", what else could it mean?

Jesus, who is this guy?

He takes the book with him to Aunt Betsy's. They sit in the living room; Betsy makes tea.

Gosh Lee, I haven't see you for a-while. I hope you've been all right? What's that you've got?

Lee holds the book up.

Oh. Where did you find that?

Do you know about it then?

Yes, I have to say I do.

Will you tell me about it? Look, there's an inscription. Who is this guy?

Aunt Betsy sips the tea. Her hand trembles. Well, maybe you've already guessed?

Lee's face reddens. The only thing I could come up with is ... is that he's my father. Then all that stuff she told me was lies. I looked this guy H.P. up at the library.

What did it say?

That he is a professor in Ireland. That he writes books: Short stories and stuff. Do you know anything about it?

Betsy takes another sip of tea. Yes, I'm afraid I do. All that I know is that Ruth met this man. She told me he was a professor. I guessed that she liked him a lot. But, he went back to Ireland. I believe she never saw or heard from him again.

Do you believe he's my father? It's too much of a coincidence if he isn't.

Yes, I believe he is. But there's no certainty. She hands the book back to Lee.

Lee, what are you thinking?

Lee shrugs. I don't know. I have to think about it.

If I were you I wouldn't do anything hasty.

Like what?

Oh, I don't know. Go and try to find him, I suppose.

Lee sits quietly for several minutes.

Thanks Aunt Betsy. They rise; Lee kisses her cheek.

Lee, don't be hard on her. She was young and impressionable. I told her that she should get in touch with him but she wouldn't.

Lee, you know how much she loved you. She wanted you to have a good life: Go to college, find a nice girl and get married. She told me so many times.

Do you think he's my father?

I don't know. I just don't know.

Chapter 16

Ruth's brother Ralph is a twenty-year veteran of the Air Force. Lee had met him several times over the years whenever Ralph was on leave. After Ruth's burial he had walked with Lee back to Calvin Street.

You know buddy, you're welcome to come out to California and stay with us. In case you want to get away, you know. We've got plenty of room. The town is small – not like what you're used to - but we're in a pretty nice spot. Anyway, think about it.

Lee did think about it. Early in the spring he called Ralph and asked if his offer was still open.

You bet it is. Get your bag packed and git on out here.

On April 15, 1958 Lee boards a Greyhound Scenic Cruiser at South Station for Los Angeles. His luggage consists of a single duffel bag containing a second pair of shoes, spare levis, two shirts and several changes of Jockey underwear. In the pocket of his Rindge and Latin baseball jacket is a U.S. map and a guide to California. Ruth's real estate partner arranged for a one-year lease of 47 Calvin Street to a young couple with a small child. The rent will be deposited monthly in a trust account. Lee stores Ruth's furniture at a moving company in Somerville.

He has dinner with Aunt Betsy the night before leaving. She says she thinks the move is a good idea. It will give you a new start, she says. But – and she hesitates – Ralph is great but he can be a little, well, undependable. Just keep that in mind. Don't breathe a word of that to anybody. I wouldn't want it to get around that I feel that way about my own nephew.

Maybe it is the promise of a new beginning or maybe enough time has gone by that the pain of Ruth's death has lessened sufficiently but Lee sleeps well the night before leaving. In the morning he catches a Red Line train to South Station.

Chapter 17

The bus ride will take three days including several stops at Greyhound stations along the way. The route across the plains is boring but Lee reads from "My Antonia" a book that he had found on Ruth's desk. The story seems pertinent especially the part about the train ride across the country.

On the first night out a Mexican woman gets on the bus in Cleveland. She sits in the back row next to Lee. My name is Maria de Jesus, she says, as the bus rolls through a spring rainstorm. Pleased to meet you. What is your name?

Her English is very good. She says she has a job in Chicago as a nanny to a wealthy family who wants their two kids to speak Spanish.

Lee asks her where she is from.

Zihautenejo. My family has a small cantina in the Square. Do you know what a cantina is?

Lee admits that he doesn't know.

A little like your tavern but not as dark.

She tells him that she has two children that she has not seen in two years. They're with my husband in Zihua, she says. We hope they can come to Chicago if my job is good. And where are you going?

California, Lee says. I'm visiting my uncle.

For some reason, maybe it is the round, open nature of Maria's face or her alert, dark eyes but Lee feels as if he can talk to her.

My mom died recently. I promised her I would go to college but I'm going to take off for a year. My uncle invited me to come to visit him in California.

The rain streaks the windows of the bus; lightning flashes in the distance. It is late.

Lee falls asleep. He wakes an hour later to find Maria asleep her head resting on his shoulder, her knee touching his knee. This conjunction is a cause for confusion. He must not move. Maria's dark hair drops across Lee's bare arm. He fights against the impulse but lets his right hand slowly descend. It feels as if hours pass during its slow descent. Lightly, ever so lightly, he lets one finger just graze her bare knee. He is prepared to retract his hand instantly at the slightest sign; but there is none. Gently and slowly his hand lights on her knee. Lee's breathing is now alarmingly loud. He thinks he should stop before disaster strikes – but he doesn't.

Maria moves then stretches. She smiles at Lee. I'm sorry, she says. I hope I didn't bother you?

Lee is happy that the bus is dark. He can feel the redness in his face. No, no. I'm ok.

Good. I fell asleep. I had the strangest dream. I was back in Mexico with my husband. It was very nice.

The bus continues on; the rain and lightning have abated. Just as the sun rises they are in the outskirts of Chicago.

It was nice to meet you says Maria. She reaches across the seat and gives Lee a kiss. That's for being such a gentleman. Adios.

Lee does not know what to think. Did she know that he touched her? Did she mind? A faint, musky smell is attached to his jacket just where her head had rested.

Lee gets breakfast in the Greyhound Terminal. There is a new driver. The bus rolls on.

Chapter 18

It is late in the afternoon when the bus reaches Los Angeles. The air outside is hot; a thermometer on the outside of a building shows 90 degrees. The air is smoggy. Lee's eyes water. The local bus to Lompoc is scheduled to leave in fifteen minutes.

One hour and thirty minutes says the driver in response to Lee's question. We'll be there in one hour and thirty minutes. You Air Force?

No, I'm visiting my uncle.

The trip north is smooth. The Pacific Ocean is on the left. The bus passes through Santa Barbara and within a half-hour stops in front of the post office in Lompoc.

Lee asks a policeman walking along where to find his uncle's address: It is in the next block.

Well, hello Lee. Looks like you made it buddy.

Chapter 19

It is in Bio 101 that Lee meets Jill. The seat beside Lee is empty. Jill slides in sideways. Lee lifts his notebook and pencil to let her get past.

Lee's sojourn with his uncle worked out well. He applied to UC Berkeley using his uncle's address. His SAT scores weren't great but they were good enough to get him admitted.

Hi, Jill says. Excuse me.

Lee smiles. He thinks there is something familiar about her but he can't quite put his finger on it.

Did I miss anything, says Jill, putting her notebook on the folding table.

Not really. He's just been shuffling some papers around.

Good afternoon ladies and gentlemen. The professor wears a jacket with alternating blue-and-white stripes and something that Lee has not seen before: A bow tie. This is Bio 101. We are going to take a little tour through the biological world including such exciting side trips as to why organisms require oxygen and how sexual reproduction works. Ok? Good. Let's get down to business.

The lecture lasts for fifty minutes. Lee has filled up several pages with notes. There is a scramble as students leave the hall on their way to the next class.

Wow, says Jill. That was a lot.

Lee agrees. Say, he says, my name is Lee.

Jill. Nice to meet you. Are you on to another class? My next class isn't until three.

Oh, me too. Well, two actually. You interested in a coffee or something?

Sure. You want to go to the Northside? I know a café there.

Sure.

They walk together through the North Gate onto Euclid Avenue.

Here it is. It's in the back of this little plaza or I don't know what to call it.

There's a small movie theatre next to the café which is under an overhang shielding the café, theatre and a small business.

The café is not crowded – mostly students and the odd professor or two (at least that's Lee's best guess).

Is this ok? says Jill.

Yea. Sure.

Lee sits in a chair opposite Jill. They put their notebooks on the table. Lee looks at the menu.

You going to get something to eat?

Yah. Maybe. I'm a little hungry. What about you?

Umm. Yes, I believe I am. Hungry, that is. See anything you like?

On the menu, you mean? The blush appears like clockwork.

Jill laughs. Good one.

The waiter appears pencil in hand. Are you ready to order?

I am, says Jill. I'll have turkey on whole wheat, mayo, lettuce, tomato. And an iced tea

Yes ma'm. And you sir?

Lee is put off by the "sir". Grilled cheese and I'll have an iced tea too.

The waiter scoops up the menus and heads toward the kitchen.

Jill smiles. Are you a freshman?

Lee nods affirmatively. Yah, this is my first year. How about you?

I'm a sophomore. Thirty-six credits so far. I went to summer school last summer. That's how I got the six credits. I wouldn't do it again but I thought I could graduate quicker.

Why wasn't it a good idea?

Well, it turns out I need my summer. When this semester started it felt like I hadn't been away at all.

Lee nods. I took last year off after high school.

Did you do anything special?

Not really. My uncle got me a job driving taxi. It was ok. Not a lot of money but you meet people.

I bet.

Some of them are nice but then there's the jerk who wants to give you a hard time.

So, you're from California?

Well, yes and no. My uncle lives in Lompoc. I stayed with him last year.

But, before that?

Boston. Actually Cambridge.

Wow. I've never been back East.

The waiter arrives with lunch. The iced tea is cold but it needs a little sugar.

How's your sandwich?

Umm. Good. And yours?

Good too, says Jill. I like this place. Sometimes if I don't feel like cooking I come here for dinner.

Where do you live? Lee feels increasingly comfortable. He thinks Jill is easy to be with.

Not far from here. On Euclid. What about you?

I'm staying in a dorm. It's like a zillion roommates.

I stayed in a dorm freshman year but I can't say I liked it. Too much noise. Somebody's music was always on.

True. Very true, says Lee. As he says it he recognizes his words to be Ruth's words.

What about your family? Apart from your uncle.

Lee's head sinks toward the table.

Oh, did I say something I shouldn't have?

Lee looks up. There are tears in his eyes.

Oh my.

You didn't ask anything that you shouldn't have. It's just – I don't know why because it's been a year now but my mother – well, she died.

Lee can't keep the tears from flowing. It's all he can do to keep from sobbing.

Jill reaches across the table. Her hand settles on top of Lee's hand.

I'm so sorry. That must be hard.

Lee shakes his head from side-to-side. I don't know: I think I should be through it. I thought I was but ...

I don't know how I would do if it happened to me. I can imagine how tough it is.

Yah. It was so quick. One minute she's alive and the next she's not. She got hit by a car. The bastard didn't even stop.

Jill takes a handkerchief from her purse. Lee wipes his eyes. The handkerchief smells good. A flowery kind of smell. Jill's hand still covers his.

The clock on the wall shows 1:45. I'd better get going, says Lee.

I'll walk you as far as Tolman, says Jill.

I'd like that.

They pay their bills.

Jill?

Yes?

Can I see you again? Outside Bio I mean?

What are you doing tonight? I could make spaghetti.

Chapter 20

Well, it went from there. Looking back now Lee can see clearly what it was. He certainly couldn't see it then. The only thing he could see then was Jill. She filled every minute.

For one thing it was the way she had of making him feel as if he was her exact center. And how long did it take? Hours, minutes even. Maybe it was on the walk across Hearst Avenue. Lee started across just as the traffic light was changing to green. Jill grabbed his hand pulling him back just as the first car barreled by.

Whoa, said Lee. Sorry. That was close.

Jill continued to hold his hand. They stopped in front of Tolman. So tonight? About 6:30? I'm at 1865 Euclid Avenue. Just ring the buzzer.

Lee went to his two o'clock class but nothing about the lecture registered. He went back to his dorm room and lay on the bed.

Jesus, I'm losing it. We don't even know each other. It's like I'm putting together a fifty-year plan. Nuts.

Nuts, maybe, but Lee saw Jill as part of every plan. Who knows, he thinks. Crazier things have happened.

With that, he falls asleep.

Chapter 21

It is a fine August day: Not too hot, not too humid. Lee has breakfast at the S&S Deli in Inman Square.

Good morning Lee. You look like your day is going good.

Marilyn the waitress stands in front of Lee holding her order pad. Lee thinks she must be in her thirty's, maybe early forty's. Still trim with an over-the-top smile.

Such an eye, such an eye. Yes, in fact, I'm taking the girls on a little trip.

Oh, where to?

New Hampshire. Keene. Well, we're going to stay in Keene but we'll be taking in the Cheshire County Fair.

Oh, neat. So you're an expert on animals?

Ha! Just the two-legged kind.

How long will you be gone? Say, that Cathy is growing up fast.

Isn't she. We'll drive up today, spend tomorrow at the fair and come back on Sunday. I'm looking forward to it.

My boss is giving me that "don't loiter" look. Is it the usual?

You know me: If it ain't broke don't fix it.

Marilyn takes the order to the kitchen. Lee opens the newspaper

Marilyn brings a plate of hash-browns and one egg over-easy. She refills his cup with coffee from a pyrex pot.

Ah, that's the ticket. I could eat shoe leather I'm so hungry.

Ugg. Don't talk like that.

Chapter 22

Lee picks up the divorce papers from the clerk, thanks his lawyer and walks through the courthouse.

Ok, it's finis. Over.

The morning was an ordeal. Lee, Jill and their lawyers sat at a small table in the rotunda of the courthouse negotiating the agreement. Lee wanted joint custody of Cathy and Sarah; Jill wanted more money. It felt unseemly to bargain over their lives in this way but there wasn't an alternative.

Lee walks up Broadway toward Inman Square. As he waits at the light Jill stops alongside in the new VW (it was part of the settlement). Come on, she says: Let me give you a lift. Lee gets in but sits stiffly in the seat.

That was rough, says Jill.

Yah, it was.

At the light on Windsor Street Lee looks over at Jill. He thinks she looks just like she did in Berkeley.

Suddenly, Jill turns to him. She smiles. A smile that he has seen many times.

Jill turns back as the light changes.

They are silent the rest of the way to Calvin Street. See ya, he says.

Jill nods.

Jill takes title to the house on Fayerweather Street; Lee is able to keep 47 Calvin Street. The tenants had moved out of Calvin Street two months earlier. For now the girls will stay where they are with Jill. Lee buys bunk beds from an upscale furniture shop in Harvard Square. Cathy and Sarah help choose the curtains and the rug. Lee thinks they will be with him six months and with Jill six months.

But, in the end, the girls stay with Lee only on weekends. Jill argues that it is too hard on them to live in two places. Lee, she says, they need a home. Ok, Lee says, why can't it be my home? In the end Lee couldn't abide a tug-of-war over the children.

Chapter 23

Jaysus, how it goes by. Like a blink o' the eye, really. Can it be that I'm going on sixty-eight? Cormack, another Guiness if you please. That's my man.

The barman gives the pint of Guiness a final touch up.

Professor, tell me what's happened to that pal of yours. What is his name? David? The one who claimed to know why these waves roll up through the Guiness.

Ah yes, David. Well, he died some months ago. Some kind of cancer got him. He was in St. James for weeks. He kind of whittled away to nothing. In the end it was all drugs to stop the pain.

He wasn't that old, now was he?

No, no. Young chap. Close to fifty. Middle fifty. I never knew exactly. Good man. Tough way to go.

The barman watches H.P.. And you Professor. Are you tip-top? I'm asking because you look like you might be a little knackered.

Do I now? Well, I am a bit. Nothing to complain about.

Cormack carries a tray of glasses down to the end of the bar. A waitress is there with an order for drinks. She nods toward H.P..

Isn't that the Professor? He hasn't been in in months.

Yep, that's him.

He doesn't look well.

That's what I was thinking. He says he's tip-top. He's still got an eye for the ladies.

H.P. has turned to a pair of young woman on his left. The near one with the long, red hair lifts a hand sweeping her hair back revealing a small, gold bell clamped to her ear.

Now, my god, who was that? … That gold bell? …

Ah now, grand, grand it is to be alive with the likes of that, says H.P..

So, you've still got an eye for the ladies Professor?

Ah God, if I lose that just pitch me overboard.

Are you still teaching then?

No, my teaching days are done. Pensioned, I am.

Now, how is that? I'm looking forward to it meself.

Are ya now. How can that be. You're not more than forty, surely.

Ah well, you're still with the blarney. Professor. I swear you've been coming in here since you were – I'm guessing now – thirty-five? And now: Seventy maybe? So what would that make me?

Cormack leans forward on the counter. Now Professor we've known each other for a power of years but I still don't know some particulars. Do you have a wife? If I'm not too brash in asking?

That you are: Brash. But I'm too gone to worry about it. No, I never married.

Children then? Surely you could still have children?

Ah no, not that I'm aware of. Of course there could be the odd accident or two but I've not been called on it. As I think on it it's too bad there haven't been any "accidents". At this stage I wouldn't mind someone that could look after me.

Cormack smiles. Now that would be something. You being led about by a pretty lass who calls you Da.

H.P. doesn't respond but the idea is charming.

Ah me. Too late, too late, I'm afraid. Time will strangle you in the end. Don't forget it.

Cormack moves toward another customer.

Cormack, one instant. Listen, send those two ladies a drink and my love, will ya then?

Cormack pours two Shanties which the waitress delivers. She points to H.P. who lifts his pint in salute. They smile but turn away.

Ah well that's it, it's all over. I'll be going. Be a good man now Cormack and call us a taxi.

Do ye need some help Professor?

Best to ye Cormack. You're a good lad.

Cormack polishes the bar as he watches H.P. shuffle toward the door.

He's looking frail, says the waitress.

Ay, that he is, that he is.

Chapter 24

The taxi pulls to the front door of H.P.'s flat in Churchtown. With difficulty he exits the car, fumbles for his keys and opens the door to number 7, Henley Court. After turning on the lights, he puts his coat on the rack and sits in the big chair by the window. He turns on the telly, flipping through the channels. He pauses briefly to look at a football match. With a sigh he turns the set off.

No, some music. A little Maria. He puts a disc on the player and turns it on. The strong, round voice of Maria Callas singing "Caro Nome" fills the room. H.P. settles into the chair propping his feet up on the ottoman.

It's come to this, he thinks. An old man sitting alone at home licking his wounds. When did it all go by?

He thinks back to his first book "Skerries". Everything seemed possible. There was that year in Cambridge. When was that? Nineteen ... Nineteen thirty-nine. Oh yes. Those jolly, young females. My little place on Brattle Street. Those readings. Today I'd be a rock star.

And who was that one? What was her name?

What did the pill pusher say? Too much ...cholesterol. And the real deal breaker: Too much alcohol. What am I supposed to do? Sit in a corner ... meditating? It's for your own good, he says. What kind of life would it be if I stopped eating eggs and bacon and went dry. The lord save us.

Well, so what if I'm checked out sooner. No one will care. My poor old Mam's gone. God, when was that? ... nineteen ... sixty? Yes, surely. All alone too. Beastly cold winter. January, wasn't it. She was out of turf.

H.P. had caught the 33a bus in Swords for a long, postponed visit with Clara. The bus driver was an old friend – classmate, really – Liam Costello.

71

Dia duit, professor. Conas ata tu?

Hello right back at you Liam. Still plugging away I see.

Aye, but more like puddling away. Going to see your auld Mam, are ye?

Aye, that I am. Will you let me off in front?

Surely.

There are only two other passengers. Neither of them is known to H.P.. The bus travels under the arcade and onto Rush Road. The Irish Sea is visible through the row of cottages facing the road. Another mile or so and Liam pulls over in front of 1 Rush Road.

And good morning to ye, Professor.

And the same to you, Liam.

The bus continues along the long, sloping road into Skerries. A wind blows off the water carrying with it a dull mist. H.P. pulls his anorak tighter around his neck.

Clara's cottage is a two story, gray shingled house bordering on the sea which is separated from the cottage by the strand.

H.P. pushes the buzzer. He hadn't told Clara that he was coming. His last visit was over a month before.

He pushes the buzzer again. There is no answer. He listens but hears nothing.

Maybe she's out back. He walks carefully through the flower beds to the side of the house. He can see nothing through the windows. The back door is unlocked.

Odd, he thinks. She never leaves the door unlocked.

The door opens into the kitchen, a small functional arrangement of cabinets and counters. What seems to be breakfast dishes in the sink are the only disorderly element. Off the kitchen is a parlor which Clara uses as a sitting room. There is a small sofa along one wall near the fireplace and a small rocker facing the sofa. There is a view through the window down to the sea. A smell of burnt turf comes from the fireplace but the room is cold. H.P. picks up a claw tool from a stand by the fireplace and pokes at the residue of what had been, presumably, Clara's morning fire.

Just as he touches the dead coals a small mouse springs up from under the coals: Explodes up is more accurate. H.P. leaps up (a surprising return of vigor) coming down with his right foot directly on top of the mouse who retaliates by squirting a tiny jet of red blood at H.P..

Reflexively, H.P. crosses himself although he hasn't been inside a church for a half-century. He steps away avoiding looking at the carnage while his heart races as if recovering from a marathon.

My god, the poor creature.

In his hurry to be rid of the evidence, H.P. sweeps up the body with the fireplace shovel into the accompanying scoop. He holds it high while carrying it to the back door. He uses an old, hurling move to toss the mouse into the weeds but the mouse slides off the scoop and lands once again at his feet.

Jaysus. It wants to haunt me.

Finally, after retrieving the shovel from the parlor and reseating the mouse on the scoop, he carries the body to the back fence dropping it into the sand. He piles sand over the tiny body.

Shaken, H.P. re-enters the parlor and sits on the sofa. His heart has stopped racing but his hands still shake. My god, he thinks, it was just a mouse keeping warm in the grate. Poor little bastard.

But Ma?

H.P. looks around the room. As tidy as always.

With a rising sense of foreboding he climbs the stairs to the second floor. As a boy H.P. would slowly climb those stairs on his way to bed. Clara would sit by the fire drinking Jameson's. H.P.'s greatest wish was for her to tuck him into bed but she never did. Sometimes he would get up and sit on the stairs in his pajamas until she came up to her bedroom.

The stairs are steep and curve back on themselves as they rise.

At the top of the stairs a small hallway leads between the two bedrooms and the loo. His old bedroom is on the left. The door is open but H.P. continues down the hall to Clara's room.

Mam? It's me.

The door there is open. Just inside he sees Clara lying face down on the floor.

Oh my God!

He hurries to her; he touches her face: It is cold, very cold. He tugs at her trying to turn her over. He feels for her pulse: There is none.

Oh my God! Mam! Mam!

Chapter 25

It's July, 1978. Lee is thirty-eight. The telephone rings. It is Jill. She says that she is moving to Oregon. Frank, the guy that they knew as a couple has moved to Oregon. She wants to go there. She says she is going to take the girls.

Lee can hardly speak. He pulls the telephone back and stares at it. What? He says. You're going to do what?

She calmly repeats herself. She says they are leaving in a week. She says that he can take the girls for a couple of days before then.

Now, just a minute. Hold on. You know the divorce settlement. You can't just take them like that. No, no, no.

Well, say what you will we are going. If you want to take them, Wednesday and Thursday would be best. Let me know.

She hangs up. Lee stands there for several minutes dumbfounded before re-cradling the telephone.

Jesus-H-Christ. She can't do that. He searches through the desk for the divorce papers. They do say "joint custody" but what in the hell does that mean? His lawyer's number is written in ink on the copy of the settlement. He dials the number. It's been disconnected.

He paces the room. He feels like getting in the car and going directly to Fayerweather Street. Confront her, that's what. She can't do this to me. Or to those girls. A picture of Cathy and Sarah is in a frame on his desk. They stand together, Sarah maybe an inch shorter than Cathy. They hold hands.

Lee grabs the car keys from the desk. The drive to Fayerweather Street takes no more than ten minutes. As the car stops he bolts from the car and bounds up the porch steps. He rings the buzzer and waits. He rings again.

There is no sound from inside. He knocks on the door. He looks around. Sarah's rag doll – what does she call it? - Skylar – is lying on the porch floor. He picks it up and lays it gently on the rocker. He opens the mailbox sorting through the letters and brochures. One of the letters is from Frank. It's postmarked from Portland, Oregon. Lee returns to the car and retrieves the small spiral notebook which he uses to record pertinent data about the car. He copies Frank's address from the letter into the notebook.

He considers writing a caustic message to Jill on the envelope but thinks better of it. He returns the mail to the mailbox and tries the buzzer again. No answer.

Back home Lee paces from the front room to the kitchen and back. Jesus Christ. She can't. It's bad. Very bad.

He goes into the girl's room. Their bunk beds are tidy. Sarah has an arm full of plush toys. He picks up Sarah's new favorite book. He thumbs through the pages. He read it aloud to her last week on their sleepover. Cathy pretended she was too old for the story but she seemed to be listening just the same.

Lee has a well-inflected reading voice with a pleasant, dynamic range. The story is about a young boy in winter whose grandmother urges him to take care of his mittens because it's so cold outside. But, in his exuberance, he loses a mitten. The mitten is found by wild animals who take shelter inside the mitten. Miraculously the mitten expands sufficiently to accommodate a bear, a weasel, a coyote and a mink. When a mouse squeezes in the capacity of the mitten is overwhelmed and the mitten pops like a balloon. Sarah giggled at this point.

Lee puts the book down and curls up on the bed. He pulls his knees up. Without intending to he begins to cry. He is astonished. He has never cried as an adult. Not even when Ruth died. It is a source of pride to him not to give way to his emotions. But here he is fully engulfed. He feels something loosen inside like a cliff giving way after a deluge of rain. A feeling of relief replaces the anger. He falls asleep on Sarah's bed surrounded by the plush toys.

Chapter 26

Lee and Jill are on vacation. They have been married for nearly two years. The real estate business prospers. Jill has a job as a social worker for the city of Cambridge. A friend recommends a place on the west coast of Mexico. Another friend who speaks Spanish makes reservations for them at a small hotel in town.

They settle into a routine: Morning coffee at the hotel, a stop at a bakery for bread and cheese. On the way to the beach they pass chickens rooting in yards, abandoned tires and young, raggedy children. They stay at the beach until mid-afternoon when they then retrace their steps to the hotel.

One evening they sit on the porch of a house and eat posole cooked, they are told, with lye.

Before dinner they sit at a table in one of the bars facing the harbor. The refreshing sea breeze matches the margaritas.

Some days they have coffee in an open-air café in a small plaza. Lee's spoon reflects the spinning of the overhead fan. He points it out to Jill but she is not impressed.

For lunch they stop at a small cafeteria with ten tables. They talk with the owner and her husband who is a retired pilot with Mexicana.

They stay two weeks acquiring deep tans and lighter wallets. Lee thinks it was the high point of their relationship except, of course, for the girls.

They fly back to Boston with a stopover in L.A.. At the airport a couple with a young daughter tell Lee that they are out of money having only the tickets to L.A. Lee normally refuses requests for money but something about the couple with the little girl persuades him to give them something. They promise to pay him back as soon as they are home.

You didn't have to do that, says Jill. You know you won't get it back? I don't know. It's ok.

They had been home for two weeks when a letter arrives with a check and expressions of gratitude. But will it cash? Says Jill.

My god, says Lee. It'll cash.

Chapter 27

Lee catches a bus from the airport to City Centre. A taxi brings him to the Shelbourne Hotel on Stephen's Green.

Ah sir, good morning to you. Checking in?

Yes, thanks. I have reservations: Lee Blake?

Ah yes, staying for two nights then?

Yes, but perhaps longer. Will that be a problem?

No sir, it shouldn't be but I urge you to let us know as soon as possible.

A bellman loads Lee's suitcase onto a cart and leads him to the elevators. The room is on the fourth floor; the windows look out on the Green. After unpacking and hanging up his clothes Lee stretches out on the bed. Despite being in a strange city, in a strange country, he thinks back to Cambridge, to Jill and the girls. A happy scene unfolds: It is Christmas. Cathy and Sarah are unwrapping presents; wrapping paper is scattered everywhere. The tree lights are on helping to dispel a little of an otherwise gloomy day. Jill sits in the big chair still wearing her pajamas. She smiles at Lee.

The sound of a lorry outside raises Lee from his reverie. It feels as if there is a large weight laid across his chest. Tears start.

He sits down at the desk. There is writing paper and a pen.

"For Jill" he writes:

I wake at five to you lying in the soft light
and I kneeling near with my mouth close and tongue
sliding along your softness breathing the Jillian smell.
I sense you in the softness building time after time
past counting. As the light grows I twist and turn

in the narrow bed at five with you and the rain.

Jesus, he thinks, get over it. Get up. Get going.

He showers and changes clothes. He takes the elevator down leaving the room key with the clerk.

I'm wanting to find Trinity College. Can you point me in the right direction?

The clerk hands Lee a map and traces out the route.

Will it rain? Says Lee.

Ah no, more likely a spot of drizzle. But here's an umbrella just in case the gods aren't with us, yet again.

Outside there is indeed a drizzle punctuated by the sun breaking through. The effect is dazzling.

Lee decides to walk through the park. Near one corner he sees Henry Moore's memorial to Yeats. It looks like a green-shaded blade of grass. A couple sit together on a bench by the memorial oblivious to the leaking sky.

Lee crosses the park to the Grafton Street entrance.

Grafton Street is lined with shops and shoppers: Bewley's has a line in from the street. A promising smell of coffee wafts out. Lee gets in line cafeteria-style choosing a roll and coffee. He pays with the Irish pounds he purchased at the airport. The ten-pound note is stationary-size.

He sits at a table. To his right two young women are talking. Lee hears one of them say that they work at a shop. Their accent is charming.

And did you know that he ... Well, I don't abide slagging but in this case we were packed-out and no mind but the bloke pushed right in.

Did he now? And then what?

The conversation goes on to detail how her revenge was exacted. The young woman across the table, the one with hair as red as Lee has ever seen, looks his way and smiles.

Lee is intimidated. He briskly manages a smile in reply. He opens the copy of the Irish Times he has brought from the hotel. He studies the print. He hears the red-haired one speak to her colleague: Jaysus, she says, is there something the matter with me?

They get up and leave.

At College Green Lee turns in at the gate to Trinity College. He isn't sure what he will do there but it is the only solid thing that he knows about H.P.. Except, that the publisher of "Skerries" is Wolf Press which is in Dublin. This gives him two places to start. He calculates that if H.P. had been about thirty years old in 1939 he would now be near seventy. If he's still alive.

Lee asks the porter at the gate for directions to the School of English. Yes sir, right you are. Now you just follow your nose straight away and you'll be finding yourself in front of what you want.

Lee points ahead.

Ay, that's right.

Lee follows his nose past Examination Hall on his right and the Buttery on his left. At the School of English he stops the first person he sees.

Can I be of help, asks the trim young fellow just emerging from the building.

Yes, thanks. I'm looking for a fellow named H.P.. I think he's on the faculty. I know he wrote a book of short stories called "Skerries" but, unfortunately, I don't know much more than that.

Hmm, H.P. you say. Well, I'm pretty new here but I'm sure there's no one like that on the current faculty. Perhaps you should go in to the office. There's a charming secretary inside; she might help.

Lee nods and enters the building. The department office is just down the hall. There is a musty smell in the corridor. Lee opens the door to the office. A dark-haired, young woman with startlingly blue eyes is standing at a desk examining some papers. Lee waits until she looks up.

Yes, can I help you?

I hope so. My name is Lee Blake. I'm looking for someone who, I believe, is on the faculty here or was on the faculty. His name is H.P.. He wrote a book called "Skerries". Do you know such a person?

Em, first off I'm the secretary of the school. Rose Dow. A wonderful smile blossoms on Rose's face.

Nice to meet you, says Lee.

Well, I can say that there is no one on the faculty now called H.P.. But, let me check. I've only been here meself for a year. Rose pulls out a folder from a file cabinet. This should have everyone who has been on the faculty since 1960.

Rose cycles through the pages her finger sliding purposely down the page.

Oh, here he is. Let's see, yes, he's on pension. Em, pensioned in 1970.

That's great. Can you tell me where to find him?

Rose studies the page. Oh, I'm sorry. It says I'm not allowed to give out his address.

Can you at least say if he's still in Ireland? It's very important that I get in touch with him.

Well, yes, according to this he's still here. Rose closes the book.

Well, you've been very helpful. Thank you. Listen, I'm staying at the Shelbourne hotel. Lee Blake. If there's any chance that you can let me have his address – I mean, without violating any rules – will you consider giving me a call? I'm desperate to get in touch with him.

Are you here for long?

Well, I'm staying until I finish my business. I only arrived yesterday. From Boston.

Boston. I visited there two years ago. We had a fine time.

There is a minute of silence. Lee shifts from one foot to the other. Rose continues to look up at him.

Well, I'd better go. Thanks so much for your time.

Outside Lee walks a few steps, then stops. Jesus, he thinks, what a dim wit. That secretary – Rose. Go on. It's now or never.

Lee walks back up the stops. Rose is typing. She looks up. That smile reforms.

Oh, did you forget something???

No. I mean, yes. Would you be willing, that is, if you're not busy, would you be willing to have lunch with me?

Oh, what a grand offer but I'm already booked.

Lee picks up his nerve. Ah, too bad. Maybe another time?

I'd like that.

Should I give you a call?

Ah, yes. Here's my tele number.

Lee folds the paper. Great. I'll call.

They shake hands.

Chapter 28

Back outside Lee turns off Grafton Street into Duke Street. According to the Blue Guide, the Bailey is a pub favored by Dublin's literary types. He requests a Guiness from the barman who introduces himself as Aedan Murphy.

From the States are ye then?

Yes, the Boston area. This is my first Guiness.

Did you hear that lads? This is his first Guiness.

A sort of roar goes up among the assembled practioners. Here's to the first jar, says a rather puckish looking fellow whom Lee judges to be somewhere in his seventies.

It takes a few sips of the Guiness before Lee decides that he likes it.

As he finishes the first pint Aedan re-appears. Another jar is it?

For sure. This is good stuff.

Did you hear that lads? The Yank says it's good stuff.

Hear, hear.

So where did you say you come from in the States?

Boston. Well, Cambridge really.

And what brings you across the water? Touring?

A bit but I've more than one mission.

Is it a secret mission then?

Lee laughs. I'm sent here by the C.I.A. to keep an eye on Irish troublemakers.

And you've got your eye on me?

No, no. You look as innocent as the day. To tell the truth I'm searching for my Dad.

Really. How did you lose him then?

I thought I was an orphan until I found out my Dad is alive. I think he might be here: In Dublin. The records at the orphanage were burned up in a fire so I don't know his name. The only thing I know is his initials: H.P.. That's because the initials were on a card from Trinity College with a picture that I was given at the orphanage. The card was with me when I was brought to the orphanage.

How old were ye?

Five.

You don't say. Well, pity us this day and night. What did you say your name is?

Lee, Lee Blake.

Well, Lee Blake, welcome to Ireland. Now that you've been baptized with the black stuff you'll be not wanting to go back.

You could be right Aedan. Anyway it's nice to make your acquaintance. Let me ask you: If you were going to take a young lady out for lunch on Friday, where would you go?

Eh, a young lady? Jaysus you blokes work fast. Think you can swoop in here and snatch up all of our fair lassies, do ye? Well, if you want to be right smart the Shelbourne Hotel can't be beat. If you're looking for something more middle-of-the-road the lunch here at the Bailey can't be beat.

Um, thanks. Actually, I'm staying at the Shelbourne.

There you are!

Look, I'm finishing here in a couple of minutes, says Aedan. What do ye say to a pint?

They walk to the Stag's Head in Dame Court.

The barman greets Aedan like a long-lost friend. My god man, he says, why I haven't set eyes on you for... what ...twenty-four hours? It's uncivilized making someone wait so long. Now, who's your friend here?

Aedan introduces Lee as a long-lost relative from the States. And what are you doing in this God-forsaken country? By Jaysus, we haven't got anything here that you don't have there. Except the unemployment.

Except the pints. Now, will you do your job or there'll be a swift kick in the backside? You'd have us die of thirst. Now Lee, this here barman-imposter is Brendan Kavanaugh. Not, mind you, the great Kavanaugh, Patrick that is. Not even close.

Now Brendan, the great unraveller, we've got a bit of a puzzle for ye.

Lee here thinks his Da is in Dublin. But – and this is the part where he needs your genius – he doesn't know his name!

Brendan stops sliding a white cloth along the bar. He looks at Lee with a mixture of astonishment and disbelief. Now, I'd sure like to know how that's possible. Look, I'd like to forget my Da's name and himself but it's seared into me memory.

Brendan slides two pints of Guinness across the bar.

Well, okay it's simple. I am an orphan. I never knew either of my parents. They told me that my mother brought me to the orphanage. They said she gave me her last name.

Then why do you think your Da's here? In Dublin?

Lee takes a generous sip from the pint. Well, there is one thing I have – only one – a little picture on a card from Trinity College with the initials H.P..

And why do you think this H.P. might be your father?

My mom kept that card locked in a box of her things.

Tell him about the fire, says Gerard.

There was a fire at the orphanage which burned up all of the records.

Well, Be-Jesus that's a power of problems.

All three are quiet for a minute. Lee looks around the room. Every stool and table is occupied. Blue smoke hangs in the air. A young black-haired woman two stools down pushes an unruly strand of hair behind her ear. She sends a brilliant smile down the bar at Lee. You're from America then?. What part would that be?

She introduces herself as Liz and her friend as Sinead. Aedan suggests that they all move to a table which has just become free.

Now then, says Liz, let's have proper introductions. I'm Liz O'Connor and this is my chum Sinead O'Malley. And who are you?

Liz's eyes are green under very dark eyebrows.

And what brings you to this besieged island, says Sinead. Slumming are ye? Sinead is fine-looking as well, very dark and lanky.

Well, I've heard good things about Ireland so I wanted to see for myself.

Lovely, tell us what they are. We've lived here all our lives but we must have missed them.

Lee says he has heard how beautiful the country-side is and adds that he hadn't reckoned on how beautiful the women are. Liz and Sinead snicker.

You must have the gene, says Sinead. You'll be right at home here.

Now, how do you know, says Aedan, that the lad is referring to you two?

Well, we don't. But, mind you, he might've been. Let's ask himself.

Lee puts his hands in front palms out. No, no, please. I plead the fifth – if you know what I mean.

Now what are you girls up to? says Aedan. Are you all taken for tonight or would you like some choice company?

It looks like we have it already, says Liz. What do you have in mind? No, I take that back: Better we don't know.

Well, my American friend and me are loose. We might have another pint or two and then seek guidance on dinner. Would that fit in with you?

We'll see, says Liz, we'll see.

Well it does fit in but they have three more pints by which time Lee has difficulty standing.

I think I'd better go home, says Lee.

Home, is it? You've got a big puddle to get across if that's what you're doing.

Liz writes her telephone number on a napkin. Here, now. Take your friend home and give us a call.

And they do call. On the following Friday they perform a strenuous pub crawl starting at Mulligans on Tara Street. If possible, Liz and Sinead seem even more attractive.

Aedan tells a story. He met Rod a month ago when Aedan answered his advert for a flat-mate. According to Aedan, Rod is a Mathematician at T.C.D..

He studies something called – if you can believe it - foliations, for God sake. And he looks the part: Slight of build, narrow shoulders, not much of a one for talk. Mostly, he sits by the fire with a paper and pencil writing down his equations.

Anyway, it was about the second day after I moved in. We were in the kitchen. Rod was trying to seat the lid on the teakettle. Well, the kettle was cheap and not well made so it was out-of-round and wouldn't seat properly. Suddenly Rod flings the lid on the floor and commences jumping up and down on top of it. You have to picture it: Rod jumping straight up and down, arms flying, eyes blazing. He jumps two or three times and then calmly picks up the lid and – a miracle – seats it on the kettle and the kettle on the fire.

Aedan tells this little story with such animation that everyone laughs even those at the next table.

After dinner at a Greek place along the canal Liz decides that it has been a grand evening but that they had better be getting on. Lee is back at the hotel and asleep by 11:30..

And so things move swiftly. A typical day starts at seven or eight; breakfast at Bewley's: Tea and a scone. Lee wanders about checking out different parts of the city; a late morning coffee; lunch somewhere near the Green; perusal of the Irish Times followed by a meet-up with Liz or Aedan or both at the Bailey on Duke Street.

He and Aedan are sitting at the bar in Mulligan's exactly one month after Lee's arrival when Aedan lifts his pint to admire the black turbulence scuttling up from below.

Lee, have you done anything about finding your Da?

Lee folds his hands together and shakes his head. Not much.

God, man, you are slow.

Lee shakes his head. That's me all right. But I'm getting ready. I'm gathering myself, or me-self as you might say. In fact, I'm thinking about cruising around Trinity this afternoon. You never know. I might spot him ambling about.

It is nearing four o'clock when Lee announces that the time has come. Gerard wants to wait for one more pint but Lee is adamant. They leave Mulligan's, walk down Grafton Street to College Green and pass through the arch at Parliament Square.

Students in knots of twos and threes are walking along the gravel paths. The low-lying sun lights the square and its Georgian buildings.

What a fine group of young talent, says Aedan looking at the female students. Notice that fine figure just ahead. I've half-a-mind to give it a go.

Lee scans the faces of those who look as if they might be professors trying to match them against the jacket picture of "Skerries". But he figures it is useless: More than twenty years have passed since the picture had been taken.

Nevertheless, walking along toward them is a man Lee judges to be in his sixties. The man is tall with black hair and black eyebrows. The eyebrows make him think of H.P. since that is the most distinctive feature of the picture on the book jacket. The eyebrows in the picture are thick and dark exactly like the fellow walking toward them. As he continues past Lee stops and turns around.

What's up!

That might be him.

That would be a miracle, surely.

I'm going to follow him.

The H.P.-possible. walks up the steps of Examination Hall. There is to be a concert according to a notice posted outside. Lee and Aedan follow the H.P.-possible inside and take a seat in the row directly behind him. The hall fills with students clutching book bags. The H.P.-possible begins a chat with a female student sitting to his right. Lee can hear some of the conversation which is about the music on the program.

Wonderful music for a late autumn day, says the H.P.-possible. Don't you think?

The conductor walks to the front of the stage and raises his baton. The first piece is the Brandenburg Concerto Number One.

After the concert Lee follows the H.P.-possible out through the front gate and then onto Grafton Street which is deluged by mothers pushing prams and towing toddlers. The H.P.-possible stops to help a mother guide her pram over a curb which results in several minutes of conversation. Finally, the H.P.-possible walks across Duke Street and enters the Bailey. Lee follows him inside taking a position at the bar three stools down. Jameson is it? asks the bartender. The H.P.-possible agrees.

Lee orders a pint of Guinness and studies the professor in the mirror.

So, are you working on my sculpture? Best side is the right.

Lee stammers: No. I mean excuse me.

No matter. American?

Lee nods.

Well, let me buy you a pint. I'm always glad to meet an American.

This is professor Nial, says the barman.

Strike three, thinks Lee.

Now, what part of the states are you from?

I'm from Massachusetts. Cambridge.

Are you now. I know it well.

What brings you back to this God-forsaken rock then, says the barman.

Lee is bothered by the resemblance of the professor to H.P.. They might be twins. At least according to the picture on the book jacket.

Chapter 29

On Thursday Lee meets Aedan at Davy Byrnes on Duke Street.

The bar is already crowded when Lee arrives; Aedan stands at the bar.

Well, well if it isn't himself. And what do you have to say for yourself? Barman a pint for my American friend here. Aedan lights a Carroll's.

Surely it's time for me to quit smoking. What about you. Did you never get going?

Lee shakes his head. I tried once in high school but it made me dizzy.

Dizzy is it? That doesn't stop me. Now I'm a pack-and-half man. Can't live without 'em.

And what happened with that – what did you call him? – ah: The H.P.-possible?

Not him. It was a little embarrassing. He caught me starring at him in The Bailey. Lucky for me he's a nice guy. The bartender said he is a professor. On the off-chance I asked him if he knew H.P..

H.P.? Yes, certainly. I haven't seen him for a few years. Retired, I believe. How do you know him?

Oh, I don't. That is … I read one of his books and liked it. I thought I would look him up as long as I'm here.

That's a fair idea. From what I know of H.P. he would probably like that.

Aedan laughs. You have the knack of landing upright. Wish I had a little of that.

Lee returns to the Shelbourne. He lies down on the bed. It is three o'clock.

He thinks that he will have to find someplace else to stay. He is spending too much money staying at the hotel.

Lee opens his eyes. The clock on the night stand reads six.

Lee sits at the desk with his journal. He reckons that it would be good to have a record of the trip although the last entry is just after Sarah was born. Life seemed to be too full after that.

Thursday, October 3, 1979. I'm in Ireland staying at the Shelbourne Hotel on St. Stephen's Green. My feelings are mixed. I'm excited to be in a new place and trying to resolve my H.P. problem but I have a real ache from missing Cathy and Sarah; Jill too, for that matter.

I went into the English Department at Trinity College where I met a charming young Irish secretary. She kindly looked up H.P. for me confirming that he is retired although she wasn't allowed to give me an address. I've been hanging out with Aedan Murphy. He tends bar at the Bailey. And I've met a stunning young Irish woman: Liz O'Connor. We've been out pub-crawling several times.

Lee has dinner in the Shelbourne dining room after having a martini at the bar. The dinner is good – roast lamb, new potatoes – if expensive. After dinner he walks around Dublin for a bit but is back in the hotel room and asleep by ten.

Chapter 30

A passing shower reminds H.P. of that umbrella that he had left in the hall basket despite the look of the sky.

But the shower passes quickly wetting the field enough to toss off reflections as if from cut glass projected by the sunlight breaking through. H.P. wipes the drops from his glasses and continues down Rush Road toward the village. It is close to five in the afternoon. He opens the door to the green grocers. Mr. Clancy is behind the counter stacking shelves.

Well, you're here in the nick of time. He looks at his watch. I'm closing in two minutes. What can I do for you?

Marmalade. I'm after a tin of marmalade.

And will it be tick or tin?

Well, tick as you say it.

Clancy places a jar of thick marmalade on the counter. H.P. hands over a pound note and Clancy delivers the change.

Staying in the old home are ye? Your Ma – God rest her soul – was a fine lass. How long has it been now since she passed on?

Twelve years. Twelve years ago.

You must be missing her?

H.P. nods, puts the marmalade jar into a side pocket of his jacket.

The faith be with you then, says Clancy.

And you.

The Home and Away is diagonally opposite the green grocers. H.P. opens the door. The room is nearly full. There is an empty stool at one end of the bar.

Ah, there he is. The bartender Sean extends his hand. Now, what will you be having this fine afternoon. A shanty is it?

Sean, enough already of your pleasantries. You know full well what I'm after. Now, be good enough to do the job you're paid to do.

Sean pours the Guiness and sets it in front of H.P..

Professor tell me the truth now: Are your pupils, the lassies that is, still as pretty as ever?

H.P. tips the pint to his mouth. Ah, liquid gold, he says, ignoring Sean's question. My cooker isn't working: Something with the gas.

Em, we can't fix the gas for you but we can take care of the cooking. Sheppard's Pie? Lamb stew? Fish stew?

Aye, the Sheppard's Pie will do.

A sign at the back of the bar announces: "Darts meeting Friday, 8:30 sharp".

I'm not there yet, thinks H.P.: Darts with the old puddles.

In fact a dart game is on. The darts fly through the air like missiles landing on the board with a satisfying thump.

Aye now, will ye look at that. Right on the bulls-eye. Fergus, you're a marvel. Give 'im a drink Sean.

Fergus downs the last of the Guiness in his pint; walks to the bar and hands Sean the empty glass. Another jar my good man. On me chief benefactor just there. May he never quit the darts.

There's a full buzz of words all around. H.P. is silent, studying the Guiness. The occupant of the next stool is a striking woman. In her forties surely, thinks H.P.. She is talking to the bloke on her right and, by the look of it, he's probably her husband. That would be a miracle surely, she says. The bloke responds but his words are mashed down by the bar din. H.P does catch: "He's a queer ol' bastard. You need to stay away." But his last words are unhearable. The presumed husband gets up heading to the loo.

H.P. glances to his right. A tear emerges from the wife.

The bloke reappears on somewhat shaky legs. Come on. Get up. We're going.

This is said loud enough that several patrons stop talking. The wife (if that's what she is) calmly finishes her drink, slides off of the barstool, straightens her skirt and walks to the door.

Sean clears away the glasses. Nothing to worry about, he says. It's not a new tale.

Husband and wife are they? says H.P..

Sean nods. Makes you want to find a mate at all costs, don't it? Whoa, I forgot whom I'm talking to. Lads the professor here has never been to that sacred alter where we all pledge to love, honor and obey. Or is it argue incessantly.

It's the last, says a red-faced bloke at a rear table. What's his secret, then?

H.P. turns around. Now chaps no sense getting hostile. I had nothing to do with your entanglements.

H.P. goes to the loo washing his hands in the sink. He draws a comb through his hair.

Jaysus, it's receding like the damn tide. There are flecks of dull gray around his ears and hideous pouches under his eyes; the skin around his neck sags toward his chin.

The Shepard's pie is tasty. H.P. makes short work of it. He has a second pint and then leaves trudging back up Rush Road. At home he takes the "Tick" marmalade from his pocket laying it on the counter: It will do for breakfast. He settles down on the couch putting his feet up on the ottoman. Yesterday's Irish Times is on the end table. He fetches his glasses from a pocket. The first story that catches his eye is a notice about the death of Robert Lowell. H.P. pulls the newspaper close. Says he had a heart attack. Just sixty, he thinks. Sixty! Well, at least I'm winning that race.

Last week H.P had felt a fluttering in his chest. He thought it was heartburn. The effect lasted a few minutes.

It has been five years since he last saw a doctor. It was a routine examination except for the execrable suggestion by the doctor that he quit drinking. Look, soon enough it will dissolve your bloody liver if you don't stop. But H.P. didn't agree. I limit myself, he said, to two pints a day and a glass or two of whiskey to relax with in the evening. No more than that. It's an absolute barrier, he said. Well, sure, there has been times when there was a breach but not that often.

Imagine a life without drink: What would be the point?

Clara's presence hovers over the room.

He retrieves the bottle of Jack Daniel's from its roost under the counter. The dark, whiskey-smell reminds him of Andrew. He is the one who got him going on Jack Daniels. Can't remember the last time I saw him. Wonder if the bugger is still above ground.

He sips the whiskey while he looks through the Times but Clara keeps intruding.

I know, he says. I disappointed you. No marriage; no children. What can I say?

There was that French woman, what was her name: Lou. She was keen on marriage. He had even met her folks in Amiens. And she was beautiful: Striking, red hair and a slim body. The topper was that she liked his work even though, at that point, he had stopped writing. The last he had heard she was involved with a cyclist who followed the tours around Europe.

That married woman in the Home and Away. She did give him a nod before the bloke returned. You never know.

He sighs: There aren't many nods anymore.

It is growing dark. He reaches for the light switch but his arm drops to the floor. The newspaper follows.

Chapter 31

Lee has lunch at the Bailey; Aedan is on duty.

Now look, he says. Have you made any progress?

Lee shrugs.

Lee looks a little guilty. There's more, he says. I should have said something before.

So, you're an ax murderer maybe?

Lee laughs. Not yet.

Well, it looks like I've got to come clean, Aedan. The story I told you is only about half-true.

Oh boy. This is getting good.

As I said I'm here in Dublin trying to find a man that I believe is my father. He was a professor at T.C.D. although I've learned that he's now retired. Anyway, I think that my mother and this professor had an affair and I was the result. She told me that my father died in WWII but after she died I found a little box hidden away with a book of short stories written by this fellow. The book is called "Skerries". There is a picture of the author whose name is H.P.. The jacket of the book says that he is a Professor at Trinity.

Do you know if he's here?.

Yes. The secretary at the School of English looked it up. He's retired but she wasn't allowed to give out his address. I went over to Wolf Press which published "Skerries" but they weren't any help. I thought of putting a notice in the newspaper but I'm not sure.

Oh, and one other thing. The inscription in the book was dated almost exactly nine months before I was born.

No.

Lee nods. Sounds pretty convincing doesn't it?

I'd say so, says Aedan.

I showed the book to my Aunt who eventually confirmed the story.

Why did it take you this long to come looking for this H.P.?

Ah, life got in the way. My daughters were born. It was always in the back of my mind to find out the truth but I never got to it. Before now.

What a story. But what will you do if you find him? Do you have any proof that he's your Da?

I don't know what I will do; I haven't got that far ahead. I don't have any proof. It's mostly one step at a time.

Chapter 32

H.P. wakes early the next morning still slumped in the chair. He pulls himself to his feet using the arms of the chair for support. His balance is shaky. He hangs on to the chair and then the wall. Tea, he thinks, I need a cuppa.

In the kitchen he turns on the electric kettle. The Lapsang Souchang tea is in the cupboard. He has trouble unscrewing the lid from the marmalade.

Merde.

He takes a table knife from the drawer. By banging the knife at an angle against the lid the lid budges. He spreads a thin crust of the marmalade over the bread. He lays the tea and the bread on the small kitchen table and sits down. Clara used to sit in the chair opposite. Some of their best conversations were at breakfast. The last time was just before she died. There had been no warning that she would die. The autopsy showed that she had a massive heart attack.

The wake was bad for H.P.. For one thing he couldn't get past the fact of her death; it was so sudden. It was like a sucker punch: One minute she was alive; the next minute she was dead.

H.P. sat beside her coffin during the wake. Her hands were crossed over her chest; a small bunch of yellow flowers wedged between her fingers. She did – H.P. thought at the time – look herself. He moved as if to touch her. Just the thought of doing that nearly made him faint. He sat back down. Mrs. Kennedy from next door tried to soothe him.

There, there, my boy, she said. She is at rest; so peaceful she looks: Lovely, just lovely.

The funeral mass was held at St. Gerard's on Strand Street. The priest read from the Bible. The casket was covered by a white cloth; a crucifix lay on top. The burial was at St. Mobhi's. H.P. stayed until the dirt had been shoveled into the pit. He walked back to town. The Guiness at the Home and Away was restorative.

Chapter 33

The last conversation H.P. had with Clara was at that kitchen table and was, as usual, about children; about a wife and children; about, as she called it, continuation.

Son, you know how much I want grandchildren. Whatever happened to that nice Irish girl? You know the one. She wanted to get married. What happened to her for god's sake?

Ma, I don't know who you're talking about.

She came from Cork, beautiful black hair. She was gone on you, wasn't she?

H.P. shrugged. The truth was that he never wanted to get married. He saw what marriage and children had done to friends: Arguments and fights, over money, over raising children. In short it was a horror show.

Son, I'm not going to be above ground too much longer.

H.P. shrugs dismissively.

No, it's so. You know it is. And when I'm under there won't be anyone here for you. No family. It will be a long, long night. But there's still time. Find yourself a nice woman who's young enough to have children. Promise me won't you?

H.P. promises. And why not. Promises are cheap and unenforceable. Still, she had a point. H.P. imagines what living with Mary Currier would have been like. At night they would sit side-by-side watching the telly and sipping Jameson's. And then, of course, there would be bed.

But then there was a baby crying. Wait sweetheart, I have to tend to him. The little bugger. And later, the folds of her skin would loosen; a ring of fat would appear around her middle. H.P. recoils.

No, he is better off this way. Clara would never understand but never mind.

It is the way it has to be.

Chapter 34

A month before Clara's burial H.P. takes the bus into city center. He has it in mind to look up Liz. He hasn't seen her for — good god — forty years or more. The last he knew she was still pumping out children. H.P. wonders if one or two of her brood might be his. That thought makes him laugh. What would Clara say about that?

The idea that one of Liz's children could actually be his sits in his mind like an insistent microbe. The thing that be-devils him is the idea that that child — boy, girl — would never know that he is its father.

H.P. is indignant. How could she keep it from the kid? And me?

She was always a diabolical bitch. God, if she could keep their affair from her husband why couldn't she keep it from the kid. And me! Of course she could; and did.

If there is a kid he would have to be ... in his middle thirties, or even late thirties. Too much. A kid — boy, let's say — who is his son and whom he hasn't met is in his thirties. Probably with kids of his own.

Jaysus, grandkids!

The bus stops just across the street from the Abbey Theatre.

The sight of the theatre re-directs H.P.'s thoughts: God, the last time I saw anything here was ... what? It must have been Synge.

He reads the billboard: What, the Erin Island? My God.

He buys a ticket for the eight o'clock performance. It is nearly five.

He crosses over O'Connell bridge. The Liffey continues its inevitable journey. A bit of rain starts up. The umbrellas unfurl like so many black mushrooms. He continues toward the College. His plan is to appear at Liz's old Department where, magically, she will still be as young and desirable as ever.

He worries that a former colleague might see him. Above all he wants to avoid that. Maybe if he didn't look so beaten down. Maybe if he didn't come close to stumbling every few steps. Maybe then he might like to meet up with somebody, Frank Flannery for instance, the Shakespeare man.

Luckily the term is over: The risk is small.

But a single glance inside the office reveals the error. A young woman with strikingly rich, red hair is busy with an electric typewriter.

Yes, can I help you?

Em, I hope so. I'm looking for the former secretary here. Liz Christy. Do you happen to know where I can find her?

Oh no, sorry, I'm new here. I don't know where she is. I believe she retired last year.

Ah, bad luck. And you don't have an address or telephone number for her?

We're not allowed to give out personal information.

Well, listen. I'm retired from the school. H.P. is my name. Would you be so kind as to send Liz a small letter with my address?

Rose shakes her head. No, I don't mind.

Right. 1 Rush Road, Skerries. You don't have to add anything. Just: H.P., 1 Rush Road, Skerries.

H.P. leaves quickly to avoid contact with any ex-colleagues lurking about. He has it in mind to get a pint and a bite to eat. On the oft chance – the extremely slim chance – that Liz might stop by Stephen's Green he exits the College in that direction.

There's still that inevitable gaggle of school girls in their little jumpers: They pay him no mind absorbed as they are by a young American looking fellow sitting on a bench feeding the pigeons. H.P. looks at the scene with envy. He remembers similar scenes when he was younger. Those girls – or their mothers! – or, god, their grandmothers –used to flit about him when he was in the park.

That's all gone, he thinks. Vanished. I'm down to the last bit.

A little tart with black hair is standing in front of the bench. Hey Grandpap, blow us a kiss then.

H.P. tries to ignore her.

Hey, are ye deaf? Blow us a kiss.

The gaggle of girls turn to H.P..

You're a cheeky bunch, he says, with your slagging.

Ah come on – the cry is taken up by the others. Come on. Come on. Come on.

H.P. finally blows the kiss.

Ah no, not to me face; to me arse!

General laughter. H.P. rises and walking slowly – by necessity – goes farther into the park. The girls, having satisfied their tribal hunger, skip off in the opposite direction.

Just as H.P. nears the Yeat's memorial a woman passes in the opposite direction. He isn't sure but she looks a lot like Liz, like an older version of Liz. If so her brilliant red hair has dulled and she has gained weight. H.P. keeps his head down as they pass. He thinks he catches a slight gesture of recognition but he isn't sure. Maybe it is just a momentary dilation of the eyes caused by a sudden decrease in sunlight.

This is turning into a disaster, he thinks. Jaysus, what next?

He feels sure that it was Liz. He's thankful that they passed with no sign. Probably she feels the same. God, what I must look like to her. What did we call them: Stumble-bums. He laughs: That's it: A stumble-bum.

Why did I give out my address? Suppose – God forbid – that she wants to meet up! Horrors! Still, maybe that wasn't her. Who knows. Maybe she's still delectable.

With that consoling thought, H.P. make his way to the theater.

Chapter 35

There are pictures of Synge, Yeats, O'Casey and Lady Gregory in the lobby of the theatre. H.P. takes his seat near the stage. He canvases his mind turning it back to an earlier trip to the Abbey but he can't remember if it was ten or even twenty years before. He does remember in somewhat sharp detail the young woman who sat next to him then.

What was her name? Christy wasn't it? or Maeve? Confounded, H.P. sits quietly until the curtain opens.

Pegeen Mike sits by herself in the pub owned by her father. She is to be married to Shawn. It is pitch black outside.

The audience is still.

Christy enters. He has murdered his da. Contrary to normal expectations this does not cause revulsion in Pageen but the opposite. Ah, but here is widow Quinn.

H.P. loses the thread; he is back in time. Vignettes of the past rise and fall. He is reading from "Skerries"in Cambridge. A bright, young woman smiles at him from the audience. A scene shift: Along a river, the Charles. That same young woman; the river is black.

Act I is over; the applause is enthusiastic. The first time it was produced Yeats himself disapproved.

H.P. looks at the time. He thinks he had better catch the bus. The bus is just loading across Bachelor's Way. He falls asleep in the bus along the way.

Chapter 36

Lee and Rose agree to meet on Saturday at 10. Lee rents a Mini from an agency. The car is delivered to the hotel. Rose arrives minutes later.

Good morning Rose I trust you've had breakfast?

Yes, thank you. Good morning to you. Did you sleep well?

Tolerably although I admit I was looking forward so much to today that it took a while to get to sleep.

I see you've got a Mini. My Da has one for getting around town. They're very economical.

I'm not used to such a small car. You know all our cars are monsters.

You'll get used to it. What about driving on the left?

That I don't know about. Please keep watch if I start drifting into the right lane.

Liz looks for a second as if she has doubts but she checks herself.

Well, shall we go?

The map says to take the N11 until the R755.

Liz nods in agreement.

Outside Dublin the country rapidly becomes green and lush. Steadily, the mountains begin to dominate.

Aren't those the Wicklow Mountains?

Yes, says Rose. Glendalough is in those mountains.

Rose are you all right?

Oh yes. I'm just a little ... ashamed.

Ashamed? Why?

Lee pulls the car over into a lay-by. I hope it's not because of me.

Oh no. Well, not entirely. I just felt I might have given you the wrong impression last night.

No, no. I think highly of you Rose. Please don't be concerned on that score. And "highly" doesn't really cover it. Technically we've only known each other for only a few days but ... honestly, I feel like I've known you for much longer.

Rose smiles. I know. It's queer but I feel the same.

Lee takes her hand.

Should we go on? I'm fine now. It just took seeing you again. I'm anxious to see Glendalough.

Chapter 37

The day following his trip to the Abbey Theatre H.P. decides to see if David is still in the Maths Department. He hasn't seen him for years.

After the bus ride in from Skerries H.P. stops at Bewley's on Grafton Street for tea and a muffin. Bewley's is crowded with shop girls on their tea break. The Irish Times is consumed by a scandal coming from the Dial: The Taoiseach is threatening to resign.

And on it goes, thinks H.P..

A young couple directly across hold hands. The boy leans close and – trying not to bring notice – kisses her ear. They laugh because the small gold bell hanging from her ear begins a faint chiming.

H.P. finishes the tea. The crowd is thinner now. Back to work, he thinks. He envies them.

The Maths Department is in a row of buildings just off the soccer pitch. David's office is on the second floor. H.P. knocks but there is no answer.

Oh, say, I believe he's in the Common Room, says a resident of the next office. Just down the hall to the left.

H.P. salutes with the tip of his finger.

The Common Room is nearly empty. David is writing symbols on a blackboard. Next to him is a bloke with sandy hair wearing a tweed coat.

So, says David, I'm not sure where to go with it from here. I've tried getting up a counter example but …

David opens his arms in a gesture of futility.

David? says H.P..

David turns. For a moment he doesn't recognize H.P..

H.P.? A miracle surely.

They shake hands.

David is withered down from his former self. Several inches of his belt dangle out of the buckle. H.P. think that a moderate gust might take him away

Look, says H.P., have you got time for a pint? We could compare notes on existence.

Ah me, says David, I would but … I can't just now. What about tomorrow? Or next week?

H.P. senses that David isn't interested. Well, there's no friends like old friends so … yes, I'll stop by again. I'm happy to see that you're well.

And you.

That, thinks H.P., was useless. He thinks he might track Liam down but then he remembers that Liam has been dead for five years.

He crosses O'Connell Bridge on his way to the bus station.

Chapter 38

They park the car at a car park; there are only two cars in the lot and there is no one anywhere to be seen.

Ah, there it is, says Rose. That tower. It's tenth century, I believe.

What is it? It doesn't look comfortable.

No, but the Vikings used to raid around here. The monks built these towers for protection. You see, they could climb up a ladder into that opening. Then they pulled the ladder up. As long as they got up there before the Vikings they were safe.

What if the Vikings brought a ladder?

Rose shrugs.

Let's have a look at that church. God, everything is made from stone.

Part of the Seven Churches of St. Kevin, says Rose.

The wind blows; water pours down into the valley from small streams on all sides.

It's beautiful, says Lee. I've never come close to anything this old.

Life was harsh, says Rose. Come on.

Sheep graze in a nearby meadow. The wind is strong: They battle to keep going.

Whoa, says Lee, as he lurches forward sharply when the gust suddenly abates.

That tower is something, says Lee. I wonder how tall it is.

There's a placard there. Let's see … It says the tower is thirty meters high. Oh, there are five floors each having one window except the top which has four for the compass points it says. The cathedral is just over there. Shall we have a look?

Ok, the cathedral is twelfth century. Wow, that makes it eight hundred years old.

Rose smiles. Imagine the people who lived here then.

Lee nods. Why on earth would they choose this place anyway?

I don't know but it might be that nearer the coast it was more dangerous. Remember those Vikings.

They wander around the grounds until Lee suggests that maybe they should find some place for lunch.

At Rose's suggestion they take the Military Road back over the Sally Gap. It is not much more than a winding track climbing up over the Liffey. There are turf cutters at work all along the route.

They stop at a pub in Roundwood. They sit by the fire and order lamb stew.

Well, that was great, says Lee. It's beautiful but I think there are ghosts there. I'm not sure that I'd want to hang around after dark.

Rose laughs. No, nor me. It would be exciting though.

Lee, when will you go to Skerries to see H.P.?

Ah me. I don't know. Now that I have the address – well, it's a quandary. I guess when you get right down to it, I'm afraid.

Part of me says to go right away and get it over with; part of me says to let it go. The main thing in favor of going is that I'm here; that's what I came for.

I'm sure it's a hard choice, says Rose. I don't know what I would do in your place.

I tell you what. Let's let the fairies decide. This is Ireland after all. Lee takes a 50p coin from his pocket. Let's call this side "heads" and this other side "tails". Rose, do the honors please and call the toss. If it's heads I'm going after H.P.; if tails, well, I'll just hang around.

Are you sure? This feels funny.

Yah, it feels funny to me too but go ahead. Rose fips the coin catching it in her palm on the way down. She looks at Lee and then turns it over on the table.

Ok, that's it, says Lee. I hope those Irish fairies know what they're doing. Will you go along as my protector?

Rose smiles. Some protection I'd be. But, if you want me to, I will.

They finish the stew and, holding hands, return to the car.

Chapter 39

Lee sits at the desk in the Shelbourne with his journal.

Saturday, October 27, 1979.

Rose and I drove to Glendalough yesterday. Pretty spectacular. Those stone ruins from the twelfth century spoke to me. Honest-to-God it felt like I had been there before. I think it was during one of the Viking raids. I thought I saw the Viking chief (or whatever he was called) shaking his fist at me and shouting some incomprehensible babble. But the ladder was safely up.

I think I'm in love with Rose. Can you believe it after only a few days, a few meetings and I'm in love! And after Jill?

Jesus (or Jaysus) what will I do about it? She's pretty and smart. Am I too old for her? God, more kids? What am I thinking?

Get a grip!

She's coming with me to Skerries tomorrow. This was decreed by the Irish fairies in a 50p coin flip. I can't say what I will do when I get there but I'm going.

The drive to Skerries is short and uneventful. They pass through Swords on the M1 turning off on the R127 through Lusk and then on to Skerries.

One Rush Road is a single detached house among a row of soldier's cottages. There are several cars parked along the road along with what appears to be a hearse.

Lee parks. Oh my god. What is this?

Not sure, says Rose. The best we can do is go in.

But what if …?

I know.

They get out of the car and walk up the short path to the house. A man and woman, both elderly, come out of the house.

She is crying, says Lee.

Rose nods.

The door to One Rush Road is open; they walk in. Through the open door they can see what appears to be a casket. There are maybe eight or nine people sitting by the open casket. The deceased is a man with grey hair and mottled skin. He wears a dark jacket and white shirt with a green tie. His hair is combed straight back. Between the body and the side of the casket is a book. The title of the book is visible. Lee sucks in a great gulp of air.

Rose takes Lee's hand which is cold. After a few more minutes they turn to go. Lee hadn't noticed the priest walking with then to the door.

Will you sign the guest book?

Lee picks up the pen. He hesitates but then writes: Lee Blake, son of H.P.. R.I.P.

1460 Days

"Anything processed by memory is fiction"

Wright Morris

It was hot that July evening when me and my buddy Grant got off the plane in San Antonio. A sign pointed the way to a bus outside the terminal filling up with sweating boys carrying suitcases. The driver was in uniform. OK Airmen, he said, your ride to hell is here. Giddy-up.

Grant and me sat together near the back of the bus. No one spoke on the ride to Lackland Air Force base. At the front gate a person who said he was Air Police checked our papers. It took about thirty, hot, sweaty minutes before he finished. The bus continued past the front gate before stopping at a building where we were told to firm up into a line.

Eighteen years old and still a virgin. God knew I didn't want to be or, if he didn't, he should have.

I wasn't even sure what it was that you needed to do to not be a virgin. Female anatomy was a total blank. In eighth grade a doctor talked to us boys about sex but none of it helped. At the time I was dating Zoe. But we never did anything but kiss once or twice and dance at the Teen Canteen. She was short, maybe five-foot-two or three. This worried me so I raised my hand to ask the doctor a question. It was the only question asked by anyone in the whole hour. Every last one of the boys turned to look at me like I was a freak. Yes? the doctor said. Does it make any difference, I said, if the woman is way shorter than the man? I guess I thought you wouldn't fit together properly if you weren't about the same size. The doctor didn't say anything for a minute. Ken Russell who was sitting a couple of desks away snickered. The doctor shook his head: If I understand your question rightly: No, it doesn't make any difference.

The closest I came to not being a virgin (and that wasn't that close)

115

was on our school's Senior Sneak. We drove several cars (my class was very small) to the Quonset huts on the Point. I brought along a cube of Gouda cheese, sausages and bread that Pauli, my Stepmother, put up for me. Grant had sneaked a six-pack of beer which he shared with Bill and me behind the hut. It was early June and unnaturally warm for that part of the world. Me, Grant, Bill, Helen, Rita and Beoma followed a path up a cliff overlooking the Bay. There were tall grasses, maybe three or four feet tall all over the cliff. As I said it was warm and sunny.

After looking at the ocean for a while we paired-up: Me and Beoma, Bill and Helen, Rita and Grant. Beoma and me wanted to get away from the others so we walked up the path to a nice spot where we tramped down the grass into a springy mattress.

Ah, it's nice here, I said. It was nice. The sun made the grass warm so it was like a heated bed.

Umm, said Beoma. It is nice.

We had been going on-and-off steady for a while. She came almost up to my shoulders. Her hair was black and pretty long for the way most girls kept their hair.

I saw a picture in Pop's newspaper. It showed a ship called the Andrea Doria sinking off the coast of Nantucket. Another picture showed this actress – I forget her name – who was on the ship. Her head was turned to the side. She had long, black hair (at least I think it was black because the picture wasn't in color) and black eyebrows and eyelashes. There was something about that picture. Anyway, Beoma looked a little bit like that actress.

I offered her a Lucky Strike from my pack but she didn't want it so I put the pack back in my shirt pocket. She took my hand which pretty nearly set me on fire. I raised up and leaned over. She smiled. I was burning up. I kissed her and this time she let me put my tongue in her mouth. Oh, Jesus! I tried to pull my right leg up over her but she blocked me with her knees. I tried again but no doing. I put my hand on her stomach. I could feel her skin through the shirt. For a minute she didn't try to stop me but as soon as I let my hand wander she said – not too loud – "don't". It didn't seem to me as if she really meant it so I kept rubbing her shirt like I was trying to see if the color would come off.

No, she said, this time louder. Don't! She got to her feet causing me to roll over like a capsized beetle. Beoma brushed off her backside and started down the path to the huts.

All I can say is that I was in a power of pain for, maybe, ten minutes. It got so bad I had to get back down on the ground. It was the worst.

Me and Grant decided we would join the Air Force after graduation. I guess it was a bunch of things – not big things, just things. We – my half-brother and me – were all doubled- up, sleeping upstairs in the same bedroom. It wasn't like there wasn't enough privacy, there wasn't any. At all.

I could never seem to do anything right. Like that time when Pop went on a honeymoon with my new Stepmom Pauli. He left me at home alone which was ok by me. Bill came over and we drank a little beer. The trouble happened when Bill lost his balance and fell over on the picket fence that the old man had put up only the day before. Two or three of the slats cracked. Man, did I get it when he got home. I tried to tell him it wasn't me but he wouldn't listen.

Or like that time I crashed the Dodge into the garage door. I only wanted to see what it felt like to start a car. I found the keys on the Old Man's dresser. I left the car door open while I put the key in the ignition. That's because I wasn't really going to do anything. If you leave a little wiggle-room, as Pop himself said, that shows you didn't mean it.

The trouble was that this car had a clutch and an automatic transmission. The shift was in reverse when I got in so when I turned the key it rocketed backward out of the garage. Luckily the garage door was open and there was no little kid playing in the driveway. Unluckily, the car door hit the side of the garage as we shot by nearly ripping the door of the car off. The Old Man came running from the pump – he was always working on that pump. There was hell to pay.

When me and Grant signed up for the Air Force we had to go to Elmendorf Air Force Base since there was no recruiter in our town. We stayed in a barracks until all of the paperwork was done. We had nothing to do but hang out when we weren't with the recruiters. We could even drink beer legally in the Airmen's Club. I said to Grant that this was the life. Yah, he said, the Life of Riley. Finally everything was ready and we took the oath. The recruiter said we were now in the Air Force and had to obey the Officers and Enlisted Men over us. We had to stay on the Base for a couple of more days before they got us a flight to Texas. Right after the oath the recruiting sergeant took us outside. We had to cut about a football field of grass and when we got that done he put us to work cleaning up the barracks. It'll be good practice for you, he said, when you start Basic Training. I mean, man, we scrubbed down those floors 'till they shined.

Is this what we got ourselves into? said Grant.

What happened to Riley? I said. He was on his knees like me scrubbing the floor with a wire brush. He shook his head.

Must have left town, I said.

Eventually we got on an airplane headed to San Antonio. It was near midnight when we landed. It was hot: I mean sizzling hot even though it was after dark. Someone said 90 degrees. There was a part of the airport where we were supposed to wait for a bus to take us to the Base. A guy with three stripes had us sit down. There was maybe twenty of us, all young guys just out of high school. Nobody said anything.

The guy with the stripes got us to our feet and into a blue Air Force bus with yellow lettering. It took maybe an hour to drive to the Base.

We piled out of the bus in single file. A Sergeant (he said his name was Sergeant Royal) said he was going to be our TI. That's "Tactical Instructor", he said. I'll be on your backs for the next six weeks. Look sharp now.

First we got dinner at the mess hall. The food wasn't bad: "Shit-on-a-shingle" they called it and potatoes and jello.

After dinner we gave a clerk the orders we got from the recruiter. Before we took the oath a Captain at the recruiting station asked me what I wanted to be, what was my ambition, he said. I told him that I wanted to be a pilot. I figured they might teach me to fly in the Air Force.

We had to file out one-at-a-time to the desk where Sergeant Royal had our papers. I stood at what I believed was attention. Well Airman, what's this? He pointed to something in the papers.

Why is one of your addresses a Navy Base?

I told him that my dad retired from the Navy.

Navy huh? What rank?

Chief Petty Officer.

Sergeant Royal kind of grunted, stamped the papers and said: Next.

We were marched to the barracks. It was a two story building in a row of barracks which seemed to go on forever. The latrine and showers were on the first floor. The barracks was already almost full. There were just enough bunk beds for us. I was asleep as soon as my head hit the pillow.

July 15, 1958: 1456 Days

The next morning Sergeant Royal rousted us at five. Man, it was already hot out. After breakfast we lined up out on the grass beside the barracks. Sergeant Royal had us sit on the grass. The company commander stood beside the sergeant.

Now listen up Airmen, said Sergeant Royal, this is your commanding officer. He's going to give you what-for. Pay attention.

All right men. You're just getting started on your training. The Air Force wants you to know that you are no longer living under civilian law. You're military and the law you're under is called the Uniform Code of Military Justice. I'm going to read it to you now so nobody can claim that they didn't know about it.

Listen-up.

Well, he read it to us all right. Maybe a half-hour's worth. It was all I could do to keep from falling asleep. Grant was next to me. His eyes kept closing as his head tilted down toward his stomach. Just as it got down as far as it could go it snapped back. His eyes were wide like the eyes I saw on a deer once when we were driving along the Coast Highway at night. Some of the Airmen who fell asleep got a prod from a baton Sergeant Royal had. Lucky I didn't go under like that.

After the Captain finished Sergeant Royal lined us up in rows and we marched to the mess hall. We must have looked sloppy because another Flight passed by marching sharp as tacks.

After breakfast we marched to Base Supply where we went through a line to get uniforms. Like everybody else I got a pair of fatigues, dress pants, shirt, a visor cap with an insignia, a soft felt cap, a belt, a pair of brogans and a tie – Air Force blue, like the sky.

Next door was the barber shop. There were twenty chairs: All full. They sat me in a chair with a blouse around my neck. The barber left maybe a quarter inch all around. It took two minutes.

Back at the barracks an Airman demonstrated the proper way to fold and store all of our belongings in a trunk at the foot of the bed. Listen up, he shouted, you all have to get this right. Sergeant Royal won't stand for sloppiness: Sharp corners, neat folds and rolls, your tooth brush clean and lined up. Y'all come and have a look. He also showed us how to fix the blankets to have hospital corners. Tight, it's got to be tight, he said. He dropped a quarter on the blanket: It bounced maybe six inches.

Next was drill. We formed up in four columns of twenty each. Sergeant Royal pulled me out of the Flight – to this day I'm not sure why. Airman, he said, I'm appointing you to be in charge of the Flight when I'm not here. You understand? Wear this on your arm. It says that you're a temporary Staff Sergeant. Now, I'm going to teach these Airmen how to march. You go along behind me. That way you'll see what to do when I'm not here. Got it?

I did get it but it scared the piss right out of me. In charge? Of eighty men?

But I did get the hang of it: Ten-Hut, Hut-2-3-4, Hut-2-3-4. Road Guards out. Column-left, Hut.

Every morning there was an inspection. We stood at attention at the foot of our bunk. Sergeant Royal came down the aisle checking that we were dressed properly and the beds were made tight.

Airman Damery, he said – it was more like a shout – what the hell is this?

He pointed to a towel which was showing out of Damery's trunk.

Sir, said Damery, I ... I

What I ...I...

Sir, I forgot, sir.

You forgot! Listen up. We don't forget in this Flight. Airman Damery will get to think this over tonight while he stands a double watch.

Nobody turned to look but we all heard.

After that we formed into a Flight which is like a platoon in the Army if you've seen any war movies. It was more drill only this time we were at the parade grounds. Sergeant Royal watched while I led the Flight. It was ninety-five degrees someone said.

After twenty or thirty minutes I put the men at ease for a cigarette and water break. Each Airman had a canteen of water and salt tablets. Just then a couple of WAF walked by (that's Women in the Air Force). I called the Flight to attention as a little joke.

We took a break outside in the shade of the barracks; Grant and me sat down with our backs against the wall.

Man, said Grant, this is hot. I thought I was going to pass out.

Yah. I was getting there myself. You think these salt tablets do any good?

Grant shrugged. I've been taking them but I haven't felt different.

Me neither.

You sorry you enlisted?

Nope.

Me neither. But maybe I should have gone to college like Pop wanted.

Why didn't you?

I shrugged. I didn't have a good answer.

Most days we did calisthenics. Except when it was too hot. A red flag was run up the flag pole when it was too hot meaning that we had to stay inside.

The calisthenics were the usual kind: More-or-less like what we did in football practice: Jumping jacks, deep knee bends, pushups. I could handle it ok but it would have been a lot easier if it wasn't so blame hot.

I was tough with the Flight. On one of the red flag days we were in the barracks sitting on the floor because nobody wanted to wreck their bunk. Falling asleep during the day was not allowed. I saw Airman Adam with his head in his arms. I got up and filled a cup with water and poured it on his head. He came up fighting mad. You know the orders, I said. No sleeping during the day.

I learned how to be tough by watching Sergeant Royal. There was a small office at the end of the barracks with a desk and a couple of chairs. The Sergeant had me call into the office an Airman who had messed up. The Airman marched in smart, saluted and stood at attention in front of the desk. Sergeant Royal seemed to be reading something on the desk. It was quiet as hell. And then, bam, he stood up knocking his chair backward. God-damn it Airman. You're in it now. The Airman almost fell over backwards. He was white as a sheet.

One time I made the Flight stay at attention outside the mess hall even though it was hot as hell. After that Grant told me he was fed up with me.

My excuse was that if I was going to be an Air Force Officer I had to be tough.

Pop pulled duty on the Midway in the Pacific. He told me about a fire-fight with Kamikazes near Guam. The Old Man, he said, was tough as nails. We took some rounds and two of those bastards just missed the Flight Deck. The Old Man never flinched.

That night before lights-out Grant came up to me. He said they were going to get me. You'd better go on sick call, he said.

There was no way I could do that so I took my canteen belt which had lots of metal buckles and clasps and wrapped it around my hand. I got down on my bunk and waited. I was going to stay awake and then fight back like hell. But the next thing I knew someone had thrown a blanket over my head and I was being hit with shoes and fists. I was so primed that I just kicked out swinging my belt like a maniac. There were five or six in on it. They scattered out of there like a bunch of scared birds. That was the end of it. It was three in the morning.

When the Flight fell in for Reveille the next morning I said that what happened was over as far as I was concerned. In the mess hall Grant said that I had gotten too big for my britches. What britches, I said.

Road-guards out. Column-right, hut.

I got the marching down pretty good. I felt like I was about ten feet tall with the Flight moving by my command. Ten-hut. Forward-harch. Right flank-harch.

August 6, 1958: 1434 Days

It was in the fourth week that we went on Bivouac. It was blazing hot. They put us in trucks and took us to the Bivouac area where we pitched tents and set up camp. The ground had dried up into pieces of broken dirt.

That first day we mostly worked on getting used to where we were. I had no trouble sleeping in a tent since I had done that plenty back home. Pop and me we would grab our sleeping bags, camp stove and some freeze-dried food and head out. We had a couple of favorite spots. One was along the Mackenzie River. We caught river trout which was real tasty cooked crisp.

I loved the woods. There was always a sharp, clean smell and I could almost taste the air.

At night we built a small camp fire. Pop would spin-out a story. He said he wanted to be a trapper in the North Woods but never got to test it out. Your mom got in the way, he said. What he meant was that they got married before he could get North. And she didn't want to go so that was that.

I used to read books about the North, about the people who did go.

Porky and me decided to run away from home. I convinced him we should go North and start a trap-line. Around Yellowknife, I said. Porky wasn't too sure but he went along with me.

We hitchhiked on the highway going North. The first ride came real quick and got us about one hundred and fifty miles out but the next ride was tougher to get. We tried a trick that Porky had heard about. We stood side-by-side with our thumbs out but I pulled my leg up at the knee so it looked like I was disabled. We gave up after an hour and hitched back home. Pop never knew.

At the firing range Grant and me were paired up. The weapon was an M16. A firing range TI showed us how to load the rifle, release the safety and fire. We had to do this five or six times in front of him before we were sent up to the actual line. We had to get down on the ground with the rifle on safety pointed at the target which was about fifty yards off.

The only time I had fired a rifle was with Pop. He said I knew all about fishing but I should know how to hunt. We drove to this gravelly field which didn't look much like a place where rabbits would hang out. The rifle was a .22 that Pop had when he was growing up in Indiana. His initials were carved into the wood.

Look son, this is how you do it. He put a shell in, brought the rifle to his shoulder and fired at a fence post a few yards off. I guess I wasn't expecting it but the sound made me jump. But the sound from that .22 was nothing compared to the M16. The M16 was like an explosion.

We took turns taking pot shots with the .22 until we ran out of shells. I never saw a single rabbit.

Grant fired first. He waited until the TI in the booth gave the signal. We were about in the middle of a row of Airmen all stretched out on the ground. The TI gave the order over a loud-speaker. It was loud enough that he could be heard up and down the line even when we were firing.

Ready on the firing line.

Commence firing.

Grant wailed away but it was hard to see if he hit anything. After about ten minutes the TI gave the cease fire.

A couple of Airmen came out from a bunker and took the targets down and put up new targets. I took aim at the center of the target which was a red bulls-eye. The rifle barrel was still scorching hot from Grant's shots. There was a cloud of blue smoke over the ground. It reminded me of the Fourth of July.

Ready on the firing line.

Commence firing.

My heart beat like the devil because of the noise and the recoil from the rifle. It was hard to concentrate. I fired all of the rounds in the magazine real quick.

Good shot, said Grant. You got a couple of them in the center.

You can see that?

Yep.

The T.I. said we could take a cigarette break. The smoking lamp is lit, he said. I fished the Luckies from my pocket and lit up. Grant did the same except he was a Camel's man.

I thought about what it would be like to fire at somebody, in a war I mean. Pop did that. He said he went ashore with the Marines in the Philippines. Nasty, he said. Very nasty. A Japanese sniper fired at him from a post in a tree. Lucky he missed and Pop was a dead-eye shot.

I've seen pictures of piles of dead people in war. I think it was the First World War, the picture I remember. The bodies were stacked up like cord wood. There was no life in any of them. It got to me that minutes, maybe seconds, before that their eyes were open and they were pulling on a cigarette thinking about their girl friend or mother back home. Bam, they were all done.

After a few more rounds we got back in the bus headed for the Bivouac area.

Hey, that was cool, said Grant. Even if it was hot as hell.

Yah, I said.

We bumped along in the back of the truck with maybe twenty guys in the Flight sitting on two benches. The top and sides of the truck were covered by a tarp.

We jumped out at the Bivouac Area and formed up. Sergeant Royal marched us to the tents where we were put at parade rest.

Now listen up Airmen: The smoking lamp is lit.

I started smoking in junior high. My buddy Ken and me went behind some bushes outside of school and he gave me a cigarette. The first couple of times I inhaled the smoke it was bad but I did get the hang of it pretty quick. My Stepmom Pauli said smoking would stunt my growth. Maybe it did because I'm all done at five foot eleven which is about two inches shorter than Pop. I heard that a boy would grow to his father's height or maybe more so there could be something to what she said.

We went back to the firing range the next day. Grant did way better this time. He should have. His family went hunting all the time. They got almost all of their meat that way.

His house was back a-ways from town down a country road. I'm not sure how many brothers and sisters he has but that house was stuffed. I kind of liked one of his sisters. She was a year younger than me and very pretty. Her hair was the color of a carrot and she had a mess of freckles. When she laughed you just couldn't help yourself. Betty was her name. She was wild. She would try anything. She played tackle football with us. And it was rough. Where we played there were rocks on the ground which hurt like hell. After one game Betty went home with a nasty cut on her cheek.

Grant didn't much like her playing with us but there wasn't a lot he could do about it. When she got home with that gash to her cheek her mom screamed at her but it didn't do any good. She was back the next day.

Well, nothing ever happened with me and Betty. Once or twice we kissed and fooled around but that was about it.

The last day of the Bivouac was what they called the "trial by fire".

There was a building with a ramp going in one side of the building and then coming out on the other side of the building. On both sides of the ramp there was fire: Real hot flames maybe seven or eight feet high coming from gas jets or something. You were supposed to walk real slow all the way through because if you got scared and ran the fire would come after you.

When I was a kid, maybe ten or eleven, I almost set the house on fire. It was the fourth of July. There was a shack that a guy set up for the Fourth every year on the corner. He sold fireworks: Rockets, firecrackers, punks, everything. My buddy Russ and I bought some fireworks and took them out to the field. It had been hot for a while so the grass was real dry. We got Russ's older brother to light the punk and we used it to light the firecrackers. We were pretty careful to toss them as soon as the fuse was lit. We also put firecrackers under tin cans with the fuse sticking out underneath. When the firecracker blew it shot the can into the air. It was great fun.

After a while Pauli called me to come in. I sat down on the floor and leaned back against the davenport. The punk I was holding must have touched the fuse of a rocket which was leaning up against the davenport. The rocket fired off like lightning. First it ricocheted off the wall, hit a window and made about two turns around the room before it fell on the rug dead as a doorknob. It was lucky that the curtains didn't catch on fire. Pauli screamed bloody murder. Lucky for me she didn't tell Pop. I would have gotten it if she had.

When I took my turn on the trial by fire I walked as slow as I could.

It was burning hot. There were no windows. The only light was from the flames. I guess it was like walking in hell. I looked straight ahead the whole way through. My head was like it was nailed down on my shoulders.

When I was about half-way through I started to think that those flames were coming after me. My brain said that I had to get out of there. But I guess my brain has more than one part because that other part kept telling me to walk slow.

It took forever but I made it through. It was about ninety-five degrees outside but it felt like after a cool rain.

Grant made it through too; the whole Flight got through. Sergeant Royal said that he was happy with us. Ok Airmen, he said, when we get through with Bivouac I'm going to give you an afternoon off.

September 5, 1958: 1404 Days

We got back to the barracks two days later. Sergeant Royal was good to his word. We had rec time from right after lunch until the dinner call. Some guys took naps; some went to the PX. Me and Grant and my element leader Merle went to the Airman's Club. We knew that you didn't have to be twenty-one to drink beer on Base. As long as you were in, you were good.

The place was jammed. We finally found a table out on the patio. We sat at ease each with a draft beer. The sun was hot but the beer was cold. The juke box played "All I Have to Do is Dream".

Man, that bivouac was tough, said Merle. I said I thought it wasn't too bad.

Are you kidding, said Merle. You were white-as-a-sheet when you walked out of that fire.

Naw, I said. I just wasn't feeling too good. That fire didn't bother me at all.

Well, it did me, said Grant. But hey, it's over. What's next on this roller coaster?

One more week and we're done.

We took a bunch of aptitude tests to decide what jobs we should do. Our next assignment would be to a training base to learn how to do the job. Sergeant Royal said we should get orders by the end of the week.

I'm getting another beer, said Grant.

The last time I had beer was with Ken, and Ken's girlfriend Sharon. Sharon picked me and Ken up in front of his house. We drove over the Interstate Bridge to the old Van Port which was once a pretty big neighborhood but the river flooded it a few years back so that all that was

129

left was the roads and the odd chimney. Sharon's father's car was a Nash which looked like an upside-down bath tub. We had a few beers so we parked in what had been a driveway. I thought about the people who had lived here. The kids probably played right where we were parked. "All-the-all-the outs in free", games like that. Ken and Sharon were necking pretty heavy in the front seat. I was what someone called a fifth wheel. The radio was on.

Sharon said she had to take a pee. She got out of the car and went off a-ways. It was so dark out that we couldn't see her anyway. Ken turned to me. Who-ee, he said. Take a sniff of this. He shoved a finger in front of my nose. Whoa, he said. I didn't say anything but I didn't like it.

When Sharon got back to the car Ken said we should drive around some more. The roads there were curvy and Ken got going pretty fast. Too fast. I could feel the car tip when we went around a curve but that didn't slow Ken down. Suddenly the tip became a roll and we turned all the way over. When we stopped we were upside-down. I must have hit my head on the door handle because there was blood dripping down my cheek.

For a couple of seconds nobody said anything.

Holy Shit, said Ken who was trying to right himself. Jesus Christ. Sharon, you ok?

Sharon said that she was but she was scared. What about Dad's car? Oh God!

Phil, you all right?

I said that I must have cut my head on the door handle.

You bleeding?

Yah, I'm bleeding.

Oh Christ, look.

A patrol car with its lights going rolled in and stopped in front of us. Two cops got out. One of them pointed a flashlight at us.

You kids all right? Here climb out.

We got out and the cop looked us over. That's a nasty gash you got there son. His partner got a first aide kit out of the cruiser. He pressed a piece of gauze against the cut and taped it in place. The cop with the flashlight checked out the inside of the car.

Jesus, he said, smells like a brewery in here.

The beer had spilled everywhere.

They checked Ken's driver's license.

None of you are old enough to drink. We're going to have to take you in.

They put us in a couple of police cars and drove to the Juvenile Jail.

The jail wasn't too bad. Well, if you like bars all around. We were in the basement of the County Court House. I don't know where they put Sharon. She was pretty scared when they took her away. I was scared too. I wasn't looking forward to Pop. Ken laughed. Hey man, he said, look at us: Jail birds. That's what we are.

He acted like it was nothing which might have been true for him because he had been in Juvenile Jail before. He once tried to hold up a car parked on Rocky Butte late at night.

There were other guys in jail with us. Maybe five or six, I don't remember exactly. The guy in the bunk next to me said he had been pinched for beating up a guy. Bastard stole my girl, he said. When I told him what we were in there for he laughed. Drinking beer, he said. Jesus Christ, did you guys hear that?

A guard came in. All right punks, he said. Lights out. If I hear another word you'll find out what Molly here is all about. He pointed at a baton clipped to his belt.

It was tough getting to sleep. I kept seeing the car spinning over.

The next day we were in Juvenile Court. Pop showed up. His face was beet red. The Judge talked to the cops that arrested us. He asked me what I had to say. I told him I was sorry that it was a bad mistake. I think he liked my saying that. Anyway, he let me go home with Pop. Remember, he said, the next time it will be much tougher.

Ken and Sharon got off with just some kind of warning. I never did hear what happened about the Nash.

When we got outside Pop really let me have it. He had to take off work to spring me. On the way home he calmed down some. How's that gash on your face? Hurt?

He wanted to know about the beer. Who got it for you?

I didn't want to say that it was Ken's older brother so I said we bought it from a guy that was coming out of the liquor store.

I got off easy that time.

131

We each had four or five beers on the patio. I figure it was the heat and the beer combined that made me a little wobbly.

I'm going back to the barracks, I said. Grant said he didn't feel too good either but Merle was ok. I slept until it was time to fall out for chow. I had a headache for the rest of the day.

My orders came the next week. I was to go to Administrative Clerk School at Amarillo Air Force Base, Texas. This suited me ok but I envied Grant a little because he was being sent to Radio Operator school in Louisiana. We didn't do any big goodbyes. We said we would keep in touch but I'm not sure either of us meant it.

September 13, 1958: 1396 Days

I was given a Greyhound bus ticket to Amarillo. It was a long ride through country that was flat as a pancake. At the bus station I bought a paperback book that Miss Pruessing had recommended in high school: "The Catcher in the Rye". I finished it off on the bus. It was good. That kid, Holden, had a lot of problems but money wasn't one of them.

I never read too much but what I read I liked.

When I got off the bus the air was about as hot as the fire during Bivouac. There was an Air Force jitney for the ride out to the Base from the bus station.

I reported in at the training squadron where they assigned me to a room in a barracks. My roommate was from Alaska: Kodiak, he said. He said his name was Danny.

I set up my bunk and hung up my gear. About ten minutes later we fell-out in formation. The TI gave us the word: Reveille at 0445, march as a Flight to the mess hall; inspection then drill. After drill we would be in classrooms for the rest of the day. Back in barracks after chow and then free until lights-out at 2130.

The classes were ok, easy really. We would be training for six weeks and then get orders to our permanent duty stations.

Before lights out Danny and me worked on our shoes. He was good at spit shining. His boots were so shiny they were like mirrors. You throw some spit on the shoe, he said, add polish and smooth it into the shoe. I don't know why it works but it does.

I told Danny that my Pop was stationed in Kodiak. It was the last station before he retired, I said.

My Pop's Navy too, he said. Did you like being a Navy brat?

Naw. But I got along ok. What about you?

Same-O.

The training went ok. We had tests on Air Force Regulations. You had to know how to fill out the forms: Which forms to use, stuff like that.

There was an Airman's Club on the Base. They did a good business. A draft beer was fifteen cents and you could get a hamburger for a quarter. There was a juke box with some pretty good music. Danny and me went there on our first weekend. I got pretty drunk but I made it back to the barracks ok.

I forgot to say that I sent in an application for the Air Force Academy before I enlisted. I didn't think my grades were good enough to get in so I checked the box for the Prep School at Fort Belvoir, Virginia. I tried for a Presidential appointment on account of Pop being Navy.

In the fifth week an order came for me to take a test for the Academy at Walker Air Force Base in Roswell, New Mexico. The TI ordered me to see the Squadron Commander, Captain Drake. I knocked on his door in the Admin building. I gave a smart salute.

Well Airman, I'm impressed that you're trying for the Academy. It's tough but well worth it.

Yes sir. Thank you sir.

What got you interested?

Well sir, my Dad was Navy so I was around military but I wanted to fly so I thought Air Force.

Good thinking. Come to see me after you get back from Walker. Tell me how it went.

I saluted, did a sharp one hundred eighty degree turn and left.

The next day I was given a round trip bus ticket from Amarillo to Roswell. It took about four hours which I mostly slept through but I sat up when I saw the Pecos River. I'm not sure but I think it was a kid's book where I first read about that river. The name kind of stuck so it was a shock when I saw the real thing.

At Walker there was about twenty-five of us. They put us in a big gym. There were different sorts of hurdles and pull-up bars. In groups of five or so we were timed going through the course. It was tough. I've never been good at pull-ups but I got to twenty-five which seemed to be ok. What I am is pretty fast so I did well in the speed trials.

The exam lasted the whole afternoon. I slept in a temp barracks that night and went back to Amarillo on the bus the next day.

The day room in the barracks had coke and candy machines. I saw an Airman kind of double-pump the handle on the coke machine and out came a bottle. He hadn't spent a dime. The news that you could get a free pop spread through the Squadron. I was checking mail when I saw an Airman trying to get a free coke but he couldn't get it to work. I went over and did the double-pump. Hey, he said, it does work.

That afternoon the TI told me to see Captain Drake. I went in thinking we were going to talk about Walker but that wasn't it. Instead, he chewed me out for stealing the coke. An Air Force Officer, he said, is not a thief. He said he was of a mind to report me to the Academy. He scared me enough that I had trouble speaking. I did say that I didn't steal the coke. I was just showing the airman what he did wrong.

You mean you didn't take one yourself? The delivery man said he saw you take one.

No sir, I didn't.

When the Captain dismissed me he said he was disappointed but the fact that I didn't take the coke for myself was better. He said he wouldn't report me this time. I hate to see a young man lose his future over a simple mistake.

That was close. How dumb can I be?

It didn't really bother me that I helped steal the coke. It was just the getting caught part. When I was sixteen I stole an Almond Joy from the Payless. I put it in my front pants' pocket and walked right by the cashier. It bothered me because I couldn't figure out why I did that. I had the money. There was like this thing popped into my head and, without thinking, I put the bar in my pocket and walked out.

I felt so bad that I went back in and put the candy back on the rack. This time the cashier looked at me funny.

When I finished the Supply and Administration School I was ordered to stay at Amarillo until there was a decision about Fort Belvoir. The T.I. put me to work in the Administrative Headquarters as a Clerk and I got my Airman Third Class Chevron.

About two days later Sergeant Reft told me that one of the squadrons was being phased out. He said that since I had experience leading a Flight they were going to make me the TI of that barracks. You will be in charge, Airman. You hold inspections, drill the Flight, march them to class, all of it. Can you do it?

I thought about it for about nine seconds. Yes sir, I said, I can. I figured this might help my chances for the Air Force Academy.

Good. The Flight is 214. Let's go over and get you introduced.

The sergeant had the Flight fall-out in the Quad.

Listen up, he said. Your new TI is standing beside me. I'll be backing him up. Follow his orders just as if they came from me. Is that clear?

There was only one or two "yes sirs".

Is that clear?

This time the "yes sirs" were over the top.

To get off on the right foot I marched the Flight around the Quad before dismissing them back to the barracks.

The next morning before class I held an inspection. The rooms were two-man rooms with two bunks, a closet and drawers. The Airmen stood at attention beside their bunk. I inspected the closets and drawers, I made sure that the bunks with their green-gray blankets were tight and I paid close attention to shoes. They had to be shined so I could see my face in them like a mirror.

There were no problems. Sergeant Reft had left me with a good Flight.

I made the rounds with the Duty Airman making sure that all was quiet and then I went back to my room.

In the morning I marched the Flight to Administration School. I was glad to be done with that myself. I had learned a lot but I was glad it was over.

I got a letter from Pop and Pauli. This was the second letter since I left. Pauli said my kid brother Pat said hello (well, he's my half-brother). I thought maybe he did and maybe he didn't. It would be more like Pauli to put that in on her own. She said he was getting ready for the start of school which surprised me that it was that soon because I wasn't paying attention. It was September already. He was going in to the tenth grade.

Pat and me didn't do much together. Actually we didn't get along even though we shared a bedroom up in the attic. Our beds were against the wall beside a window which looked out on the breezeway between the garage and the house. When it rained – and it rained a lot – it pounded on the roof and against the window. I still hear – many, many years later – that rain. If there was enough wind the rain sounded like rapid-fire gun shots on the window. At night I lay awake listening to it as if it was music.

Our water came from a well with a pump. Pop was always working on that pump. He had to keep adjusting it. He must have pulled it completely apart and put it back together fifty times.

In his part of the letter Pop said the pump was working well, that the Dodge had been fixed and work was going good.

When I was little I got Appendicitis which my folks thought was just a stomach problem until my temperature shot way up. Then it was a race to the hospital. I remember those white gowns and bright lights in the operating room. I guess I wasn't that close to dying.

The thing was I couldn't figure out what came after death. I couldn't just not be anymore.

Pat is two years younger than me so we weren't interested in the same things at the same time. He liked cars. He got a job at Nohlgren's All-You-Can-Eat-For-Ninety-Nine Cents. He was their dishwasher. Well, he made enough money to buy a dark blue 1952 Chevy from Ron Blankenship. I have to admit that that was one sweet car. It didn't have a radio when he bought it so he went to a supply store on Main Street and bought one which he installed in the dash himself. It sounded good. I asked him a couple of times if I could borrow the car but he never let me.

I liked being alone. I did have a couple of friends: Grant for one. But I mostly liked being by myself. In the woods across the street from our place there was a small stream running through. I called it "Beaver Creek". I practiced being a fur trapper along that creek. I scouted for signs in the woods. It was beautiful in the winter after a snow storm. Pop had a pair of old skis which I used. If it was real cold I tested myself by staying outside as long as I could. Sometimes I only wore a tee-shirt. Pop thought I was nuts. What's the matter with you? he said. The crazy police will be down on you.

I never told him or anyone else that I was practicing to move north, way up north. Alaska or the Northwest Territories. You had to be tough to be there so I tested myself.

Flight 214 had only a week left of training. The routine stayed the same: Reveille, inspection, mess hall, Administration School, lights out. The best thing that happened was when the Flight graduated. There was a parade in front of the Base Commander. We were the lead Flight. There must have been twenty Flights in all stretching back as far as I could see. I marched the Flight past the reviewing stand. We stood tall. When we came to the General I called out "Eyes-Right" and saluted. He returned the salute. That was something to write home about but I don't think I did.

In the Flight there were two Airmen from Queens, New York: Leonardo and Francesco. They were Air Force Reserve on summer training. They were going home in two days. They told me they were giving a party at a motel in Amarillo on the weekend and they wanted me to come. They were both brokers, they said, in New York, so I guess they had money.

The party was on Saturday night at the All Rest Motel. They had rented a bunch of rooms and when I got there about four in the afternoon the party was already going good.

Hey boss, Francesco said when he saw me, come in, come in.

The room was full of people sitting on the floor, lying on the bed, standing around with drinks of some kind.

Hey, the frig has plenty of beer. Help yourself.

I got a Pabst Blue Ribbon out of the frig and sat down on the floor next to a girl wearing a white skirt and a blue shirt. She had a nice smell.

Boss, this is Angel. She's native here. Nice, huh?

And she was but I found that my tongue had gotten tied up pretty good.

Nice to meet you, she said.

Hot isn't it? I said.

Umm.

She was very pretty. Her hair was ink-black but her eyes were perfectly blue, like her shirt. Her smile was tops, I mean tops. When she smiled at you it was all you could do not to melt down in a puddle at her feet.

You have beautiful eyes, she said.

Leonardo and Francesco were definitely prepared: An Elvis Pressley record started up.

Don't be cruel to a heart that's true.
I don't want no other love
Baby it's just you I'm thinkin' of

You want to dance? Said Angel.

There was a little space in the room for dancing but most of the dancing was outside on the balcony.

Angel was real light on her feet. Maybe one hundred pounds soaking wet. She pulled in real close. Her hair smelled like the powder that my mother used to have. I hadn't smelled that since she died. I wanted to ask Angel what it was called so I could get some but I was too shy. I never came across it again, sad to say.

I wasn't very good at dancing. I was scared that I would mess up. Miss Kirsten gave dance lessons at Mac Junior High in the eighth grade. I must have learned enough from her because I did ok dancing with Angel. I started to think I was maybe Fred Astaire.

After the song we got another beer and decided to visit one of the other rooms. The balcony in front of the rooms made a short, right turn. Leonardo had said that 203 and 204 were rented.

When Angel opened the door of 203 there were two people in bed but under the covers. Hey Caroline, Angel said.

Caroline just smiled. This is Rick.

Rick waved before turning back to Caroline. They were lying on their sides facing each other. It made me nervous. The blanket they were under kind of rippled like waves on a pond.

Come on, said Angel. She pulled me to a little alcove away from the bed. She sat down on the floor and patted a place beside her.

When I was twelve Pop was stationed in Hawaii at Pearl. This was after Mom died. He said that we were going to have dinner at Chief Gorman's house. The Chief was Pop's buddy. His house was in the Enlisted Men's Housing not far from where we lived. Pop said the Chief's wife wouldn't be there. Just you, me and the Chief, he said.

From day one I was told to call Navy people "sir" so that's what I did when the Chief opened the door. Come in, come in, he said. Nice to see you.

He asked me about school, what grade I was in and like that. I told him school was fine. He asked what my favorite subject was. Well, I said, I guess science. Really? he said.

When I was about ten I hung out at the library. I just liked the place. There were all of those books with stories inside. I would go down the rows pulling out books and opening them.

The library was in an old, brick building with an odd number of steps up to the front door. The way I knew it was an odd number was if you take the first step with your left foot and it ends up that the last step is with the left foot, then it's odd. Alongside the door were two statues of women sitting on pedestals but looking at each other. One had a painters' palette in one hand and the other one held a scale.

One day I was in the library just looking around. I took down a book called "Nuclear Physics". There was a diagram that looked like a picture of the sun and planets. The sun in this picture was called the nucleus and the planets were called electrons. According to the book this was a picture of an atom. Atoms, it said, were what everything was made of but they were so small that they couldn't be seen even with a microscope. I was amazed at how something so small could look like something so big, like the sun and planets.

I started reading. Most of it was Mathematics that I could not understand but there were bits and pieces of writing which kept me going.

Well, for some reason I wanted to figure it out so I came back to the library nearly every day after school. I sat in that same place in the basement trying to figure it out.

Anyway, we got up from the chairs in the Chief's living room and sat down at the dinner table. My Pop and the Chief had been talking about a fishing trip they were going to take when the Chief said to me: Did you ever have a piece of tail?

I thought he was talking about some kind of fish that we were having for dinner. I said, no, I never have.

Then he started talking about women and their getting pregnant and so on. I bet my face was as red as a stoplight. I didn't say a thing.

After dinner Pop said that I should thank the Chief and not just for the dinner but the other thing. At least now, he said, you know what it's all about.

But I didn't. I couldn't remember a word of what the Chief said.

Pop put his arm over my shoulder on our way out to the car.

So Angel and me were making out on the floor. Rick and Caroline were making little grunting noises like someone pushing a heavy load up a hill.

Angel and me were kissing pretty good. I got so excited I was climbing all over her. This is it, popped into my head: This is it. But Angel shoved me off. No, she said, not now.

I felt like a used-up dishrag.

I caught the bus back to the Base about ten. The brokers said goodbye before I left and that-was-that. It was the last time I saw them or Angel.

November 2, 1958: 1346 Days

Three days later I got my orders. I had to report to the 1st Missile Division Headquarters at Vandenberg Air Force Base, California. I didn't get in to Fort Belvoir after all.

I took a Greyhound bus from Amarillo going to Los Angeles on Route 66. It was an ok trip. I slept on the way and read a Popular Mechanics magazine that I bought in one of the bus stations. My uniforms were packed in my duffel. I wore my jeans and a tee-shirt which I had bought at the PX for the motel party. A guy across the aisle from me had his hair in a duck's tail. It was a good one flat on top but the sides were swept back like the fins on a Caddy. My hair was just like that until they got me in Basic Training.

We stopped at the Greyhound Terminal for lunch in Kingman, Arizona. The station looked old. There was a small restaurant inside the terminal. I sat on a stool at the counter. The counter reminded me of the place that Ken's dad owned out on N.E 47th street. I used to hang out there with Ken after school. His mother was the waitress and his dad did the cooking. Mostly hamburgers, fries, small stuff like that. My best spot was the counter stool at the far end. I played tunes on the juke box and joked with Ken and his sister who was supposed to help out but I don't think she did a lick. Ken told me that her boyfriend was a class-A jerk. Man, he must have crawled out of a hole somewhere, he said. If he isn't careful I'll bust him up-side the head.

In the Men's Room somebody had written little messages on the walls. "A rolling stone gathers momentum" was about the best one. Even if I could think of a good one I wouldn't have had the nerve to write it like that.

In the Greyhound Terminal in Kingman the menus were posted on the wall up over the cook stove. I got a cheeseburger, fries and a Coke for twenty-five cents. The same price as at Ken's place. The fellow sitting on the stool next to me was also from my bus. He said his name was Jimmy. He wanted to know where I was going. I told him that I was going to Vandenburg AFB.

The missile base?

Yep, I said.

So you're in the Air Force?

I said I was.

Do you fly those B52's?

I laughed. No, I'm just an Airman 3d class. You have to be an officer to do that.

Well, 3d class is something, he said.

The waitress gave us our lunches. The cheeseburger was good.

After lunch there was still fifteen minutes before the bus was supposed to leave. Just across the street was an old hotel made out of some kind of stone. I thought it looked like pictures that I'd seen of the Alamo.

After sunset we passed by a place called the Blue Swallow Motel. It had a beautiful sign with "Motel" in bright-red, blinking letters and on the top a picture of a Swallow in ice-blue. I had a little daydream about staying there: With Beoma or Angel.

We rolled into L.A. about ten at night. The bus to Lompoc, which was the closest town to the Base, didn't leave until the next morning. The U.S.O. told me to stay at the Y.M.C.A. which was only two blocks away. The clerk at check-in told me I was lucky because I was getting the last single room. That was not a surprise because my luck always holds out. Well, I guess it depends on what you mean. In things like that room I do get what I need but it's mostly things like that.

The next morning the bus ride took about three hours. We headed up the coast on Route One past Santa Barbara to Lompoc. The bus dropped me off outside the main gate. I got my duffle and walked across the highway to the gate. I showed my orders to the A.P. on duty who said there would be a bus in about ten minutes.

He was right. The bus let me off in front of a neat, blue-and-white sign of the Strategic Air Command. On the shield was blue sky and clouds and

143

a fist holding three lightning bolts. I signed in with the Airman on duty in the Dayroom. He gave me blankets and pointed me to the barracks.

The barracks was a two story, white building opposite the Dayroom. At the end of each floor there were showers and latrines. My roommate was lying on the bunk asleep. I tried not to wake him but there was too much shuffling around to do. Hey, he said: I'm Tom from L.A.

Tom got up and we shook hands. He was maybe six inches taller than me. He looked strong. His jaw reminded me of that Bulldog I saw once which had been left outside Ken's restaurant. It looked like if you hit him in the face you might break your hand. I unloaded my stuff, hung up my uniforms and made the bed.

It's about time for chow, said Tom. You interested?

I was starving. My stomach growled like that Bulldog. The Mess Hall was only a quarter- mile away. There were barracks all the way down as far as I could see.

Tom said he wasn't really from L.A.. My parents live in Fullerton, in Orange County, he said, so that's not really L.A.. He said he drove his Chevy nearly every weekend to Fullerton to see his girl.

The next day, which was a Monday, I reported to the Command Post. I reported to Major Zimmer who got me in past the Air Police who had charge of building security.

The Command Post was the place where if there was a war the order from the President to launch would be given. The missiles were always on standby. One inside wall of the CP was glass which separated it from the Scheduling Room. There were three officers working there. Their job was to approve all of the stuff to be done around the launch pads. One whole wall of the Scheduling Room was covered by a board which listed what was taking place and when and where.

In the CP the Officers sat on chairs in front of a console. A bright red telephone was on the console which Major Zimmer said was connected to SAC headquarters in Omaha. Usually there were two officers on duty twenty-four hours a day.

I had to fill out paperwork to get a Top Secret clearance. This was going to take several days and I could not work at the CP until then. While I waited for the clearance I had to go through training at the Base Motor

Pool. My job was to check out a pickup truck each day at the Motor Pool and drive it to the CP.

The training was pretty boring. Mostly we had to watch films on how to load heavy equipment or how to service the trucks. None of which was good for me since I was just going to drive a pickup.

There were about fifteen Airmen sitting in chairs facing a movie screen. And, it was hot. There was a fan in the corner but it barely stirred the air. Between a movie showing how to check the oil and lubrication levels in a two-and-a-half ton rig and the safe way of driving on the left in England (I had no clue why we had that one) a movie started showing a man and a woman swimming in a pool. It was tough to figure out how this was going to be something about vehicle safety. They got out of the pool and went through a door. The next shot was in a room. It was supposed to be a motel room. After about a tenth of a second they started kissing and then taking off each other's clothes. The sound of heavy breathing in the Motor Pool was deafening. I'm sure you can guess where the movie was going.

Nobody said a word after the movie was over but it was tough to go back to how to check air pressure on an eighteen wheeler.

That movie sat in my head for the longest time. At least I knew a little more about what happens between a man and a woman because of that movie. It was way more than I knew before.

My Top Secret clearance came through at the same time as the Motor Pool training finished. From then on I walked to the Motor Pool after breakfast at the Mess Hall, got the keys to one of the pickup trucks and drove to the CP. I now had an I.D. card with my picture on it that got me through Security at the check point.

I was introduced to the new secretary who had started work the previous week. My desk and her desk faced each other. Her name was Betsy K (she said she liked just the first letter for her last name). I guessed she was in her late twenties maybe early thirties. Betsy asked me where I was from. She said she was originally from New Jersey. I liked her right away. She was easy to talk to. She had black hair and a little black mole on one cheek. She was wearing a bright, red dress which matched the color of her lip stick.

It's Philip, isn't it? she said. Can I call you Phil?

Sure, everybody does.

Our office was next door to the CP. The Commander was Colonel Bain and Major Zimmer was his deputy. Their desks were screened off from the rest of the room. Betsy K and me were close to the door.

My job was to take care of the CP's documents which were mostly Top Secret plans and War Orders. Naturally, there were Defense Department forms and other things which had to be filed and sometimes I had to help out in either the CP itself or Scheduling. We were in the same building as MOD II Guidance. We shared Security with Guidance.

The people in MOD II Guidance were mainly civilians along with Air Force Liaison Officers. The antennas on the roof were their connection to the missiles. At meal times a truck brought out the food and we shared it in a kind of mini, mess hall.

At the end of the first week Betsy said that she still had some things to move in to her room from the trunk of her car. She had two rooms in quarters for civilian, female employees not far from the Base PX. She asked me if I would help her finish moving.

I'll drive you over, she said. There'll be a couple of beers.

Betsy's car was a green Chevy with a small dent in the rear bumper. When she stepped on the clutch or the brake her dress would slide up a-ways. She didn't seem to mind because she never tried to pull it back down.

So, she said, what do you like to do? Girlfriend? or girlfriends? I bet. How old are you anyway?

I said I was eighteen and that I didn't have a girlfriend.

No? Doesn't seem likely to me. Do you want one?

I don't know why but this embarrassed me. I just nodded my head.

Well, there's a cute young woman in my building. I'll introduce you.

She parked in the front of the building. In the trunk were two boxes of books. I followed her up the steps. Her rooms were in the front of the building. There was a long hallway down the middle separating the rooms.

I carried the boxes in and put them on a small table in the first room. The bed was in the next room. It was a single bed with two posts at the foot and a head board made out of metal. That bed made me think of my Mother's bed. I used to sit on that bed with her when she read me stories.

There was a kitchen about half-way down the long hall. Betsy took two bottles of Olympia beer out of the refrigerator and opened them.

Thanks for helping out, she said. We're going to do well together.

She had a great smile. Her teeth were white like new snow. She smiled a lot.

She didn't want to sit in the front room because, she said, the books were on the couch and she didn't feel like taking care of them just then. Let's sit on the bed why don't we?

Betsy sat on the bed and I sat in a chair facing her. It was hot in the room so the cold beer tasted good.

What do you think of Major Zimmer?

I guess he's ok, I said. I hadn't thought much about it.

Mmm. He's very good looking, she said.

Well, I could say nothing about that.

He tried to sell me shares in a mutual fund, she said. He pretty much guaranteed I'd make money but I don't know. It put me in debt just to get here. Take your jacket off if it's too hot. Unbutton your shirt.

I was getting pretty steamy but not all of it was caused by the heat. I took off my jacket and unbuttoned my shirt.

I guess the first time it happened to me was when I was about thirteen. Pop was stationed at China Lake Naval Air Station which is in the California desert. His job was as an Air Controlman. They fired test rockets at drone aircraft.

It was one night – hot like this one – when I was lying in bed wearing my shorts looking at a magazine. I don't know, maybe "Life" magazine. There were pictures of Marilyn Monroe. In one of the pictures she was standing on a grate or something and her dress blew up above her hips. You could see her panties. Suddenly I felt something warm and sticky. I looked down and there was this milky-looking stuff all over my leg. I didn't know what to think about it. I never told anyone.

Betsy smiled and patted a place next to her on the bed.

You're very handsome, she said. She turned toward me. She looked like she was expecting something. I was too scared to make a move. That's when she reached over and kissed me. Well, I kissed her back.

This kiss was like fire. There was nothing I could do. It was like I wasn't in charge. With Beoma I always knew it was me calling the shots. Not this time.

I got to thinking one day about this kissing stuff. It's really pretty funny when you think about it. Two people locked on each other, mouth-to-mouth. It probably isn't even sanitary as Pauli would say. You can probably pass thousands of germs that way. Maybe there's a kissing sickness or if there isn't there should be.

We kissed again and it was even hotter. She put her hand between my legs. It was like fire. I tried to get on top of her but she made me stop.

Phil, Phil. I have to go and get protection. Understand?

I said yes but I wasn't sure. It seemed like hours before she came back.

When I walked to the barracks afterward I did a little jig step until a Captain came toward me on the pavement. I pulled myself together and gave one of my best salutes ever.

When I went in to work at the CP on Monday I was a little nervous. Betsy was sitting at her desk. She gave me a big smile and a little wave of her hand. Hi, she said.

The rest of the day went good. We didn't talk much but she filled up the whole room. Major Zimmer called to me from behind the partition. I didn't hear him until Betsy said something.

Yes sir, I said, and went to his desk. Sorry sir, I didn't hear you.

I want you to take this folder down to Colonel Anderson at Hq. Wait there until he gives you something to bring back.

He handed me the folder. Yes sir, I said.

I drove the pickup past the Thor blockhouse and followed the road to Division Hq. Colonel Anderson's secretary was sitting at a desk outside the Colonel's office.

Ah, I see you have something, she said.

I'm not sure but maybe she was about fifty. She had grey hair but no wrinkles. Not like my friend's mother who had so many wrinkles on her face that she looked like a piece of broken china.

She told me to sit down in a chair beside her desk. She took the folder in to the Colonel.. She came out in about a minute and sat dawn behind her typewriter. I think, she said, he'll have something in a minute or two. Would you like something? Tea? Coffee?

I shook my head. No, I'm good.

What's your name Airman?

Phil, I said.

Well Airman Phil, I'm Vi. We'll probably be seeing a lot of each other. Where do you come from?

I told her my Pop was retired Navy. We moved a lot, I said.

She said she knew all about that. My husband is Air Force, she said. It does take getting used to. What are you going to do when your enlistment is up? College? Or maybe you'll stay in?

I told her I didn't know yet but that I was thinking of College.

You like school?

I said yes but that wasn't all true. Some of it I liked; some I didn't.

You know, she said, there's a program here on the Base. You can take courses right here which get you college credit. It's Allan Hancock Junior College in Santa Maria which runs the program. Keep it in mind. And you've got a new secretary at the CP. How's she working out?

Read good, I said, real good. I don't know if I did or not but I might have blushed. It's a real curse.

Vi went back to her typing and I twiddled my thumbs. The Colonel came to the door with a new folder. I jumped to my feet and saluted. Good Airman, he said. Take this back pronto to Major Zimmer.

Yes sir, I said as he went back into his office.

There now, said Vi. Nice to meet you.

After I gave the folder to Major Zimmer I had a lot of filing to do. Mostly it was routine but there was one with a Top Secret mark called "Emergency War Orders". I read some of it. It listed the targets in the Soviet Union if there was an attack. Naturally, this was filed in a safe next to the red telephone of the duty officer in the CP. Major Riley was on duty.

Howdy son, he said. Almost from the first day he called me "son". You know, he said, when you get to college you're going to want some cool transportation. Do you know what an MG is?

Well, I did. I guess I was about fifteen. There was this tv program about a photographer. He made pictures of beautiful women and he drove an MG. One night me and Russ were hanging out at the Holland restaurant on Main Street. Just across the street was a used car lot. As soon as we walked out of the door I saw it. It was white and it had leather seats. There was nobody around so I reached in and opened the door. The latch inside was a loop of wire that you pulled down to open the door. I sat in the seat for about fifteen minutes turning the steering wheel and trying out the shift. I stepped on the clutch and changed gears. I imagined I was in California driving to the beach. A beautiful woman sitting beside me. We were flying down the road.

I told Major Riley that I did know about the MG. Well son, I'm going to sell mine for $1100. If you want it it's yours. Here's the keys. It's outside. Take her for a spin.

And there it was. It looked like a duplicate of the one outside the Holland. I got in and started it up. I drove around the parking lot a couple of times. It felt great. I could really see myself with this car. The trouble was that I had about $27. Oh, did it hurt that I couldn't have it.

So what do you think Airman? Do you like it?

Yes sir, I do, I said. But I don't have the money.

Do you know about the Base Credit Union? I bet they'll loan you the money with the car as surety. I'll not try to sell it for a couple of days to give you time. After that I'll have to find a buyer.

It did work out: The Credit Union loaned me the money, I gave the check to Major Riley and he gave me the keys and registration. As soon as I was off duty at the CP I went out and got in the car. It was raining. I sat there listening to the rain on the roof and looking at everything. It was hard to believe it was mine.

One Saturday in July, Aunt Betsy and me drove to the house of a friend of hers in Santa Barbara. It was pure joy to be chugging along in that car with the top down and Betsy beside me. It was a dream come true.

Sometimes it feels like my heart has filled up with so much air that it lifts me up like a balloon. Betsy reached across the seat to put her arm around my shoulders. Who-eee.

Betsy's friend Elsie lived in a small house. Her yard was pretty much overgrown with weeds. Elsie was sitting on the porch when we pulled up. Betsy gave her a big hug. She introduced me as a co-worker. She said she had promised my mother to keep an eye on me. Well, that surprised me but Betsy shot me a wink as soon as Elsie turned around.

What about your Mom. I thought of her a lot after what happened to your Dad, said Elsie.'

She's fine. Still in New Jersey.

So, let's go to the beach, said Betsy. What do you say? I've got to get rid of this pale skin.

We drove in Elsie's car to a beach in Goleta. We spread blankets out near the pier. I didn't bother with sun screen but I should have. The sun was fierce. I walked down to the water. I was standing there trying to get my nerve up to go in when Betsy came running up behind. She pushed me hard enough in the back to drop me into the water. I kept going and after a couple of minutes the water felt good.

Well, I got her back. I used my hands like paddles splashing her all over. After that I turned and swam out away from shore. Betsy followed.

Mmm. The water is nice.

It was nice. Warm, but not too warm.

Betsy swam on her back. Her toenails – which were bright red – stuck up out of the water like little sea creatures. I rolled over on my back. There was a row of palm trees just beyond the beach.

Yah, it's good. Betsy …?

Now look, she said, Elsie is an old friend. She knew my father. I don't want her to figure us out. You hear?

It was the first time she said "us". It sounded weird.

What about your father?

She didn't say anything for a couple of minutes.

A tall guy came roaring down toward us. He dove in and started swimming out like his life depended on it.

My Dad is dead, said Betsy. He killed himself. In the garage hanging from a rope. I was just nine years old.

That was a downer. I didn't know what to say.

Hey, she said. Let's not let anything spoil the day.

She whacked me on the butt underwater. Man, she was something.

Around five o'clock Elsie said she knew of a small, Italian place not far from her house. Pizza, chicken cacciatore, you know. It's not bad.

Sounds good to me, I said.

We took turns in the shower. When I came out Betsy was sitting on the bed with just a towel around her. She smiled at me but wagged here finger back-and-forth. I gave her my best hang-dog look.

All along the walk there were lots of flowers. Some were bright red and some were a pale blue. The sun was blocked by the houses on the other side of the street but it was still plenty warm.

Phil, how old are you? Elsie said.

Nineteen. Well, I'll be nineteen this month..

Nineteen, my my. Do you remember nineteen Betsy?

Umm. New Jersey. You remember that time we went to the fairgrounds. I was scared out-of-my-mind by the roller coaster.

Yes I do. And I was too. We both had dates. My God I can't remember his name.

Jordan, I think.

We got down to the corner where the restaurant was. There were maybe five or six people inside. We sat down; a waiter brought menus. I went for a pepperoni pizza, Betsy and Elsie ordered some chicken dish. They got a carafe of wine. Betsy signaled to me that we could share as long as the waiter didn't see.

Everybody was pretty tired by the time we got back to Elsie's place. Elsie said good night almost right away. Aunt Betsy slept in a second bedroom and I was to sleep on the couch in the living room. We said good night and the lights went off. It was very quiet. I waited a few minutes. I couldn't wait any longer. I crept as quietly as I could to Betsy's room.

December 27, 1958: 1291 Days

It was just after Christmas when Aunt Betsy introduced me to Sheila who had moved in to the women's quarters. Her rooms were on the other side of the hall from Aunt Betsy's but more toward the kitchen. Aunt Betsy said that Sheila was getting a divorce.

Sheila was about my age. The top of her head came up to about the middle of my chest. She had short, black hair and black eyes. She had a few freckles and a real nice smile. She was from someplace in New York.

Sheila was different. The way she was, I mean.

One day we drove up Highway 1 to 101 and over to Pismo Beach in my MG. We hung out in town until it got dark. Sheila saw a poster outside a place called the Rose Garden Ballroom. Oh look, she said, it's Fats. Fats Domino was on that night. Let's get tickets. I've got to see him.

My buddy Ken was big on Fats. He would be insane if he knew that I had gone to see him.

The thing didn't start until nine.

We took our shoes off and I rolled up my pants' leg to wade in the surf. Sheila had on a short skirt so there was no worry about getting our clothes wet.

The water was cold at first. I have always had to tough it out but eventually I can stand cold water. Sheila nearly slipped on a rock or something but I grabbed her hand in time.

Thanks. You saved me.

The thing was we kept on holding hands even though she was ok.

It was dark and the sun was going down over the ocean. It was perfect with the light and the waves which made a crackling sound on the sand as they went back out.

The ballroom opened at nine. Fats started singing and the dancing got going. You may remember that I wasn't a good dancer. I did learn a little from Mrs. Roberts in eighth grade and I went to the senior prom with Jill when I was a junior.

The way that happened was that it was a cold, wet day so I decided to take the bus. Normally I rode my bike because that way I could sleep in a little more. You know: Ten minutes more was a life-saver.

In high school we had to take a bus from one building to the next on account of the City was building a new high school but it wasn't finished. There was only one open seat and that was next to Jill. Hi, she said, my name is Jill. From then on she saved a place for me. My buddy told me that her old boyfriend was one of the school's best football players. He's joining the Marines, he said.

I started riding the bus regular after that.

One day she turned to me and said: You have the most beautiful eyes. Will you be my date for the Prom?

I could have dropped through the floor boards.

Well, I said yes.

Pop wouldn't let me use the car because he was still gun-shy because of the garage door trouble so Jill (who was a senior) asked another couple if we could ride with them. I did find out in time that I had to get Jill a corsage and that I had to wear a tie. The old man let me borrow one of his ties and a jacket. We were about the same size then – in height, I mean. I had to walk to Jill's house which was in town. Maybe a half-hour's walk. But I got there. I gave Jill the corsage and she gave me a boutonniere which she stuck in my lapel. She looked real cute. Her pink dress went down below her knees.

The dance was ok. Her boyfriend was there with someone else. He gave me a dirty look like I had stolen something from him which, I guess, I had.

You dance well, said Jill.

I must have looked surprised.

No, I mean it. You haven't stepped on my toes once.

I liked dancing with her. I felt brave so I tried that thing where I bend her over backwards and back up. No problem. She knew just what to do.

At the end of one dance she got up on her toes and whispered in my ear: We're going to Paddy's after. Her breath in my ear reminded me of that Popular Mechanics' story on a wind tunnel for testing things. Well, it probably wasn't that strong.

I liked the slow songs the best. Jill and me fit together like two pieces in a jigsaw puzzle. The top of her head was right below my chin. I could feel all of her up against me. She was breathing pretty hard which just about sent me to the moon.

Around midnight we got back into Jim's Ford. It turned out that Paddy's was a kind of hangout down by the river. There were booths all along the walls. The waitresses were dressed in black. Right away I knew I was in trouble because I had only a quarter to my name. That was the one thing I hadn't counted on: Money.

Jim and Lorraine said they were going to get cheeseburgers which were twenty-five cents and a cherry coke which was another dime. Jill said she wanted the same.

I did know that it was up to me to pay for Jill. The man always pays which is something that Pop and the movies taught me.

I felt crummy.

What's the matter? said Jill.

I said that I didn't have any money. I said that I didn't know we would be coming to a place like this. Jim said that everybody knows we come here. I pulled out my quarter. It's all I have, I said.

They decided they would drive me home and then come back. Which they did.

Jim gunned the Ford so hard that I got hit in the stomach by a piece of gravel kicked up by the tires when they pulled away.

I was bummed.

The house was dark. I practically tip-toed up the stairs scarred Pop would hear me and I'd have to say something about the Prom. My half-brother was out cold. I got in bed and pulled the covers over my head.

From then on there was always someone else sitting next to Jill on the bus. I went back to my bike and my ten minutes.

February 2, 1959 1254 DAYS

The winter had lots of rain which I didn't mind but there weren't many days that I could put the hood down on the MG. Christmas came and went. I called Pop and Pauli on Christmas Day. The Dayroom had a tree and decorations but that was about it except for a turkey dinner in the Mess Hall.

Sheila and I started hanging out together. She was secretary to the Base Commander. Betsy didn't seem to mind. Sheila told me that Betsy was going out with a bartender at the Officer's Club. Sheila said he was married.

Across the hall from Betsy was Maria. Betsy said she was about fifty. She had real black hair except for a few gray spots. She was funny. When she laughed I couldn't help myself. It reminded me of my friend Porky in junior high school. One day we were in his house lying on the living room floor. His Mom was outside doing something. Maybe hanging clothes on the line. It was summer vacation. Anyway, she kept going in and out of the house. She didn't say anything except stuff like: "Oh, tsh-tsh" or "darn". Porky and me watched her. We couldn't help ourselves. He pointed to her on her way out the door. This made me laugh which got Porky going. Pretty soon we were rolling on the floor holding our sides. It got so bad it hurt. When she came through again she stopped in the doorway.

What's the matter with you two?

Well, that got us going even more. She stood there for a minute more and then went into the back somewhere. We quieted down after awhile.

I didn't ask Betsy about the bartender.

A couple of months after she came to the CP she had to take a leave to go home to New Jersey. She asked me to take care of her car while she was gone. – this was before I got the MG.

Just take good care of it, she said. I need it.

My friends from the barracks Gary and Rob were both from Indian River, Florida where, they told me, they grew oranges. It's so beautiful, said Gary. Nothing like it anywhere.

We were in the barracks sitting in my room. Gary said that his father was in the wholesale fruit business. I got the idea that they had a lot of money.

I knew I shouldn't but I told them that my father was a retired Rear Admiral. Their eyes kind of popped out.

I told them I had Betsy's car for a week.

Hey, said Rob, how about we drive down to Tijuana. Man I hear good things about that place.

Tijuana? I don't know, I said.

Why not, said Gary. TJ's only five or six hours away. We drive down on Saturday and come back on Sunday. What do you say?

Well, I didn't see anything wrong with it. Betsy wouldn't know anyway.

On Saturday we drove out of the Main Gate headed south toward L.A..

Man, this is going to be fun, said Rob. What I hear about T.J. is far out. There's strip clubs and girls all over the place.

What about me, I said. I'm not twenty-one.

No problem. The Mexicans don't care how old you are. As long as you've got the dough, you're in. In like Flynn.

Betsy's car handled real well and didn't use much gas. We drove straight through L.A.. Gary offered to drive but I said it wouldn't be right. They slept most of the way. We got to the border around noon. We were in line behind a bunch of cars going through the border-check. Gary said most of the tourists were sailors from San Diego.

We parked on a side street just off the main drag which was called Avenida Revolucion, or something. There were plenty of tough looking hombres around. I said a little prayer that nobody would touch the car.

A sign said: "Girls, girls, girls".

Whoa, said Rob. This is the real deal. He patted me on the back. This is it, old buddy. This is it, and he swung his arm around like he wanted all of it.

Hola hombres, come on in, said a guy at the entrance to one of the clubs. We got the best looking girls. They show it all.

We walked on.

A bunch of sailors dressed in their whites went by. One of them was so drunk he had to be held up by two of his buddies. Oh, oh, said one. Don't look now but it's the Shore Patrol.

Rob liked the looks of a place about half-way down the block. Not sure why. Maybe it was the sign that showed a dancer kicking up her legs. Her legs went up and down in the lights.

Whoa, said Rob. Let's give it a go.

We walked down some stairs and at the bottom there was a big bar in the shape of a horse shoe. A couple of bartenders and five or six girls were sitting on stools. I didn't see anybody dancing. When we came down the stairs they all turned to look.

Rob was right: Nobody asked me for an I.D..

Hey, handsome, one of the girls said, buy me a drink?

I said sure.

You're a big boy, she said. Come sit here.

She took me by the hand into a little alcove with a bench. It smelled like perfume, some kind of flowery perfume but I didn't mind. She pulled the curtain shut. We sat down.

I'm Maria, she said. You're real good looking. Sailor boy?

Air Force.

Oh, you fly them big planes?

Sometimes, I said.

You mean like those really big ones? You know, the ones that look like this: She held up her thumb.

B-52s, I said. Yes. I mean, yes I do fly them.

But, you're so young.

I shrugged.

It didn't matter much but I hated that I had said that about flying B-52s. I do that sometimes. I say I'm something that I'm not or I might say that my father was a Navy Officer when he was only a Chief Petty Officer. I know I shouldn't but I do it anyway.

Maria had on a real short dress and a blouse that showed a lot of her breasts. She pulled one part of the way down.

You like?

I nodded.

You like me?

I mumbled a "yes". She put her hand on my leg. Then she unbuttoned her blouse letting one of them out of its cage.

It's alright. You can touch.

Which I did.

You want to see more?

I said that I did.

Come on, she said. We can go upstairs.

For some reason it came into my head that she was probably a prostitute and this was going to cost money which I didn't have a lot of. Not only that but I heard stories of guys getting rolled in places like this.

I don't think I will, I said.

No? You scared? Maybe you don't like?

I shook my head which I guess could have meant anything.

I can't stay with you if you don't like me.

Maria opened the curtains. I took my beer back to the bar. She sat down with the others on the opposite side. Gary and Rob were nowhere to be seen. I ordered another beer for fifty centavos.

Hey Amigo, said the bartender. Something wrong with Maria? You want someone better maybe?

No, no, nothing wrong with her, I said. I didn't want her to get in trouble. It's just that … I didn't know what to say.

Did you give her a tip?

He wasn't acting friendly anymore

No, you little prick?

Lucky for me a whole bus load of sailors came stomping down the stairs just then. I think it was the same bunch we saw on the street but without the drunk one. Maybe the Shore Patrol got him. The bartender's smile came back.

Hey Amigos, bienvenido a casa.

The whole crew got busy with the sailors. Just then Rob and Gary came halfway down the stairs and signaled to me to come. I left the rest of the beer and made for the exit.

We spent the rest of the night in a bar getting drunk. After that thing with Maria I wasn't much in the mood but after a few beers it got better. There was a strip show where the girls danced on a long raised platform.

159

One of the girls danced right in front of me. She took off everything but her panties. I could see right through them: I mean: Right through. She turned around and bent over. She looked back at me through her legs and smiled. Without thinking on it I reached up to touch her. She pulled back. No, no, she said. No touch.

I wondered about her. Did she have a family? I don't know: Maybe a kid? I would have liked to talk to her, ask her some things but there wasn't any way to do that. Rob and Gary would have said I was cracked if I told them.

That happens to me a lot. There's things I think which I can't tell anybody. It's just inside my head.

Maybe I could have told Mom but I never got the chance. Besides, I was too young then to have anything like that in my head.

There was never any way I could tell Pop. He did tell me once that he wanted to know what was happening with me but I never took him up on it.

I did say something once to him but it never panned out. I said this before about how I didn't understand how things work with a man and a woman. I desperately wanted to know but I couldn't figure out what to ask. So one day – I must have been about twelve or thirteen – I said it out loud: Pop, how does it work? You know? I guess I wasn't clear. We were standing outside by the pump. He thought I was talking about how the pump worked. He started telling me the whole thing. That was the last time I tried that.

We slept in the car that night. It was tight. I got the front seat and the steering wheel; Rob and Gary got the back seat. Mostly we didn't sleep.

The next day was bad. I had the worst headache of my life and the sun was fierce. We drove back to the Base without stopping. I left the car outside Betsy's quarters and walked back to the Barracks. It was Sunday.

The next morning at the CP Aunt Betsy came in carrying a glass. Look what I found in the glove box, she said.

It was a beer glass with "Club Tijuana" in gold letters.

You drove my car to Tijuana?

I didn't know what to say. After a couple of minutes she laughed. That got me going too.

All right, she said. I don't want to know about it.
I went over to her place after work. We made out; it felt good.
I hope you didn't catch anything down there, she said.
I didn't tell her that there was no chance of that.

June 28, 1959: 1108 Days

The civilian women's quarters were pretty crazy. One day I was sitting in Maria's front room waiting for Betsy to come home. Maria was in the bedroom.

You young guys, she said, you just kill me. All you can think about is ... well, you know what it is. What do you think happens when a woman gets older? Not that I'm old but later. What do you think?

She brought me a beer from the fridge and went back to the bedroom.

Well, you just toss us away when we get old. What would your mother say to that?

Mom's dead, I said.

She was quiet for a couple of minutes. I heard a zipper zipping.

Philly, be a good boy and bring me that shirt that's hanging on the chair.

I got the shirt and took it into the bedroom. What a shock! Maria was naked. I stood there not knowing what to do; my mouth was wide-open.

Ah, that's it. Hand it here please.

I reached across.

That's good. You can go back to your beer now.

And I did but I admit I was a little pumped up. In a few minutes she came through the doorway dressed. She had a big smile.

Mind if I sit her, she said.

I shook my head like a crazy fool.

So, she said, have you met Sheila? She's available you know. But I hear she's been going out with a 2d lieutenant.

You all are lucky, she said. Nineteen, twenty years old, living in Southern California.

162

September 9, 1959: 1035 Days

It was a big day. An Atlas missile was to be launched down range as if we were going to war. General Power, the commander of SAC, flew his KC135 down from SAC headquarters in Omaha. The aircraft was packed full of staff officers. General Power was at the controls of the airplane. This trip was his third. All of the other launch dates had to be scrubbed at the last minute. Betsy and I stood outside MOD II guidance during the countdown waiting for liftoff. She had her blood red dress on. It's the one where it is hard to see how she gets it on.

You think it's going to go this time? she said.

Major Riley said that most of the problems had been worked out. I think it's a go, he said.

It was a beautiful day: No clouds, total blue. From MOD II we could see the rocket on its launch pad. Little wisps of fuel came up from the fueling vents.

5 – 4 – 3 – 2 – 1, engine ignition.

The rocket was held down by metal arms which fell back when the proper thrust was reached. The Atlas lifted off its engines blazing. The noise was terrific. The ground started to shake as if there was an earthquake. It felt almost exactly like that time when I was about seven and walking home from school. I didn't know what it was. My knees felt like rubber like they wouldn't hold me up. I was scared. When I got home Mom said what it was. I never thought that the whole earth could shake like that. It made me think that nothing was safe.

It seemed like it took many minutes before the rocket was even a couple of hundred feet off the ground. Suddenly, the thrusters began to swing back and forth causing the rocket to pinwheel in the air. I mean this was a six story building turning a circle like it was a pin wheel.

Finally the controllers must have got back some control and the Atlas went higher but at a angle toward the ocean. After another minute or two the rocket exploded like it was a part of a 4th of July show. The pieces fell into the ocean off Pt. Arguello. It took another couple of minutes before anyone spoke.

Wow, said Betsy.

Double-wow, said Major Riley.

General Power raced off to the airfield he was so angry. He left a plane full of officers behind.

After work Aunt Betsy said I should come by. I'll get us a beer, she said.

I didn't need a second invitation. She looked that good.

My buddy Bruce was from Chicago. He lived two barracks down toward the mess hell. He said he was getting out of the Air Force to study architecture as soon as his enlistment was up. In eighty-seven days, he said. He already had a ton of drawings which he said were going to revolutionize building. I looked at the drawings but I couldn't figure out what he was talking about.

You heard of Frank Lloyd Wright? he said.

No.

He's only the world's greatest architect. I'm going to study with him when I'm done with the Air Force.

In school?

Sort-of. He takes certain students to his place in Arizona. He calls it "Taliesin West" because he has a home in Wisconsin called "Taliesin". You're kind of an apprentice. You work on projects that he's interested in.

Are you going to re-up?

I don't know, I said.

You have to go to college if you're going to get anywhere.

But you didn't finish college.

True, so true. But I did two years.

Did you get good grades?

Grades, I don't know. I never looked at them.

No kidding. You never looked at them?

Nope. Waste of time. I didn't want to know.

Was this in Chicago?

Bruce nodded. Yah, University of Chicago.

Was it tough to get in?

Very tough. There's a bunch of assholes there. They think they're the tops. Most of them come from rich families. Me, I was the scholarship kid from the wrong side of town.

I liked Bruce but there were times when he was a little too much.

He showed me the drawings that he was going to send to Taliesin. Some of them looked like Buck Rogers. There was one that looked like part of an Atlas rocket. Well, it was like a kind of a nose cone with steps. Bruce liked it that I paid attention to his stuff.

Hey, he said. Let's go to town for a beer.

That would be great but I'm not twenty-one.

Not a problem. You look a lot like Craig. You can borrow his I.D..

It was true, Craig did look like me. But he wasn't ready to loan me his I.D. until Bruce said he had a bottle of "Old Grandad" for him. Bruce said that Craig was on his way to being an alky.

You ever notice how his hands shake? he said. And there's nicotine all over his fingers.

That was true.

It's a short drive from the main gate to Lompoc over a twisty road. The top was down and the sun was coming in at us from the ocean. I felt good.

Lompoc isn't much to write home about. There's a main street with a J.C. Penny and a couple of bars. We parked on Main.

Let's check out the "Do Drop Inn", said Bruce.

This was my first time in a bar. Except for Tijuana where it didn't matter how old you were. I was nervous, I don't mind saying. What happens if they see you have a fake I.D? Do they call the cops? Man, that would be a hassle.

The bar was in a long room. In the back beyond the bar there was a small stage and some tables. Bruce said there was music and dancing on the weekends. If you call "country music", "music". There were booths along one wall opposite the bar. We sat on stools at the bar.

Howdy gents. You boys got I.D.s?

Bruce showed his; I gave him Craig's. He looked at the picture as if he didn't believe it but then he smiled and said: Ok Craig, you're ok. What'll it be? Bruce ordered a Bud and I said I'd have the same.

The juke box played a Hank Williams tune. My Pop has all of his records. The mirror in the back of the bar had a string of Christmas tree lights from one end to the other just above the rows of liquor bottles.

Oh well, 87 days and I'll be back in Chicago.

I thought you were going to that place: Tail spin?

Taliesin. Yah, but I can't start until next fall. I'll be in Chicago until then. I'm going back to the University. If it works out I'll finish before. I don't have too much more to go.

There was a big curve at one end of the bar. A woman came in and sat down along the curve. I'm not much good at judging age but I guess she was forty or, maybe, even fifty. Like Maria.

Hey my girl. It's been a coon's age since you've been in, said the bartender. What is it? Your old man on the warpath again?

The bartender brought her a drink called a "Manhattan". I don't know what was in it but it looked pretty strong. She smiled at me.

What are you boys up to on Saturday night?

Bruce said we were just having a beer; hanging out, you know.

Yes, I do know.

Say, do you boys want to sit in a booth? My name's Dore, with an accent. What's yours?

I'm Phil; he's Bruce.

I looked at Bruce who gave me a twisted sort of smile. I hunched my shoulders because I couldn't see anything wrong with it.

We moved to a booth: Bruce and me slid in opposite Dore. We ordered two more beers.

Oh hey, Dore said, I'll get that. My pleasure to help out two young, handsome Airmen.

An Airman 1st Class named Jose from the Squadron sat down with us. I knew that he lived off Base in Lompoc. Bruce didn't look too happy. When both Dore and Jose got up he looked at me with a sneer on his face.

Let's get out of here.

Why? It's cool.

The bar was filling up. A band was warming up on the stage at the back. It must have been about nine.

No kidding, let's go.

Let's stay until the band gets going. Might be good.

Naw, I'm out-of-here. I'll catch the shuttle back.

And he left.

Where's your friend? Said Dore.

He wasn't feeling too good. He's going back to the Base.

Dore sat down next to me.

Oh, that's too bad. I hope it wasn't me.

No, no, I said. No way.

Her perfume was like flowers, or, maybe, raspberries.

Jose came back.

Hey, where's that queer friend of yours? Didn't like the competition, hey.

I knew what "queer" meant it's just that I didn't see it about Bruce. It was odd, anyway, because at different times I had been followed by guys. One time on my way home this guy followed me for maybe ten or fifteen minutes. He stayed back far enough that I wasn't worried but I couldn't figure out if it was my imagination or what.

A guy was on stage working his guitar. He was dressed like Elvis. His hair was streaked back like a duck. It was a little cakey – his hair – like he had used a lot of Wildroot on it. My hair was never like that. My Pop wouldn't stand for it. The men in this family aren't pansies, he said. His hair was so short you couldn't hide a pea in it if you tried. My hair was almost as short. I like it that way. It keeps my head cool.

Say, said Dore, want to dance?

It was a slow song: "Send me the pillow that you dream on", real slow. We got going pretty good. I even tried that fancy thing where you spin her around with your arm and then catch her.

Hey, you're good, she said.

We danced a couple of more songs.

Say, why don't we ditch your friend and go back to my place?

Ditch him?

Yah, you know: Two's company, three's a crowd. We could have a drink at my place. It's only around the block.

When we got back to the booth Jose said he wanted us to go over to his place. I looked at Dore who looked like she might have bit down on a real hot pepper.

It's close, Jose said. I've got a fridge full of beer.

Jose's wife and kids were gone but there were kids' toys everywhere. There was a fire truck with a ladder that could be raised by turning a handle. There were a couple of soft animals with huge eyes. For a little girl I guessed.

Jose brought beer from the refrigerator. Dore went to the bathroom.

Hey man, said Jose, his voice real soft. She's got the hots for you. Let me in on it.

I don't know about that, I said.

Oh come on man. Let's do it. Look, I'll disappear for awhile like I'm sacking out. You get it going and when she's all set I'll come back. What do you say?

Jose unscrewed a light bulb from the lamp and replaced it with a red bulb which made it look like we were in Tijuana.

Hey, said Dore, what gives? What's with the light?

She sat down next to me. I think I'm gonna be sick, said Jose. He disappeared into the back of the house. I put my arm along the back of the couch just touching Dore's shoulder. She leaned back against me.

Cozy, she said. And I do like the red light. Makes me think of something hot.

And then she did something that floored me. She reached over and put her hand between my legs. That was like starting a fire.

I turned toward her. In a second we were flat out on the couch, me on top.

We were sailing along when out of the blue (or out of the red, I guess), she screamed.

What? I said raising up thinking I had done something wrong.

Jose was on all fours beside the couch. He must have crawled in like a dog.

You creep!

Dore picked up her purse and headed to the door. Aren't you going to walk me home? I'm scared. I've been violated.

I looked at Jose. I'm sorry, I said. I've got to walk her home.

And I did.

Her house was on Pleasant Street. She unlocked the door and switched on a light. Sorry, no red here. Too bad because I did like that light. It was like anything could happen.

She took my hand and led me to a bedroom. I saw work clothes on the back of a chair and a man's shoes by the closet.

Oh, don't worry about that. He's working at Antelope Lake Dam. He won't be home for two days.

She pulled me toward her on the bed. Do you like me?

I didn't say anything. We kissed and then undressed. As old as she was she was still in good shape.

Afterward she said that her old man was never around. He's either working or tired, she said.

I didn't say anything. What could I say?

Anytime you want to get together just give me a call. She handed me a slip of paper with her telephone number on it. If he answers you can say you've got a wrong number. I sure would like to see you again.

I got out of there as quick as I could.

At the Motor Pool the next day I saw Jose who was checking out a two-and-a-half ton for the Blockhouse.

Hey man, did you score?

I shook my head yes along with a big smile.

She sure was hot. Too bad I scared her off. She could have handled both of us.

Aunt Betsy wouldn't let me near her. She was friendly and we worked together but every time I tried to come over she said no. According to Maria the reason was her new boyfriend, that bartender. Maria said he was married. She didn't think it would last much longer.

It was ok because I was spending more time with Sheila.

One Saturday in November we drove to Santa Maria over the Hill Road. It was warm and the top was down. It's not like this where I come from, Sheila said. It's already cold there.

Where's that.

New York State. Saranac Lake. In the Adirondacks?

It gets cold there? Snow?

Plenty. We get hammered. I've seen months where the snow gets six feet or more deep.

God, what do you do? Just stay-in?

Mostly. We play games. Hide-and-go-seek. You know. Grown-up games.

We came down off of the ridge curling around the hill. Santa Maria was down in the valley maybe five or six miles off. Sheila looked good. Her black hair was blown back like those wind socks at small airports. She smiled: Made me smile back. It felt like we were as free as birds. But then I remembered that I had to report back to Major Zimmer on Monday. For the first time I felt like I wanted to get out of the Air Force. It was an idea that just popped into my head. I wasn't sure. Maybe college. Maybe something else.

What about you and Betsy?

For a few seconds I had forgotten Sheila, Santa Maria and the road. I wasn't sure what she knew so I decided to play it easy.

Me and Betsy? We work together.

Yah, yah, that I know. But isn't there something more?

Something more?

Are you going to repeat everything I say? Look out there's a truck in this lane.

I swerved but it was close.

Maybe you don't want to talk about her?

No, no, I was thinking of something else.

Like?

An answer just opened up inside my head. I don't know where it came from: I was thinking about you.

Sheila said nothing. I saw her look at me out of the corner of my eye. She seemed to lean a little closer in but the gear shift was in the way.

In Santa Maria we passed by Allan Hancock Junior College.

There's a sign to a park. Want to stop? I said.

We snagged a bench at Mueller Park, me on one side, Sheila on the other. The bench was beside a tree. The shade kept us cool.

Eucalyptus, said Sheila. It's a Eucalyptus tree. Here: Smell this.

The leaf did smell. Asphalt, maybe, like the asphalt plant when my cousin worked.

You didn't answer my question, she said.

Which one?

About Betsy K.

I thought I did. We work together. She's a friend. Ask Maria.

She gave me a look like she didn't believe me.

Ok I guess that's all I'll get. Mind if I sit over there?

Before I could say anything she came around the table and sat next to me.

You're real cute, she said.

No lie?

No lie.

Sheila's arms were bare. The dress she wore didn't have any sleeves. Our arms touched just at the elbow. Little electric shocks sped up my arm and into my hair.

You want to kiss? she said.

We kissed all right. She swung her legs over the bench so that she was facing me. I saw a little pink thing as her legs came over.

I guess after that we were going together.

We stopped at a Dairy Queen for a hotdog and coke and then back to the Base. It was late in the afternoon, almost dark. We went to her rooms which were a few doors down from Aunt Betsy's and Maria's rooms. I was scared they'd see us.

We sat on the Davenport in her room. It was about enough for two-and-a-half people so it wasn't long before we were scrunched together and it wasn't long after that before we fell to kissing and such.

Well, the bed was only a couple of feet away and it doesn't take long if you're in a hurry to get your clothes off. I liked the way she looked even better without clothes. Sheila isn't tall: She about comes up to my shoulders. I guess you could say she's compact. Compact and curved.

It was dark before I knew it. We lay in bed together her left leg over my right. It felt real good.

We could make a couple, she said.

That alarmed me: I wasn't sure what she meant by that.

How old are you Phil?

I'll be twenty next month. In July.

Oh good, we're the same age. That's a good sign.

A good sign?

You know, couples should be about the same age. Not too far apart. My husband was almost ten years older than me.

Where is he? Your husband, I mean.

I had heard stories about husbands catching their wives with another guy. There was hell to pay.

Oh, he's still here but we're finished. He's a staff sergeant.

Pop and me used to take what we called wind-therapy. When the weather was good and he wasn't working on the pump we stretched out on the lawn and let the wind blow over us. Pop said it was like therapy. I saw what he meant. I didn't think of a thing. I never fell asleep but it was close.

Psst. Sheila: It's me.

Well, I nearly jumped out of my skin. There was somebody outside the window. I couldn't see who because the window was a-ways off of the ground. Sheila put her finger to her mouth to keep me still.

What is it Dean? I'm in bed half asleep. If the APs see you, you won't be happy.

They won't see me. Let me come in. I won't stay long. I just have to talk to you. Please?

No. No, you can't come in. Remember the last time? That was it for me.

Well, they kept talking like that for awhile. I don't know maybe ten or fifteen minutes. Finally Dean - or whatever his name is – decided to go.

What was that all about?

I went out with him a couple of times. That's all. He's a Lieutenant. I'm sorry I ever encouraged him. Are you all right?

Yah, but I'd better go.

Oh no, stay a little longer. Please?

So I did stay a little longer but I sure wasn't comfortable. Suppose he had hoisted himself up on the sill. We would have been looking straight at each other. Him in his Lieutenant's gold bar and me in my sailor suit, as Pop would say. What would have happened? It was a real close call.

Mrs. Torongo – the librarian at Mac Junior High – had me work for her during third period. I shelved books and checked out books to the students. There was a kind of knob which had the dates on a roller. I pressed the date into an ink pad and then stamped the due date on to a paper glued inside the book. I liked Mrs. T. I'm not sure how old she was because her hair was grey but the rest of her didn't look old. She had those big green eyes that stared straight at you.

The library was in a part of the school building that jutted out from the rest of the building. The shelves were along two walls and there were tables and chairs in the middle. At one end were windows onto the football field and the woods where Russ and Ken and me used to smoke after class. At the other end of the room was the office where Mrs. T had her desk and a counter for check-out.

Oh, that's such a good book, she might say to a student. Is this for History or Civics?

The library had a movie projector. The theater was in a room with dark shades that could be pulled down for movies. Mrs. T. said she wanted me to learn how to set up and play the projector.

Now come in close Phil. Watch how I'm threading it. See, right through here and then loop around this way.

We were standing very close together in the dark. Her hip accidentally touched mine. She smiled. Oh, pardon me.

I never saw Mrs. T. after 9th grade but I still think about her. She wrote a good report on my report card which I still have. She said my work was executed in a most satisfactory manner. "I have enjoyed having him on the staff", she said. "I have thoroughly enjoyed knowing Phil... He has contributed much to Mac Junior High."

Well, I'm not sure I was that great but I'll take it. I don't know whether or not she got another student assistant.

Maybe I have a thing for librarians.

Sheila and me became a couple. Or sort of one. I still had it in for Aunt Betsy but she was all in with her bartender boy friend. Whenever we talked she only wanted to talk about Sheila.

Isn't she the best, she'd say. And so pretty. I think you two are made for each other.

Several times I tried to put my arm around her but she always pulled away. Oh no, she'd say. That wouldn't be right.

You'll get over me, she said. I'm too old for you.

She was way wrong about that. Even to this day I'm not over her.

I got promoted to A1C after I got good evaluations from the CP.

Colonel Evdokimoff stopped me when I delivered some papers to HQ.

Airman, how'd you like to come to work here? I saw your recommendations. I think you would fit right in.

I didn't know exactly what to say.

Major Zimmer and the others won't like losing you but I mean to pull rank. We'll arrange it so you get started on Monday.

He introduced me to Master Sergeant Willis who was the Chief Administrative Clerk. His desk was just outside General Crow's office. General Crow was the Deputy Commander and General Preston was the Commanding Officer.

Sergeant Willis was spit-and-polish. His hair was cut as short as Pop's and his shoes were like two mirrors. He was about my height, stocky, not fat. It was like he was always standing at attention. His back was straight and he looked you in the eye. But he smiled a lot. At least when things went well.

Welcome aboard Airman. I think you'll like it here. He showed me where my desk was just outside the big room and off the hall leading to the other offices in HQ. There were two secretaries one for General Crow and Colonel Rasmussen together who sat in the big room across from Sergeant Willis and opposite Colonel Ev's desk. General Preston's secretary had her own office which was just outside the General's office. They both had IBM Selectrix typewriters. There was a little ball which you put into a slot on the typewriter. The ball rotated to the right number or letter as you typed on the keyboard. Real cool.

Part of my job was to set up the conference room whenever there was to be a meeting. I had a list of who was coming and we had a box with name plates which had to be set around the big conference table. Everything was done in order. If General Preston was going to be there he sat at the head of the table. General Crow and Colonel Rasmussen were next sitting across from each other. Then came any Colonel, Major, etc.. I set out ashtrays, big amber colored ashtrays, around the table. Everybody smoked. Fresh coffee and ice water was on a table by the windows. Sometimes I had to set up a projector if they were going to show a movie. Thanks Mrs. T.

The Headquarters building was big. I had to deliver stuff – letters, orders, plans – to the other units in the building so, naturally, I got to know the other administrative people, mostly civilians. One afternoon the secretary from the 1st Missile Squadron came into the big room. I was talking to Sergeant Willis about what I should do with a batch of letters that I found in my basket when he turned and, I swear, lit up like a Christmas tree.

Ah, Neva, where have you been? It's been a coon's age.

Sergeant Willis was originally from Georgia. He said things like that.

Neva was Colonel Martin's secretary. Her office was just down the hall and around the corner. We had already met but I didn't know anything about her.

So, Airman, Neva here is Texas. The Pan Handle aren't you darlin'? What is the name of that town?

You know perfectly well. You just want me to repeat it.

Ah yes, Muleshoe. Muleshoe, Texas. Now how about that Airman?

Neva was very pretty. I guess you could say that her face was perfect as if it came right out of a magazine. She had a beautiful smile with the whitest teeth I've ever seen.

What can we do for you my dear?

Neva seemed a bit flustered from all of the attention. I don't blame her.

Sergeant Willis, Colonel Martin wants a copy of that letter on Tuesday from General Preston. The one that went out to SAC Hq.

Why sure enough Miss.. Airman Greevey will fetch it for you. If you care to follow him to his private suite?

And she did: Follow me.

It's nice to meet you, she said. I'm Neva.

Phil, call me Phil. We shook hands. Her hand was cool.

Let me check the file. I think I filed that letter yesterday.

My, you've done a lot of work in here. This place used to be a mess. I don't know how anybody ever found anything.

Thanks. Yah, it was a mess. I think I've got it under control. Here it is.

My heavens, that was quick.

I'll make you a copy on that new machine.

It was nice meeting you. I'm sure we'll see a lot of each other. She gave a big smile.

I hope so, I said, bold as brass.

So, what did you think, said Sergeant Willis when I walked back to the big office. She's somethin' isn't she?

I nodded.

But, he said, she's married. Not that that would stop me but she can't be bought. I've tried.

I don't know why I said what I said next and I still regret it some.

I bet I could if I tried.

Now, why I said that I don't know. The most I had to go on was that smile. But she probably smiled at everybody like that.

Oh, said the Sergeant. Now I wonder if you'd like to make a little bet? Think about it. She's a married, Christian woman from Muleshoe, Texas not some strumpet from God knows where.

I swear that the Sergeant was a little angry but I went right on in.

Can we make it just a friendly bet?

Sure, sure anyway you want it.

Well, that started it. I wasn't all too serious especially since Sheila and me were still going strong but I guess I felt like it was a challenge.

It might seem a little odd especially but sometimes I say I'm going to do something which I don't have any reason to think I can. I kind of step-in without knowing how deep it is.

May 11, 1961: 425 Days

We sat in Sheila's room, me on the chair and her on the bed. There was a pretty steady rain outside but not like the rain at home. The room was getting dark; we hadn't turned on a light. We both liked it like that: Everything in shadows and the rain kicking against the window.

I got a letter from my sister, Sheila said. She says that Mum and Pop are sorry we got in that fight.

Fight? Did you tell me about that?

I don't know if I did. Anyway, I left home because of it. My Pop especially. They were always fighting. Mostly it was the beer. They sat around watching tv and drinking beer. And then one of them would say something that the other didn't like and that would get it going. I pretty much had enough. When my husband came back on leave and asked me to marry him, well, I did. My folks never liked Benny which, I guess, might have been part of the reason I married him.

What does your sister say now.

Oh, she says they're sorry. She says they've sobered up.

Somebody walked by in the hall. Probably on their way to the ladies'. There wasn't a mens'. If you had to go someone had to stand guard. Once in the middle of the night I decided to risk it without waking Betsy. That caused an uproar when somebody came in while I was in there. It took days to settle it all back down.

So, do you still want to do it? said Sheila. I still do.

Well, what that was was that she wanted us to get a place together off Base. Santa Maria maybe. She had talked about it a few times. Me, I didn't know. I did like the idea of living off Base but I wasn't too sure about living like a married person. I told Sheila that I didn't know for sure.

177

It would be so cool, she said.

I just nodded.

I got my final divorce papers today, she said. I'm free as a bird.

What I thought about that was that I was still free as a bird. But living together did have its good part. I could see sleeping together every night, eating dinner together and other stuff which I knew must be a part of it but that I couldn't quite pin down. It's like you see stuff in the movies about the way people live so you have an idea but it's not like you've done it so until then it's not real.

When I got back to the barracks Tom was just coming back from Fullerton. As usual he wasn't too happy to be back.

Jesus-H-Christ, he said. The fuckin' freeway was a mess.

He was lying flat on his bunk with his feet propped up on the bedrail. His hands were crossed under his head.

What's with you? he said. Girlfriend blues?

Pretty much, I said. She wants us to move in together.

That got him to sit straight up. No shit? Are you going to?

I shrugged. Maybe. There's good and bad about it.

Where's the bad man? You get off the Base almost like you're civilian. If my girl was here I'd do it in a flash. Oh boy, would I. Instead I have to haul ass down to Fullerton every weekend for a few hours of what you would get every day. You kiddin' me?

Yah, I guess. But, I'm not ready to get married not like you are. Maybe I'm going to college after this. Maybe I'll travel. You know, Europe, South America.

You can do that married. My buddy in high school did it. He and his wife hitch-hiked across country.

When I got to thinking about what I'd do after the Air Force I got a little scared. If I was with someone – like Sheila – that wouldn't happen.

I laid awake for awhile thinking it all over. Tom was asleep about as soon as his head hit the pillow. Pop told me to think things through before doing something. He said I should picture the possibles and what they would mean. Kind of weigh one thing against another. Well, when I did that it seemed to come down on the side of living with Sheila. I went to sleep on that.

Colonel Ev said he wanted to give me some advice. I was standing by his desk in the big room waiting for some papers that he wanted me to deliver to the CP. Even though I had changed jobs I kept going to the motor pool for a vehicle each day. The Colonel talked to me while he was going through a big pile of papers.

You know, he said, you should go to college when you finish your enlistment. If you want to get anywhere in life you have to do it. It got me started.

Where did you go to school, sir?

For undergraduate I went to Michigan. Then I did some graduate work at Cornell. I can tell you that both were top-notch.

But you, he said, should go to UC. There's a fine campus in Berkeley. Got any idea what you'd like to study?

I told him that I had been reading some books in Philosophy from the Base Library but they were hard to understand. When I was young, I said, I did read about Nuclear Physics.

You'd need a lot of Mathematics. How did you do in high school? In Math?

That was a sore subject with me. My best friend Ron Blankenship and me were in the same Algebra class in tenth grade. The teacher Mr. Glover had a bald head and a weird smile. He liked to call on us without warning.

Phil Greevey: You have thirty seconds. What are the solutions to the equation $x^2 + x - 6 = 0$?

Well, at first I wasn't sure what to do. I thought I should use the quadratic formula because that's what I had worked on the night before. It took a few seconds to get it set up and it was coming but then Mr. Glover rang this little bell. Just as the bell went off and I was getting close, Ron said: $x = 2, x = 3$.

And how did you get that? Mr. Greevey here is laboring mightily.

Factoring, sir, he said.

Ah yes, factoring. Well, Mr. Greevey you would do well to remember that.

I told Colonel Ev that I did ok in Math in high school. I thought I might take a course at Allan Hancock in September.

Good idea. Deliver these to Major Zimmer. Make sure he gets them personally and have him sign the receipt.

Yes sir.

Colonel Ev was short and stocky. He had yellow hair which was combed straight back over his head. He had some kind of bracelet on his wrist which jangled when he moved. His voice was smooth, like silk, Sergeant Willis said. But I thought it was kind of grainy like small pebbles bouncing off each other, if you know what I mean.

BMOC, he said. That's what you'll be.

BMOC?

Big Man On Campus. The world will be your oyster.

I couldn't get what he meant by that but it sounded good.

Sergeant Willis told me what to do to get permission to live off base. He said it shouldn't be a problem.

The trouble was that I was getting less-and-less sure about it but I had pretty much told Sheila I'd do it. She checked out an ad in the Santa Maria Times. It's a one bed, she said, furnished. Can we take a look this weekend?

I didn't see my way clear to say no but I didn't feel good about it. If I had had the nerve I would have broken up with her then and there. But I didn't want to hurt her.

I had the same problem in high school. It was hard for me to say no. The chance that I might hurt her feelings was just too much. I knew how it would be if somebody turned me down.

I took the papers from Colonel Ev and went down stairs. Neva was just coming back from lunch. Hey, she said.

Hi. I'm on a mission, I said.

Don't let me stop you.

She had the darndest smile. I wanted to turn around and watch her walk upstairs but I didn't.

At the guard station a tv was turned to the news. The announcer said that the Soviet Union had just launched the first man into space. General Crow was just coming in. I gave him my sharpest salute.

Aunt Betsy was at her desk when I walked into Major Zimmer's office. She looked up kind of sudden-like. Her face turned red.

Oh, she said, Philly. I wasn't expecting you.

I'm delivering some papers to Major Zimmer.

Betsy half-smiled. So how are you? I hear you and Sheila are moving?

Yah I guess.

Well, that's nice.

I wanted to ask her about her bartender boyfriend but Major Zimmer walked in.

Well, Airman Greevey. What have you got for me?

I gave him the papers and asked him to sign.

Colonel Ev keeping you busy? We do miss you here, don't we Miss K.?

Major Zimmer went into his office.

Well, I said, I guess I had better get going.

Nice to see you Philly. I hope it works out with Sheila.

She has a mole on her cheek just to the left of her mouth. I can still picture it after all these years.

I don't know how I did it but I said that I thought she looked beautiful but I kind of swallowed "beautiful". This time both of us got the blush-curse.

On Saturday Sheila and I drove into Santa Maria.

What's the address of the place?

592 Boone Street. It's supposed to be close to Allan Hancock.

How much for the rent?

It's a little steep but if we split it 50-50 it shouldn't be too bad: $175 per month.

It sounded like a lot to me. My paycheck was around $210 and I had to make payments to the Credit Union for the MG.

The apartment was in a house with a separate entrance and a driveway. The owner met us at the door.

Oh, she said, so nice to see a young couple. Are you Air Force?

Sheila said we were.

Well, come on in and look around.

There was a small kitchen with a frig and stove, a living room with a Davenport and a couple of chairs. Except for the bedroom, which had a queen-size bed, I don't remember too much detail.

What do you think? Do you like it?

Sheila said yes but we would need to talk about it.

Yes, of course, you go right ahead. Young couples need to talk it over.

Sheila said we would call later in the day.

We drove to a Dairy Queen. For a couple of minutes we were quiet drinking the milkshakes. Finally, just as I was slurping the last drop, Sheila asked me what I thought.

I don't know. It's pretty expensive.

Sheila looked hurt. Well, she said, if you don't want to, that's that.

No, I didn't say that. I mean, I do want to it's just … the money.

I stopped but Sheila didn't look up.

Ok, I said, let's give it a go. It will be fun. What do you say?

She looked at me with a big smile.

Mmm, good. I'd better call the landlady. There's a pay phone inside

Idiot, I thought to myself. Now you've done it.

But then I thought: What's so bad? We live together, make dinner, sleep together and … What's so bad about that. I could see Sheila talking on the phone.

Mrs. Bender says we can move in on the First which is Tuesday. We have to leave a month's deposit.

Well, I didn't have a month's deposit. I guess that showed on my face.

Its ok, said Sheila. I have it.

Well, we did move in on Tuesday. It felt right to be doing this even if I didn't know how it would turn out.

I had permission to live off-base so all I had to do was load my clothes in the boot, tell Tom what I was doing and drive to Boone Street.

That first night Sheila cooked a chicken. She put a candle on the table. Like I said: It wasn't so bad.

Slante, she said, raising her glass.

I figured it meant the same thing as "cheers".

After dinner we watched the tv that was in the apartment. We were just like an old married couple sitting on the Davenport with our feet up on the hassock.

Around 1030 we got into bed. The bed was a little lumpy but neither of us minded. All-in-all we got off to a good start.

Colonel Ev didn't much like my living off-base. He said I should keep my eyes on the main thing which was to go to college. Look, he said, girlfriends are fine but it's easy to get in too far.

Boy was he ever right.

For a while it was ok but then I started to feel trapped. Every morning we drove to the Base and home again at the end of the day. We had dinner, watched tv and then went to bed. One problem was that we didn't have enough money to do anything else. Another was that Sheila kept talking as if everything was settled. She thought we would get married and go from there.

Oh Philly, she once said, we'll have such a beautiful life together. We make a great couple.

I didn't know about that. There were just too many things I hadn't done yet and I didn't see myself the same way she saw me.

But I had an idea.

Sheila, I said, you know the way you talked about your family, your parents? The way you left it?

Yes?

Wouldn't it be better – I mean before we ... we ... Well, if you straightened it out with them. Just so we start with everything in the past ok?

It is ok, at least as far as I'm concerned. What do you mean?

I wasn't too sure what I meant either but I said: Maybe you should go back to New York to see your parents. Kind of straighten it all out. Then ... then you could come back and we would, well, be together. And there'd be no hard feelings with your family. See what I mean?

No, I don't see. Why do I need to make up with them?

You said yourself that your parents were sorry about what happened and that they wanted to fix it. If that were me I'd want to fix it.

Sheila wasn't convinced. I can't go back to New York. I don't have the money. It costs a lot to fly.

She had me there.

The next day I saw an ad from Beneficial Finance in the sports' section of the Santa Maria Times. The ad said they would give personal loans instantly if you had a co-signer. I showed the ad to Sheila.

You mean borrow the money? Who would co-sign?

I pointed at my chest.

Really?

Really.

You'd do that for me?

I said that I would. This put her in the right frame of mind.

And then I'd come back and we'd still be together?

I nodded: Sure, for sure.

On Saturday she said she would need about $100 to make the trip.

The Beneficial Finance office was in the middle of a block in downtown Santa Maria. When we walked in a guy wearing a plaid shirt and one of those cowboy ties got up real quick.

Hello, hello, he said. Come right in. How can I help you? Please sit down.

He corralled another chair to go with the one by the side of his desk.

Jimmy O'Brien, he said. Please, can I get you a coffee? Tea?

We said we were good.

He sat back in his chair. What can I do for you?

Sheila said she wanted a personal loan. $100, she said.

May I ask what it's for?

It's just to tide me over for a month or two. Until I get back on budget.

This surprised me until I realized they might not give a loan to someone who was going to use it to leave. Smart, I thought.

Well, Jimmy said, I might be able to help you there. You both work? Sheila said she was civil service at the Base.

And you're Air Force?

Yes. A1C. Headquarters 1st Strategic Missile Division. I thought this sounded important.

Ok. E-3 pay grade and civil service. I'm sure we can work this out.

And he did. We filled out a couple of forms and we both signed, me as the co-signer which meant, according to Jimmy, that if she couldn't or wouldn't pay Beneficial back then I would have to. I'm sure that won't happen, he said.

We shook hands and took the check around the corner to a bank where Sheila cashed it.

Well, that's done, I said.

Sheila looked pale like she wasn't feeling well.

You ok? I said.

Oh Philly, I hope we're doing the right thing.

So do I, I thought.

Two days later Sheila made reservations to fly home.

She gave two weeks notice at her job. The landlady wasn't happy. She gave us a hard time about the deposit. Sheila told her that she had a family emergency in New York and that seemed to fix it. We did get the deposit back.

The night before she left we had dinner at a place in Santa Maria. It was a restaurant, a bar and a night club or, at least, that's what I thought it looked like because there was a band getting ready. It felt like I was going to be free again. I hadn't thought it through but my plan was to write Sheila a letter breaking it off. I'd find some excuse to make it easier. I thought it would be better for her too. It felt like the right way to do it.

That last night we stayed awake a while. A pretty strong wind blew in around eleven o'clock. It shook the windows which weren't very tight. Sheila held on to me; she cried. It was all I could do not to tell her to stay.

We went to the airport. Sheila checked her bag and got her ticket. We stood waiting for the announcement. Neither of us said anything. For a minute the idea that this was the last time I would ever see her made me choke up.

The flight was announced. We hugged and kissed. She started up the ramp. About half-way she turned around to wave. Then she was inside.

I waited until the plane took off. It was like a weight had been lifted off my chest.

I got in the MG and drove back to town.

I don't know if it was a plan I had or not but I drove straight to that club. It was just getting dark out. A plane flew by overhead; its lights kind of winked. I don't know if it was Sheila's plane or not; probably not.

The club was going strong. The band was playing and the place was packed but just as I came in a table opened up. Lucky I had an ID from one of the guys in the mail room. I ordered an Oly from a beautiful, young waitress. Ok, sir, she said as she poured the beer into a glass. Are you running a tab?

I said I was. She smiled and went back to the bar.

About ten minutes later two young women came in looking for a table. One of them – the taller one with red hair – came over.

Mind if we join you. This place is jammed.

Of course I said yes.

The red-headed one said that her name was Amy and that her friend was Joyce.

Do you come here a lot? said Amy.

It's my first time, I said, not counting yesterday with Sheila.

The waitress came by. Fast-worker, she said, pointing at me.

185

Do you dance? said Joyce.

Yes, but I'm not too good.

Let's give it a go.

She was just about as tall as me. Her breasts were big, like balloons. They pushed against my chest. Not that I complained.

Philly, she said, you're cute and a good dancer.

They told me that they were from Buellton but worked in Santa Maria. Amy was a dentist's helper and Joyce was a secretary.

We grew up together, said Amy.

A little later Amy said she was ready to leave. We promised we would be back by ten, she said.

Joyce didn't want to leave. Give us another hour, she said.

No, I'm going to keep my word, said Amy.

She got up to go. How will you get home?

Joyce looked at me.

I'll give you a ride, I said. No sweat.

Joyce and me danced some more and then I said – I don't know how I did it – I asked her if she would like to come to my place. "My place"? I believe that was the first time in my life that I said that. Well, I know it was because I had never had a place before.

Joyce said she didn't know. She said she wasn't that kind of girl.

I said I wasn't that kind of guy. That seemed to make it ok.

Oh, you're got a sports car. How nice.

The top was down and there was this super, big moon right on top. Her long hair went flying out behind as we picked up speed.

Oh, this is great, she said. She put her hand on my leg which made me step on the gas even more. Lucky there were no cops along the way.

I parked by the garage. I still had the keys because we were supposed to leave them inside for Mrs. Bender.

What a cute little place. You live here all by yourself?

I gave her my best shrug.

She took a look inside a couple of cupboards.

Hmm, she said. Doesn't look like you do much cooking.

She opened the refrigerator. No wonder. There's nothing to cook unless you cook beer. She laughed.

Here's an opener, I said.

We sat down on the Davenport with the beer. She sat real close.

I like you, she said.

Ditto, I said.

She wore a red skirt which hiked north of her knees when she sat back. Like it was all planned, we started closing in on each other. It was like an explosion. After a few minutes – or, maybe, it was seconds – we got up and headed to the bedroom. That's when I saw it – Sheila had forgotten one of her panties which was lying on top of the bedspread. Joyce saw it too.

What's this, she said. You aren't strange are you?

There was nothing I could say so I didn't. Anyway, the panties were soon forgotten as we fell together on the bed. I admit it was strange – a little – being in the bed with her when it had been Sheila only the night before.

The next day I put what little stuff I had in the MG and moved back to the Base. It was lucky that nobody had moved in so I got my old room back with Tom.

Oh my god, he said, as I walked in the door with my duffel. Don't tell me, let me guess. You just couldn't stand it not to see me. So you broke up with your girlfriend?

You got it.

No, seriously, what gives?

Sheila flew back to New York. She said she wanted to see her parents.

That must mean that you weren't quite up to it?

No, no. Her mother or someone was sick.

Ah, I see. Well, welcome back.

I told Colonel Ev that I was back in the barracks. He said he thought that was a good move. You're too young to get tangled up, he said.

I got a letter from Sheila the next week. She said she missed me but everything was now ok with her parents. She thought she might come back in a couple of weeks. That made me super nervous.

I sat down right away and wrote her back.

Dear Sheila,

I'm glad to hear that you and your parents are ok again. I'm good. Back in the barracks with Tom.

But there is something I have to tell you. I've been thinking about it. About you and me, I mean.

Well, I think we're too young to get married or like that. Colonel Ev told me he thought so too. I wasn't sure before but now I am. I want to go to college when I get discharged. I don't see how that could be if we were together.

So, I hope you won't take this the wrong way.

Good luck in the future.

Phil

I read it over a couple of times, put it in an envelope and mailed it. I didn't want to risk her getting back here before she knew.

July 11, 1961: 364 Days

I t was my twenty-first birthday. Aunt Betsy said she wanted to celebrate. We drove in her Chevy to the bowling alley in Lompoc. We sat across from each other in a booth in the bar. The seats had that kind of shiny, purple covering that I've seen in a couple of movies and a nice carpet and lots of lights.

Naturally the waitress carded me but when she saw it was my birthday she said the first drink was on the house. I started to order a beer but Betsy wouldn't go along.

No, no Philly. It's your birthday. You must have champagne. Champagne for the birthday boy, she said.

The waitress brought this tiny glass shaped like a knife and full of bubbles. I can't say I liked it but it wasn't too bad. After that I went back to beer.

I told her what had happened. She didn't seem too surprised.

Philly, you're too good for her. It's true. You need to go to college, get somewhere. Sheila would hold you back.

What about you? I said. Your boyfriend? That bartender?

She looked at me. Her eyes got big and then tears came out. Her mascara, or whatever you call it, started to run down her face in little black rivers.

Aunt Betsy, I didn't mean that. I'm sorry I said that.

Oh, it's ok. I guess I'm not over it yet.

You mean you've broken up?

She nodded.

He went back to his wife.

It struck me as funny that me and Sheila had just broken up too. It was strange like it had all been written down. Betsy and her boyfriend, me and Sheila. Naturally, of course, Sheila didn't know about it yet unless the post office was super quick.

I surprised myself because I reached across the table and took Betsy's hand.

She looked at me. Oh Philly, we're a pair we are. You're so sweet to me.

We talked some about the CP and Maria. We had a few more beers and then we left.

You want to come over? said Betsy.

Boy, did I.

Betsy went to the kitchen and brought back two beers. She gave me a cigarette: A Lucky Strike. I got my Zippo lighter out and lit both cigarettes. Betsy wears a lot of bright, red lipstick which left a red ring around her cigarette. It was sexy.

We smoked for awhile and then Betsy put her cigarette out. Be right back, she said.

I heard her in the bedroom. It sounded like she was undressing.

Then she came back. She was naked. And crying.

I got up.

Oh Philly, she said. She said that over and over. Just: Oh Philly.

I tried to put my arm around her but she wouldn't let me.

No, don't she said. She went back in the bedroom. I didn't know what to do. After a minute I went in the bedroom. She was lying on the bed crying. I laid down beside her. The only thing I could think of was that she wanted to do it but when I put my arms around her she turned away and she kept her knees tight together.

Betsy, I said. What?...

No, she said, don't mind me.

After a while she fell asleep. Just like that. I dressed and went back to the barracks.

A week later I got a letter from Sheila. It was in the mail room but I didn't want to open it there so I folded it and put it in my pocket.

Part of my job was to go into General Preston's office in the morning before he came in. I had to make sure the office was just the way he liked it: Nothing out of place, desk cleared, curtains open full.

When I came out of the office Neva was talking to Sergeant Willis.

SKERRIES AND 1460 DAYS

She had come for a copy of some correspondence between General Preston and SAC Hq. I told her to wait there and I would go get it.

No, no, she said. I'll come with you.

She followed me into my little office. I opened up the folder with the General's letters.

Here it is, I said.

Ok good. I'll take it to the Colonel. Will you walk me back?

That seemed strange but I said I would. It was maybe only fifty or sixty steps from my desk to hers. She sat down at her desk and then looked up.

She wore a huge diamond on her left finger which when it caught the light just right sent sparks in my eyes.

Thanks Philly. Thanks a lot.

You're welcome, I said.

I thought about it on the way back to the office. It was strange. Why would she want me to do that? The more I thought about it the more I thought she was flirting. But then, I thought, she's married. That ring. That flashy ring.

Sergeant Willis came to the door. Did you take care of Neva?

I told him that I gave her a copy of the letter from General Preston to General Power.

She's somethin' isn't she? Too bad she isn't on the market.

Well, I said, I thought she was flirting with me just now.

What. No way kemo sabe. No way.

It looked that way to me.

Now you've lost it Airman. Tell you what. If you can get a date with her there's a cool $20 in your pocket. If you can't, it's in mine.

I wasn't as sure as I sounded but there was no way I could back out so I said ok.

All right Airman. It's a bet.

I thought about the bet the rest of the afternoon. Pop always said that vanity was the downfall of fools. I guessed he was right.

Sheila's letter burned me. She said I was a bastard, that I never meant to be with her and that I had tricked her into going home. Goodbye you double-bastard, she wrote.

"Double-bastard"? I couldn't figure out what that meant but it was bad.

I showed Tom the letter. He was lying on his bunk but he sat straight up as he read.

Wow, he said. She wants to fry you.

Yah, I know. Actually, she's about right. I do feel like a heel.

Are you going to write back?

I shook my head no.

I tore the letter into little pieces and when I was on the road to Santa Maria threw the pieces out the back.

I didn't really think I could get anywhere with Neva but because of the bet with the sergeant I had to try. What I did was stop by her office at least once a day. She was real friendly. She told me about Muleshoe. She said the country was flat and the wind tried to blow you away. There was a church, a tavern and a diner and that was all except for a few houses. Her father distributed propane gas in a fifty-mile radius of Muleshoe. Her mother stayed home and, as Neva said, worked at staying sane. She said it was about a million miles from anywhere.

I didn't ask but she told me about her husband. They both were from Muleshoe. They had gone to school together. Everyone assumed they would get married and they did. She said they got married right after high school and then he enlisted. She was happy to leave Muleshoe. Except for her parents.

I told her a little about my family.

What about Sheila? she said.

Sheila? What about her?

She works on the first floor, she said, in procurement. My best friend works with her.

That set me back a little. I said that Sheila had decided to go back to New York.

Does that mean you're not dating?

I said that it did.

She smiled.

I think it was a couple of weeks later as I was heading out the door after closing up the office. Sergeant Willis had already left for the day. General Preston's secretary came by my office to say good night which meant I was cleared to close up. When I got to the main entrance Neva was standing by the door.

Anything wrong?

My car won't start. I don't know how I'll get home.

No problem: I can give you a ride.

Really?

Come on. I hope you don't mind a little wind. The top is down.

Mind? I love it.

Which was funny coming from Muleshoe.

Neva wore a red sweater that fitted her very well.

Where are you heading? I said.

Lompoc.

Ok. How about a little spin first?

Great.

I drove down to the beach at Point Arguello. We got out and started walking along the beach.

It's nice here, she said. I like the ocean. It's so different than in Texas.

I told her that all I knew about Texas was the basic training I did at San Antonio and Administrative School in Amarillo.

Amarillo is in the same part of Texas as Muleshoe. Except it's a whole lot bigger. What did you think?

I shrugged. I didn't get much of a chance to look around. I think I wouldn't like some place where there aren't any trees. I mean, to speak of.

She agreed with me.

We walked a little more but then sat down on a big driftwood log that had washed way up on the beach. It was as smooth as paper.

We were quiet for a few minutes looking at the ocean. The waves were pretty big. They rolled in and then smashed against the sand making a kind of hissing sound as they went back out.

I guess I'd better go, she said. You sure you won't mind driving me?

Oh no.

She had me pull over a couple of blocks away from her house. She said she needed the exercise. That seemed strange since we had just walked a bunch on the beach.

This is swell, she said. Thanks Philly.

I watched her as she walked away. She turned and waved.

I wondered if this counted as a date.

So, there I was: Neva on the one hand and Sheila on the other not to speak of Aunt Betsy. Looking back on it now I think it was a dream. There's only a feeling that it really did happen but there's nothing to back it up. Besides a memory sprinkle or two. It's like a kind of fog which I can't touch. Was that really me? Did those things really happen?

I'm inclined to believe that they didn't happen. What I see out this window, the lake, the trees those small children running on the lawn – that's real. The rest is just ghosts.

July 26, 1961: 349 Days

Neva would step into my little room at Hq from time-to-time just to have a chat. Sergeant Willis noticed.

Jesus airman, are you serious? Are you getting to first base?

I told him that I had given her a ride home when her car broke down. She was just being nice, I said.

No kidding. Did you see her old man? I hear that he's a jealous s.o.b..

That jealousy business did worry me. In high school I had a date with someone who had just broken up with her steady. When we got to the dance he was waiting outside. He was a big bastard, a right tackle on the football team. He grabbed my date by the arm. I moved toward him but he stuck a big hand on my chest. Get lost punk, he said.

I stayed clear which wasn't what my date wanted.

What? You're letting him take me? Chicken, are you chicken?

I guess it was because I backed right away. I rationalized it by saying that they deserved each other. A couple of years ago I was visiting my Stepmom when I saw the pair of them on the street. He was as big as a small house and she looked like she had been put through the rungs of an old-fashioned washing machine like the one my Stepmom used. Neither of them saw me or, if they did, made any move to stop.

Colonel Ev said he was going to be the pilot for a trip General Preston was taking to England to see the Thor facilities. He wanted me to go along as an orderly. You don't have to know much about it, he said. It should be fun.

Tom couldn't believe it. Jesus, he said, you're a lucky bastard.

He was right. It's true: I was riding pretty high.

August 3, 1961: 344 Days

We left Vandenburg at five in the morning. We flew to Goose Bay where we spent the night. The aircraft was a VC-121C which had separate compartments for the General and his staff and seats in the rear for everyone else. I didn't have much to do on the flight. Colonel Ev called me up to the cockpit where he said that he and the co-pilot wanted coffee.

Later on I brought box lunches to Colonel Ev and the rest of the crew. I'm not sure what General Preston and that bunch had for lunch. Mine was a chicken leg with a salad, milk and a cookie. I was nearly thirty-five before I stopped drinking milk and I only stopped then because I thought it was bad for me. I used to buy milk by the quart. I loved it.

I sat next to an Airman from Wisconsin. He said he had hitched a ride with us because he had an English wife who was still in England.

Man, he said, will I be glad to see her. It will be a big surprise. I was supposed to get leave next month.

He said his name was Adam and that he had gone to UC Berkeley for three years before enlisting. I asked him why he didn't finish.

Long story, he said. It boils down to meeting my wife who was working at the Mediterranean Café on Telegraph Avenue. I've always had a thing for English accents. We hit it off right away and two months later we were married. The trouble was that she couldn't stay in the U.S.. She had to go back to the U.K. and apply for a visa from there. That's when I decided to enlist. I thought it would make it easier to get her a visa.

Jimmy Latham sat across the aisle from us. He said he worked at the Thor sites as part of a team making sure that there were no problems with the practice launch – kind of a graduation exercise, he said. When he heard that the Old Man was flying to the U.K. he jumped at the chance to go.

Adam had a portable chess set. You play? he said.

I used to play with Pop. When I was about ten he put me in a competition with about a hundred kids. A photographer from the newspaper took pictures. There's one of me looking kind of sideways at the kid I was playing. I had just made a foolish move and I was waiting to see if he would see it. He didn't and I won the game. I made it to the final round.

We played speed chess with Adam's chess clock. It was move, bang, move, bang right to the end. I won once or twice but Adam was definitely better.

When we landed at Goose Bay there were vehicles waiting to take us to the transit barracks.

We had dinner in the mess hall. It was a short walk from there to the barracks. I fell asleep about as soon as my head hit the pillow.

August 3, 1961: 343 Days

We were airborne by 0530 headed to High Wycombe an RAF base north of London.

You can stay at the Union Jack Club in London, said Adam. It's just for military and it's cheap.

Sounds good to me, said Latham.

We landed after dark. The next day Colonel Ev said I could take off for the next four days. Be back here by 1700 on the tenth, he said. There's a bus from the Base to London.

I snapped to attention and gave him a sharp salute.

We found the London bus. It turned out that one of the stops was the Union Jack Club so that was easy.

There were small villages or towns along the route: Old-fashioned houses, kids playing in the street and pubs.

We checked into the Union Jack but we only stayed long enough to park our gear in the room.

Jesus, London was noisy. There were cabs and buses everywhere. The desk clerk gave us a map of the underground and pointed us to the nearest stop. The train came into the station like it was shot out of a cannon. The crowd on the platform – including Latham and me – jammed through the doors. I wanted to see Big Ben – about the only thing I knew about in London – so we got out at the Westminster Station and there it was.

We looked at it for a few minutes and then Latham said it was time to eat. We walked about a mile before we found a small sandwich shop with four or five tables. The only thing on the menu that I could be sure of was a ham sandwich on white bread. Latham said he had to try the fish and chips.

At the next table were two English girls. We checked each other out a few times.

Are you chaps American? the closest one said. We said we were and that we were looking around London. They said they were from London.

Where are you from in the States?

Latham said he was from New York, upstate, he said. But we're in the Air Force stationed at Vandenburg Air Force Base in California. Have you heard of it? The RAF train there.

Neither girl had heard of Vandenburg. Diane – she was the one who spoke first – asked what we were doing in London. She had the best accent: All little squibbles and quirks.

We're just hanging out, I said. We flew over on a training mission but we've got a couple of days off.

That's pretty smart, said Jillian. You chaps are keeping us free. We need that.

What are you girls up to? said Latham.

Diane said they were going to a dance at the Regent.

She stopped and looked at her friend. Some word must have passed between them because she asked if we would like to go along.

It took no more than half-a-second for Latham to say that we would. He didn't bother to check with me. I would have said the same if he had.

The girls said it wasn't far to the Regent. We sort of naturally paired up on the walk: Me with Diane and Latham with Jillian.

Diane said she was a secretary for an insurance company. I'm just a little wheel in a big machine, she said. My Mum and Da live in Brighton, she said, not far from the sea. Do you know where that is?

I shook my head no. Is that where you grew up?

They moved there after I was out of the flat. We lived in Aldgate. My Sis and me both went to school there. One of my Profs said I should try for 6th form but I got a job instead.

I didn't know what the 6th form was but I didn't ask.

It was a few more blocks until the Regent. I was expecting something like that dance bar in Pismo which was pretty big but this place was gigantic. There were hundreds of people. Even though the dance floor was big the dancers were all crowded together. That's how many people there were. I recently saw a picture in "Life" of the Regent. It looked just the way I remembered: Crowds of Bobby-Soxers and guys with ties. I believe it was torn down in the '80s.

The first song was slow. I held out my hand with a little bow to Diane.

Do you like it? she said.

I wasn't too sure if she meant the place, the music or dancing with her.

Sure, I said. I sure do.

It was impossible not to bump into people. I said "excuse-me" several times but then gave up.

The next dance was the Twist which I had tried only once or twice. But I went into it like I knew what I was doing. Actually, I think I did pretty well. Diane confirmed it by her smile.

The band was at one end of the dance floor. Just as we came in the bandstand turned all the way around like a carousel. There was another band on the other half which swung into view as the first band disappeared.

Diane was only a little shorter than me. Her long red hair was tied up in back somehow.

We danced and then switched off with Latham. It was ok with Jillian but I really wanted to be with Diane.

You two are getting along, said Jillian.

I nodded. She had some kind of perfume in her hair. I didn't like it that much.

I got Diane back at the next dance. We kind of glided together.

Did you like dancing with Jillian?

Yes, but I like it better with you.

She didn't say anything but I think she liked that.

After about an hour Jillian said she was getting thirsty. Will you not join me, she said. My local is not far. Latham said he was in. I looked at Diane. We seemed to think the same thing.

I don't think so, Diane said.

Me neither.

Latham and Jillian left. Diane and I went back to dancing only this time much closer together. Her perfume was to my liking.

We danced until midnight. I said I would walk her home even though I was worried about how to get back to the Union Jack.

Diane said she wanted to show me something. We stopped at a pond in the middle of a park. The water was as black as the night. There were two big, white swans swimming in the pond. Not exactly swimming. More like floating. They looked like they were asleep. In all of that blackness the swans looked like a king and queen.

They're mute swans, said Diane. She whispered this even though there was nobody around but the swans. They belong to the Queen.

No kidding, I whispered.

We sat down on a stone bench beside the pond.

I have to go, said Diane. I have to be at work at half-eight in the morning.

I walked her to the Tube station. She waited until I was headed to the right train. We kissed and kissed again. She slipped a piece of paper into my hand. Call me, she said.

You bet, I said.

August 5, 1961: 339 Days

When I woke up the next morning Latham wasn't in his bed. About half-past nine he rolled in singing. He flopped onto his bed.

Who-ee. Man alive. I thought I was coming here just to see the sights.

Well, I said, did you?

Did I?

See the sights?

Hell yes, I did. And they're right pretty. Mm-mm.

He said that Jillian lived in a small flat. Small, he said, but cozy. Two cats, he said. Both of them sleep with her.

Now she has three cats who sleep with her, I said. Latham laughed.

What about you? What was her name? Diane?

I showed him the piece of paper with her telephone number.

Right on, he said. You can't be stopped.

Me? If I can't be stopped what do you have to say about yourself?

Look, I said, I'm ready for some breakfast and to look around. There's only two days left.

Not for me. I'm going AWOL.

For a second I thought he meant it but then he flashed a smile.

Yah, sure: AWOL. You could get away with that for, maybe, a day.

I'll grab a quick wash-up. Can you wait?

I said I would wait in the lobby. But get it going, will you?

In the lobby I picked up a magazine called "Country Life" and flipped through the pages. There were ads for what looked like mansions or castles.

Jesus, I thought, if Pop could see me now. I thought that maybe, someday, someway, I could live in one of those places. When Latham came into the lobby I was pretty much floating on air.

Latham and me had breakfast at a small place on the corner. We walked around for the rest of the day. I called Diane from a red telephone kiosk. She said she had borrowed her parent's car. I want to show you the country, she said.

She picked me up at the Union Jack in a black Mini. We were packed in pretty good. I told her about the MG.

Oh, that's good, she said. You see, we Brits are good for something.

I asked where we were going.

Just a way out of London. It's in a lovely spot. She said her aunt lived in the village.

The Green Man: That's the pub, she said. We parked and went in. It was pretty dark in the pub but we got a table in the back near a window. There was a small stream just outside. I thought of the creek out back of Pop's place.

Diane recommended the Shepherd's Pie which she said was on the menu in every pub in England. We each had a glass of beer.

So, would you like to see something nearby?

Sure. What is it?

Well, I'll keep it as a surprise. We can walk from here.

Ok by me.

The lunch was terrific. Diane told me about her aunt. Some might call her eccentric, she said. She does dress strangely. She lives by herself in a big house with almost no furniture. She sold most of it to keep herself going. I think she's down to a bed and maybe a table. And, oh yes: Cats. I'm not sure how many there are. She's a big fan of Virginia Wolf. Do you know of her?

I said that I didn't.

She was an author. Two of her books that I really like are "To The Lighthouse" and "Mrs. Dalloway".

Are they good? I mean, are they good stories? I haven't read much but I do like good stories.

Well, I wouldn't say they are stories. More like impressions. They tell what happened in a single day by a kind of listening in on the thoughts of the main characters.

I felt stupid that I had never even heard of either book. In fact, next to Diane I felt really dumb.

Are we going to see your Aunt?

Oh no, I wouldn't put that on anybody and certainly not you.

That was a relief.

Tell me about yourself Phil. What about your parents

Oh, there's not much to tell. My Pop was Navy. He's retired. He lives with my Stepmom and Step-Brother. Mom died when I was nine. She got hit by a car when she was crossing the street. The driver took off. They never caught him.

How terrible and you so young.

Yah, she was special. She read to me every night. She would sit on the floor with me for hours while I played with my blocks. She was beautiful. I have a picture of her.

I took out my wallet. I had a small picture: Just her face. She had a big smile.

Oh, you're right. She was beautiful. What was her name?

Ruth. Her name was Ruth.

We left the Mini in the parking lot of the Green Man.

It's only a short walk, said Diane. Maybe ten or fifteen minutes.

We walked on a path alongside the river. It was very nice. Whenever I think of England I think of that small river and that walk. We stopped to look across the river at a gigantic tree. Diane said it was a Sweet Chestnut. It would have been a perfect tree to climb. When I was a kid I used to climb an apple tree out back. I imagined that that tree was an airplane and I was flying a mission over France like my Uncle John did when he was shot down. Only, I never did get shot down.

A little farther on we saw a church just over the top of the trees.

That's where we're going, said Diane. It's the Cathedral. It's very beautiful inside, especially the windows. I hope the light is right to show them off. It's the Seat of the Bishop.

I smiled. Me in a Cathedral.

The last time I was in any kind of church was Mom's Methodist Church. It was painful having to sit still on those cold, hard benches. After she died Pop never went near a church again. So much for God, he said. Knocking her off like that.

When we got to the Cathedral there was a small sign outside: Rehearsal, it said, 1300-1500.

Oh, said Diane. We might be lucky.

The roof of the church was a mile high. I don't know how high but it was way up there. Diane was right about the windows. They were like cartoons only made out of colored glass: Angels and people from the Bible.

The building was shaped like a cross. Diane called the cross bar the "Nave". That's where the orchestra was.

Let's listen, said Diane. Shall we?

We sat down a little way away from the orchestra.

This was my first time listening to an orchestra. Oh, maybe, I don't know, maybe on the radio without knowing it. The conductor stood on a little platform in front. He counted the orchestra down and the music started. He stopped almost right away to tell them to do it differently. He said he wanted a lot more second violins. He said: Let's have the cellos alone at 60, or something like that.

It's Franck, I think, said Diane. Cesar Franck: The symphony in D minor.

Whatever it was I liked it. The sound from all of those violins filled the whole church. It made me shiver a little.

The conductor stopped the orchestra again.

Diane laughed: Did you hear what he said to the cellos?

I did hear but I couldn't make heads-or-tails of it. It was something about "piano" but there wasn't a piano that I could see.

Diane took my hand and we walked around the church. There were little niches or side-churches. She said that that was where the oldest families were buried. In the chapels, she called them.

On one of the tombs it said:

What wee gave, wee have,
What wee spent, we had;
What we left, we lost.

It was confusing why they put "wee" three times and then switched to "we". Maybe I don't remember it right. It's possible. I couldn't figure it out to be honest. But that marker in the floor for those people who died in 1419 made me nervous.

Are you all right Phil?

Yah, but I'm a little cold.

Me too.

We left the cathedral while the orchestra played through the symphony once more.

On the walk back to the Mini it started to rain. At first it was just a few drops. You could easily count them. They were big and wet. In a minute more the rain came down like crazy. We got lucky because there was a bus shelter right where we were. Diane shivered. I put my arm around her. It took about two seconds before we were kissing. I said a little prayer to thank the rain. It was coming down so hard that I thought the shelter might give way. It was impossible to hear anything but the rain banging down on the roof. Diane tried to say something but I couldn't make it out.

You're nice Phil.

That caused a big smile.

The rain suddenly stopped like somebody had thrown a switch. There were big puddles everywhere. We got up and walked back to the car.

When we got to the Union Jack, Diane pulled up at the curb and shut off the motor. It took about two seconds to start kissing again. After awhile I said I had to go in but I didn't really want to. I said that the bus for High Wycombe was leaving in an hour.

Oh no, she said.

Will you give me your address, I said, and telephone number?

You'll call? That's expensive.

I think I can use the Air Force system as long as I call from Headquarters. I'll try.

It was very sad to leave. I waved and she waved back.

That was the last time I saw Diane.

Adam and Latham were already waiting for the bus.

Better hurry it up, said Adam. He's about to split.

I got to the room p.d.q. put on my uniform, threw everything into the duffel and sprinted downstairs. The door to the bus was just starting to close. I wedged my foot in and pulled the door back. The bus driver didn't look at me.

As soon as General Preston was on board we taxied out to runway 35 and took off.

Latham sat next to me. Are we going to stop at Goose Bay? he said.

I told him we were flying to Barksdale in Louisiana. Near Shreveport, I said. It will be an overnight.

Good, he said. You want to go into town?

I said that I did.

Now, what's the story with … what was her name?

Diane. Her name is Diane. No story. We went to a concert. Well, not really a concert. It was a rehearsal in a Cathedral.

No shit. You went to a concert? Weird. That's the last thing I would have guessed.

I laughed. Yah, me too but I did. I liked it. I'm guessing that you've never been to one?

Me. You kidding. I wouldn't be seen dead or alive there. It's too high and mighty as my Old Man would say. We're just common folk. You know: The salt of the earth. Concerts?

It was pretty good, actually. I wouldn't mind going again. But I'd have to learn more.

My Ma had me taking piano lessons when I was little, said Latham. What a joke. My piano teacher was this little old lady, about a hundred and five: Mrs. Silverstein. I hated going there on Saturday mornings. I mean she hovered over me. Ma never got me to practice enough to satisfy her. It still takes me awhile on Saturday morning to remember that I'm not going for a lesson.

Have you played since?

Naw. If I see a piano, I speed up.

I wish I'd had the chance to take lessons.

I had a lot of time to think on the Flight. Latham fell asleep and Adam talked to a sergeant from Guidance. The engine noise was a loud hum or, maybe, like a long snore.

I thought about Diane. She was smart. And educated. It was dumb of me not to go to college after high school but it never entered my head. None of my friends went. Grant, Beoma, Bill: None of them. Grant got a job after high school at a McDonald's; Beoma went to work at her mother's store. I don't know about Bill. My brother Pat still works at Noghlgren's. He makes enough to rent an apartment near Esther Short park and keep his Chevy in gas. I could re-up in the Air Force, make sergeant, see the world. Wouldn't be bad. But that music. That … Franck. It was like from another place. Planet even. And Diane. Amazing that she liked me. She's way up there.

Latham woke up. He stared at me like he didn't know who I was. Then he turned and was snoring again along with the engines.

College? I could. BMOC says Colonel Ev. I could go to Berkeley. Except I'm not a resident.

I thought of Jose. I could use his address. They would think I was a resident.

I let that percolate.

Study? Study what? You had to pick a major. Maybe Philosophy? That course in Philosophy I took at Allan Hancock was interesting: Why am I here? What's the point? Mom died. I'll die.

I thought I had a plan now. Anyway, I rested my head on the seat back.

Diane …. Philosophy.

August 6, 1961: 338 Days

Latham woke me.

Hey man, we're coming in.

I looked out the window. There was a big lake just to the North (I guessed it was North). The plane touched down without a bump.

Jesus, our pilots are good, said Latham.

That's Col Ev, I said.

A Base bus was waiting to take us to our quarters. The three of us got set up and then walked to the Mess Hall. It wasn't bad. In fact, the S.O.S. was good.

I've had worse, said Latham.

We asked an A1C at the table how to get in to Shreveport. He said there was a shuttle that went about every twenty minutes.

The stop is just outside. You can also hitch-hike. People around here are friendly. No problem to get a ride.

We went back to Quarters and changed into civvies.

The bus ride was quick. We got off before downtown. Adam said he heard of this place from an Airman in the latrine. The Stray Dog, he said. It's cool, he said.

It wasn't much to look at: A regular building like a warehouse with a big neon sign out front. The parking lot was full of cars.

We paid and went in.

It was dark inside except for the light show. They had strobe lights flickering on and off making everyone stop-start.

We hung around by the bar trying to get our bearings. There were lots of girls standing around in twos and threes.

Hell man, said Adam, I'm game.

He went over to the closest bunch. He smiled and twiddled his fingers in a "let's dance" circle. A cute red-head wearing a flouncy white skirt and a brown sweater took his hand.

Latham went for the one left behind. I was feeling guilty about Diane. The third girl gave me a look like: What's the matter with you? I had no choice, Diane.

She said her name was Penney. She had a pretty thick southern accent. What with the music which was way over the top, I could hardly make out what she said.

Y'll from around here? Shreveport, I mean?

I said we were on our way to California.

Air Force, I guess?

Yep.

She kind of lost interest once she knew that. We finished the dance and the three girls regrouped farther down the bar.

Did you tell her we were Air Force? said Adam. Boy was that a dumb move. They figure we're long gone. Our chances are screwed. I mean …

A guy wearing a cowboy hat came over. He got right on top of Adam.

Hey, you're messin' with my girl. I don't tolerate that.

Adam said he didn't know she was taken.

You makin' me out a liar, you little quibble.

No, no. I'm not.

Several others came over so we were surrounded by a rough circle.

They're chicken-shit Air Force, somebody said. They're always comin' for our women.

That's right, someone shouted.

The strobe lights made everyone seem huge. I thought that dude in front of Adam was about six-foot-five.

Show 'em who's boss, said someone.

Yah, take 'em out.

Now look, said Adam, we don't want trouble.

That so? You came to the wrong place, buster.

The dude grabbed the lapels on Adam's jacket and shoved him against the bar. Adam must have been about fifty pounds lighter that the guy and a half-foot shorter but he had gumption. He swung both of his arms up from his sides until they hit the dude's arms knocking them away. Then he swung an uppercut right on to his jaw. I thought I saw a tooth fly out and blood. The dude stood there with this dazed look like he didn't know what had just happened. Then he lowered his head like a bull and rammed Adam. The two of them fell in a sort of heap on the floor. There was screaming: Kill him Red, get the dirty sucker.

Somebody grabbed me and spun me around. The next thing I knew I was lying on the floor. The side of my head ached like nothing.

From then on it was all chaos. We must have started up some other battles because all around there were fights. I tried to crawl away afraid I might get trampled. I didn't know where Latham and Adam were.

I heard sirens. Cops and APs came in through the door. They started pulling people apart using batons on anybody who didn't move. I saw the dude take a baton across his shoulders. That let Adam get up and head for the door which is where I found Latham. The APs hustled us out the door and into a paddy wagon. Once we were out of the driveway the Sergeant said we were definitely in the wrong place.

This is the third night in a row, he said. They've got it in for Air Force. You're lucky we got there right away.

I told the Staff Sergeant AP that we were crew on a plane to California the next day. He said we might not make it. That flat-out scared me.

Sergeant we've got to make that Flight, said Latham. We had nothing to do with the fight. They're a bunch of crazies back there.

That's for sure. Look, I might do you boys a good turn. What Base did you say you're stationed at.

Vandenburg.

What are you doing at Barksdale?

I told him we were crew on General Preston's plane. I said we stopped at Barksdale on our way back from High Wycombe.

That right. Jesus, I was there myself back when. Ok you're good to go. He turned to Adam: You want to go by the dispensary?

No Serg, I'm good. Any chance you could drop us by the temp barracks?

The Sergeant told the driver to drop us there. Now boys, he said, you stay out of Shreveport.

No problem, said Latham. It's off my list of the ten best cities.

The Sergeant laughed as we headed into the barracks.

August 7, 1961; 337 Days

The flight next day was easy but the box lunch was terrible: Stale bread and cheese; an apple that was soft as mush.

I got a shock the next day. Colonel Ev told me to come by his quarters after work. There's something I want to talk to you about, he said.

Colonel Ev had moved out of the Married Officers' Quarters a few months before. He and his wife had split up so he was back in Bachelor Quarters.

When I got there Colonel Ev told me to come in. He was in civvies. It was the first time I saw him in civvies.

Colonel Ev is a little stout – I think that's the word. He's not fat exactly but he does have a stomach. His hair – which is blond – is combed back over his head. It is so blond that it always reminded me of straw, the kind you see in photographs.

Come in Phil, come in. Here, have a seat.

His voice is very smooth as if he just swallowed cough medicine.

Would you like something? A soda?

Now I was very nervous. It felt strange to be in a Lieutenant Colonel's quarters to start with. Whatever it was about I didn't think it could be good.

Colonel Ev sat down across from me. It was tough to see him because the sunlight was coming in straight across through a window. His face was blurry. Not exactly blurry, more like erased.

Ah, you see, he said, well … Sheila's come back.

Well, that was like a blow to the head.

She's come back?

Right away I thought she had gone to him to get him to talk to me

212

about her and me getting back together. I tried to think what I would say to that but I couldn't think of anything.

Yes Phil, she's back. Now I want you to know that neither of us intended this to happen but, well, she and I ...

"She and I!" I couldn't take it in. Was he saying that he and Sheila were ...?

So we both wanted you to know – well, mostly I wanted you to know – that nothing was planned and, certainly, nothing against you. Do you see what I mean?

Are you ok?

He probably asked that because I must have had a look on my face like that deer that stepped onto the road that night when Pop was driving home from the tavern. That deer didn't make it.

Finally, I mumbled something and then got up to go. I wanted to get out of there as quick as I could. Anyway, what was I supposed to say: Hell, it's ok if you steal my girlfriend. No sweat Colonel.

Colonel Ev got up and offered his hand which I shook. Honest-to-goodness it felt as soft as butter.

No hard feelings Phil?

I said no and got out of there as quick as I could.

I found out later that Sheila had moved in with Colonel Ev. Now, that really got me. Whenever I saw Colonel Ev – which was pretty much every day – I had to think that he had just come from her. She might have been in bed blowing him a kiss as he went out the door. Jesus, that made me crazy thinking about it.

I mean I know it wasn't right that it was me that broke up with her and all but still I couldn't get it out of my head that this was a dirty trick – by both of them. And how did it happen? Did Sheila meet up with him somewhere? I thought of the O-Club, like Betsy and the bartender. I heard that they liked to have single girls come to the Club. Maybe she went with somebody and Col Ev was there. A little talking, a little touching. That's how that goes.

Boy was I lucky to be done with that. Never again. I told myself that I would not hook up with someone ever. It was too painful. Such treachery!

I didn't know where I was going. I just walked. She's a two-timer,

I thought. She's doing this to get back at me. Colonel Ev and her: Jesus-H-Christ.

I was going to walk past the Base PX but I went in without a clue why. Just inside the door was a counter with movie cameras on display. I thought right away of Pop. He would love to get one.

The clerk showed me an 8mm camera. He said it had the latest stuff. It had a black housing and an adjustable lens. I could see Pop going ape over it. I bought it.

I felt a little better after that. Without exactly planning it I ended up in front of Aunt Betsy's Quarters. I wasn't sure I wanted to go in so I stood there trying to think it through. But then Betsy came out on the porch.

Phil? … What are you doing out here?

I shrugged.

Well come in. How are you? You look like you could use a beer? What's up? Aren't you feeling well? Cat got your tongue?

It's Sheila, I said.

Sheila? Is she back?

She and Colonel Ev are shacking up.

She looked about as stunned as I looked when he told me.

No. Colonel Ev? I don't believe it.

He told me himself. Just now.

My Lord. He must be, what … thirty years older than her.

I hadn't thought about that but she was right.

Well, well, well. I never. Have you seen her?

I told her that I hadn't that it was the first time I heard that she was back.

Betsy looked at me like she couldn't figure me out.

Phil? Why did she go home? I thought you two were hitting it off.

I wasn't sure what to say. For one, I thought she would see Sheila and whatever I said would get back to her.

What I can't figure out, she said, is why she didn't come back to you. Did you two break up?

Yah, we did.

Umm. Well, what do you think about Colonel Ev and her?

I don't know, Aunt Betsy. I honestly don't know. I mean, I'm still a little … stunned, I guess.

So you thought she'd be coming back to you. Wow, what perfidy.

I wasn't exactly sure what she meant by that but I guessed I agreed with it.

I wonder how this all came about, she said. Did she just bump into the Colonel and they got together? Doesn't seem likely. There must have been a plan.

She gave me a kind of hang-dog look. Oh Philly, I'm so sorry.

I wasn't sure if what she was saying was right but right away I saw it was a good story. Sheila (and Colonel Ev) were the ones in the wrong, not me.

I stayed a little longer. Betsy gave me a kiss on the cheek and a bit of a hug.

Buck up Phily, she said. There's lots more fish in the sea.

When I got back to the barracks I told Tom about it.

Man alive, he said. That is impossible.

Then he told me that he and his girl in Fullerton had broken up which was a shock because they were planning to get married.

She's going out behind my back, he said. Can you believe it?

I didn't say anything. I felt sorry for him I really did.

He was still steaming about it while we walked to the Mess Hall.

Jesus, he said, the guy was a buddy. We played high school ball together. Can you believe it? I helped him out of a jam once. Bad jam. Man, if I run into him he's gone.

Tom has a belt that they give in judo. He was pretty high up.

At chow I asked him if he had any clue about it. Were there any, you know, signs? I said.

Hell no. I told you Phil we were getting married. Next summer! We talked about kids.

He looked like he could cry. Then I remembered: Colonel Ev and Sheila. Man, I didn't deserve it. Why come back here. Then I had the idea that the whole thing had been planned like Betsy said. They may have got together before and figured out how to get rid of me. It made sense. She only pretended to not to want to go back home. Just to keep me off guard.

When I thought of it she wasn't all that broken up about leaving. She got on that plane real easy.

Jesus, I said. Tom, I think we've both been had.

215

September 6, 1961: 307 Days

I had to see Colonel Ev almost every day. We only talked about what had to be done: Nothing about Sheila. I didn't see her for it must have been a month even though I was on my guard all the time. But then I did see her.

Tom and me were having a beer at the Canteen. He was having a hard time getting over his smash-up. Hey, I said, UCLA is doing pretty good.

Yah, not bad. Ron Lawson is right there.

Have you been to any games?

I went once with my girl ...

He stopped like he had just run into a wall.

Didn't you play ball in high school? I said. He didn't answer.

Hell, he finally said, I've got to get this out of my system. Phil, how about you and me taking a trip?

A trip? To where?

I don't know. San Francisco? Definitely not L.A..

I had never been to San Francisco. Hey, that's not a bad idea, I said. When?

Next weekend? We could drive up right after work. We could probably make it in — I don't know — five hours or so.

We shook hands on it.

September 16, 1961: 297 Days

The weather was pretty good. The top was down. We rolled up 101 North through Santa Maria. I couldn't see Boone Street from the highway but I felt it.

Hey, where's that place that you and what's-her-name rented?

I pointed. That direction. You can't see it from here.

How was that? Being shacked up like that?

I don't know.

Phil: It's hard to get stuff out of you.

Huh?

To talk. You don't open up.

He was right about that. Other people have said the same thing. Not sure how I got that way. My Pop is like that too. I tried to get him to talk about Mom but all he said was that she was a good woman. A real, good woman, he said.

I once told my buddy Grant that I got scared that time we climbed Mt. Barometer in the fog. By that cliff, I told him. I thought I might fall over. Naw, he said. There was no chance. Maybe, maybe not. After we got back he told Bill that I was scared on the mountain. Bill laughed.

We rolled past Pismo Beach. I could just see the Rose Garden. More Sheila reminders.

You been up this way? said Tom.

Yah, me and Sheila. We were here for Fats. Fats Domino.

Oh yah? How was that?

Good, real good.

The miles rolled by. I can get in a groove driving. It's like I'm a part of the MG. I'm sitting comfortable, back against the seat, steering wheel at just the right place, foot on the pedal. The wind rolls around the windshield. The tires zing over the pavement.

Hey man, I'm getting hungry.

Yah, me too. San Luis Obispo is just ahead.

What say we stop there?

We pulled off the highway into town. We spotted a restaurant which had a picture of a hamburger on the billboard.

Ok, said Tom, I'm up for one.

Me too.

There was a cute waitress behind the counter. College girl, I guessed. Blond hair in a pony tail. As she walked the tail swung back-and-forth like wiper blades.

Well boys, what'll it be?

We both ordered cheeseburgers. I asked for everything on it; Tom said to hold the onions.

French fries?

You bet.

You boys from around here?

Tom gave me a half-look. We're checking out the College, he said. Might like to go there.

Oh, I'm a sophomore. Pre-med. Well, I think I am.

Tom asked her about the Campus. She gave him the low-down. She leaned her elbows on the counter while we talked. I didn't do any of the talking but her and Tom were talking up a storm. Before we left she gave Tom her telephone number. He was riding high the rest of the way. Must have forgot about his Fullerton problem.

We got back in the MG and headed north.

You got it going with that waitress.

Big smile from Tom. Yah, she was nice. Hey, can we stop there on the way back? On Sunday?

Sure. That was a pretty good cheeseburger.

You bet it was.

We didn't talk for awhile. We passed up King City and Salinas. The sun was off-and-on blocked by some clouds coming across the ocean. I swore to God, one of those clouds had the face of Colonel Ev. It even had a yellow patch on top but that could have been from the angle of the sun. I don't know.

You got an idea where we can stay?

Tom shrugged. I heard that there are some cheap places in Chinatown. Chinatown?

Chinatown, North Beach. Joe Ferguson told me about it. He's from San Francisco.

Ok by me, I said.

The radio played "Heartbreak Hotel", one of my favorites. That bit about "down at the end of Lonely Street" always got me. Especially now. With Sheila. Jesus, I shouldn't have let her go. That was a mistake.

But by the time the song was over, Neva came to mind. Must be with her husband. Who knows what they're up to.

We drove past San Jose and Palo Alto. We could see tall buildings ahead and a bridge.

Hey man, this is going to be great.

We took an off-ramp marked "Downtown" and pulled over at a gas station. Tom got out to get directions to Chinatown. When he got back in the car he said to stay on California Street and we'd find it sure.

Luckily, we found a place to park right in front of a sign in Chinese letters that said: "Hotel". Let's check it out, said Tom.

Inside there was a little Chinese guy behind a counter. There were stairs which went almost straight up behind the clerk. We asked if we could see the rooms. He gave us a key, pointed to the stairs.

The room was tiny: Two narrow beds with the bathroom down the hall.

Let's take it, said Tom.

We paid for two nights, got two keys and went out. I checked the street sign. The car was ok for the rest of the day.

Let's look around, said Tom.

There were lots of people, mostly Chinese. You had to weave around people to get anywhere. I liked it right away.

About half-way down the block from the hotel was a bar and restaurant: The Hunan. We went in. The bar was four or five steps down. It was pretty crowded but a couple got up to leave as we came in. They gave a little bow and we did the same. The waitress came over and right away wanted to see

219

my i.d.. This happened to me until I was in my early thirties. It bothered me no end.

Almost everyone was Chinese in the restaurant: The bartenders and waitresses were Chinese; the customers were Chinese. Me and Tom were the only Whites but nobody paid us any attention. We had beers but it seemed like everyone else had some kind of mixed drink with what looked like a little umbrella perched on the rim of the glass. There was talking going on all over the room – in Chinese, naturally. It seemed very strange, almost like exotic. I kind of liked it.

Many of the women wore skirts with a slit up the leg. I guess that made it easier to walk but it was sexy too. Me and Tom were like giants in that room.

Are you boys' tourists? asked the fellow at the next table. I reckon he was about forty but it was hard to tell. He sat by himself with a tall, yellow drink with what might have been a lime. His English was perfect.

Yah, I guess you could say that, said Tom. We're Air Force on a holiday.

Where are you stationed, if you don't mind my asking?

Vandenburg Air Force Base. Down the coast? The missile base?

I know of it. You guys work on missiles?

Well I don't, said Tom, but my buddy here does. Well, not on the missiles: The support. We're part of the Strategic Air Command, SAC.

Oh, Top Secret stuff, I suppose. My name is Kai Kong.

We shook hands. You guys are doing so much already. Let me buy you a drink.

Waitress, another round for these gentlemen.

The waitress brought two more beers; Kai paid.

So, can you tell me more about what you do? At Vandenburg, I mean?

Well, my job is boring, Said Tom. But Phil here works in the Command Post. Top secret stuff.

No kidding.

I gave Tom a sign to shut up but either he didn't catch it or he ignored me.

Yah, top secret. We're tied to SAC. You know, if we have to go to war, Phil here will be in on it.

I'm impressed, said Kai. Phil, is this true?

I said it was.

Kai said he was born in China but that he has lived in San Francisco for a long time. I asked him if he had folks in China.

Yes, my father is there.

I knew almost nothing about China. About all I knew was from Geography in ninth grade. Mr. Daniel had a pull-down map of China. I remember that he said it was across the date-line and they dressed different than us. I looked it up in Pop's World Book encyclopedia. It looked interesting.

So, said Kai, if there is a war – I mean with nuclear weapons – you would be in on it? In what way?

No, it's not quite like that, I said. I don't think I should be talking about it. I gave Tom a look like you wouldn't believe.

Oh, I see. Well that's all right. I'm just curious. You don't think I'm a spy do you?

Tom laughed. Hell no. Spies don't look like you.

How do they look?

Well, dark, you know, bushy eyebrows, dark skin. When they're outside they wear a – what do you call it – trench coat. Probably packin' a weapon inside the trench coat.

I see. Well, sorry to disappoint. What are you boys up to this evening?

We just got here. This is the first place we've been.

Do you know your way around?

Not at all.

I don't suppose you're interested in - girls?

Tom and me looked at each other.

Well … maybe.

You like Chinese girls? I know a couple who live not far from here.

I wasn't sure what to say but Tom didn't hesitate.

You bet.

Ok. They're not home until around ten so we can hang out here until then; unless you want to go somewhere else?

Well, we stayed put. Kai ordered some Chinese food. I'm not sure what it was but it was pretty good. At home we used to go out for Chinese on Fridays: Pork chow mien, fried rice, stuff like that. This was way different. Kai showed us how to use chopsticks but I can't say I ever got the hang of it.

By the time we were ready to go I was feeling no pain. Kai paid for everything. He asked me again about my job.

Are they all ready to go? I mean: Are the missile operational?

I'm a little hazy about what I said but I think it went like this: The missiles were ready but sometimes there are problems. I even think I told him about General Power.

Oh really. So, they aren't ready?

Well it went on about like that. I don't have a clear memory and when I asked Tom later about it he was no better. The one thing I remember and which scares the hell out of me was, somehow, the words "Emergency War Order" was out there. Jesus, I hope I didn't say anything. My goose could be cooked. Later on I thought that Kai might be a spy or, I don't know, CIA or FBI. Jesus.

Around ten we got up and followed Kai.

It's just around the corner, he said.

We had to walk up four Flights of stairs. Kai knocked on number 402 and a cute Chinese girl opened the door. This is Lilly, he said, like the flower. She is like a flower, isn't she?

I couldn't disagree.

She was short like Sheila with very black hair. Black like the darkest night, Tom said. She wore bright-red lipstick almost the reddest color I had ever seen.

She bowed slightly and opened the door. A second girl was sitting on a kind of sofa. Kai introduced her as Caelan. It means "thin", he said. But she wasn't really thin.

Kai said that Lilly and Caelan didn't speak much English. Only the words, he said, that you need. Please, he said, sit down. No, no, Tom you're here beside Caelan, Phil right next to Lilly.

Kai took a bottle from the table and poured two glasses. Now watch it boys. This is Baijiu. It's strong so I'm only pouring a little.

He was right. That whiskey burned my throat something fierce. I offered the glass to Lilly but she shook her head no. She had a beautiful laugh.

Kai said that he had to go but he would see us tomorrow. At the bar? he said. Around six?

We said we'd be there.

After Kai left Lilly and me turned to talk but it was hard. Pretty soon Tom and Caelan got up. She led him through a door which I figured was to a bedroom. Lilly smiled at me. I guessed I was supposed to do something. About the only thing I could think of was to kiss her, which is what I did. Man, we got going like you wouldn't believe. Like a house-a-fire. In no time she had my belt undone and my zipper down.

A couple of hours later Tom came back from the bedroom. Lilly and me were huddled up tight. Hey man, he said, we should scram.

I guessed he was right. I got dressed and we left. Lilly was still on the couch looking like that picture I saw in "Life" magazine. I still think of her every once in a while. Well, like now.

In the morning Tom and me talked about Kai. I told him that I wished he hadn't said anything about the CP or SAC. Jesus, I said, we don't know who he is. We could get in a shit-load of trouble.

Yah, he said. You're right. What do we do now?

I said we should head back. Right away, I said.

Tom said he was game to go. But, I wouldn't mind seeing Caelan again. No sir-ee-bob. She was somethin'.

I felt the same way about Lilly.

Hey, said Tom, you said we could stop in San Luis.

Well we did stop in San Luis. Unfortunately for Tom his waitress wasn't working that day. At least, she wasn't anywhere in sight.

We did get a hamburg but that was it. We rolled into the Base in good time.

December 15, 1961: 207 Days

hristmas was coming on. I had some leave time but I didn't want to use it. If you have any leave left over when you get discharged you get paid for it. I figured I would need every dime I could for college (I had pretty much decided on UC Berkeley). I got applications and I set up the SAT test in Santa Barbara for the spring. I used Jose's address in Lompoc on everything.

Aunt Betsy said I should come over for Christmas. Her and Maria were going to cook a turkey. They even got a small tree which I helped decorate.

On Christmas Eve I drove into Lompoc to do a little shopping. I wanted to get something for Betsy but I didn't have any ideas. There were Christmas lights on the lampposts and the Salvation Army was out on a couple of corners. I dropped a dollar in the bucket. For California it was a bit cold. Nothing harsh but when you're used to seventy plus a little drop seems cold. I liked it. Put me in mind of back home where there was probably a ton of snow already.

As a kid I liked to go skiing. Not at a resort or anything, just across the road. I took Pop's wooden skis and went across the road to the Kunze's field. I strapped on the skis and headed for a little hill about a quarter mile back. All I knew how to do was the snowplow where you keep the skis out in front of you like a fan. To get up the hill I had to turn and go sideways.

On the other side there was a clear shot down to a little valley with no trees blocking the way. I pretended I was on winter patrol with the Army Rangers. There was a hair-raising quick slide down. I never got all the way without falling at least once.

I parked the MG on Main Street in Lompoc and walked the block to

Sparks department store which is pretty much right next to the Do Drop Inn. I hoped I wouldn't bump into Dore.

The store was crowded. I headed to the Ladies' section. I was thinking of lingerie but when I looked at what they had I wasn't sure.

A saleslady came over. Can I help, she said.

Jesus, I couldn't stop my face from getting red-hot. No, no thanks, I said. Just looking.

Well, these are real nice, she said, holding up something that you could see right through. How could I give Aunt Betsy something like that. Especially if she opened it around Maria.

Let me know if you need help.

She moved away, thank god.

I saw some bathrobes that looked like they might work. They weren't too – I don't know – personal. I could give Pauli one and nobody would think anything of it.

I picked one out which had red, white and green stripes. It looked like it would be very warm. The woman at the cash register was the same one who asked me if she could help with lingerie. When I handed her the bathrobe she smiled. Well, what a nice choice. I'm sure she's going to like this. I know I would. Should I gift wrap it for you?

Oh sure, I said. I hadn't really thought about getting it wrapped. That was a load off.

Merry Christmas, she said as she handed me the robe.

I was glad to get out of there.

I was on my way back to the MG when I saw Neva walking on the other side of the street. I hadn't talked to her since the trip to England. I crossed over.

Oh hi, she said. The long-lost stranger turns up.

Yah, it's me in person. Can I give you a lift? The MG's just right there.

Well, I don't have far to go … but, ok, thanks.

Neva saw the present: Oh, you shouldn't have. She said.

That flustered me. Oh, it's not for you, I said. I mean …

She laughed. You don't have to say who it's for. It's none of my business.

I put the present in the boot. Neva looked real good. You have time for a coffee or something, I said.

Or something, she said, and laughed. Jesus her teeth were as white as new snow.

Where to? I said.

Hey, it's up to you but there's a coffee shop at the bowling alley.

Ok that sounds good. We can always bowl if we have to.

Neva laughed. You're cute, she said.

The bowling alley was just outside city limits. The last time I was there was with Aunt Betsy.

We sat at the counter.

You want something to eat, I said. It's on me.

Whoa. No kidding.

Well, I'll have the roast beef plate with a side of hash browns. Maybe a slice of cherry pie for desert.

You look shocked, she said. Thought you were going to get by on the cheap?

She laughed. I was just kidding. Don't look so stricken.

Then she reached over and put her hand on mine. I was cool about it.

We had a coffee and split a Danish with lemon filing.

How's it going in Operations, I said.

The Colonel's daughter is getting married. I don't think he's too happy with her beau.

Why?

Not sure. I get the feeling he's a lot older. Maybe married before. Married couples should be close in age. Don't you agree?

I shrugged. Why do you think so?

Well, one problem if they are far apart is that they won't be interested in the same things at the same time. Know what I mean?

Not really, I said.

Ok, take my friend Janey and her husband Oscar. They live in Dallas. He's almost twenty years older than her. She likes to get out, go to parties, you know, stuff like that. All he wants to do is watch tv and go hunting. Basically, they don't do anything together. Except sleep, of course.

I see what you mean.

Can I ask you something? I said.

Sure, Ask away.

What if the man is younger than the woman? Would that make a difference?

Neva didn't say anything for awhile. She looked at me with those big, black eyes of hers.

Anyone you know? she said.

No, no, just curious.

Well, I guess it would be about the same, she said. I mean it would still be off-center, if you know what I mean.

How is Betsy these days?

She's good, I guess.

She still live in the women's quarters?

As usual my face was getting hot.

Yah: I mean, I think so.

Neva nodded. Well, anyway, she said.

We stayed another five minutes. I paid the check.

You got by pretty cheap, she said.

I shot a little smile her way.

We got back in the MG. It was getting dark. Without asking, I drove down one of the gravel roads outside town. There was a little turnout looking over the highway maybe fifty feet below.

It didn't take much. Almost before I could take my hands off the steering wheel we were kissing. I mean: Kissing. It was like we were both on fire.

If you've ever ridden in an MG you can probably guess my problem. I tried getting over on her side but it was hard to get past the shift. After a lot of squeezing and pulling I made it so we were in the bucket seat together, me facing Neva. We were pulling and pushing each other in some kind of frenzy.

Well, somehow we managed it but it wasn't the best. On the drive back to Lompoc neither one of us said much. She told me to let her out two blocks from her place. Before she got out she turned toward me.

Well, she said. I didn't expect that.

I didn't know what to say so I kept my mouth shut. She started to get out but then she leaned over and kissed me.

The drive back to the Base took a long time.

Well, from then on it was just Neva. Once or twice she would pretend that she needed a file so she would come to my office. She would close the door and we got into a clinch. We had to be careful that it didn't last long but I got wired up real fast. When she left she always did the same thing. She opened the door and started out but then she turned toward me with this big smile on her face. I can say it took some time after for me to cool down. Once, Sergeant Willis came looking for me just as Neva was leaving.

Hello there Mrs. Smith, he said. Getting caught up on your paperwork with Airman Greevey? I hope he's been helpful?

Oh yes Sergeant. Airman Greevey is always helpful.

I'm sure, said Sergeant Willis.

After she left he looked at me kind of funny like he figured something was up. I never did tell him that Neva and I had gotten together. The bet wasn't big enough to make me do that. I never told Tom or anyone else, ever – well, until I wrote this down.

Neva would find some excuse with her husband so I could drive her home after work. We stopped at that same place above the road – we called it "The Bends" because of all the curves getting to it. I'd see her in the Headquarter's Building – in the hall, or her office, or mine – and I'd just say – real quiet like – The Bends? And she'd either nod her head, yes, or she'd shake it, no, depending on what else was going on.

She once went on a leave with her husband down to Muleshoe. Some relative was real sick.

I don't mind saying that I got a little jealous about that. I don't know why because I knew that she was with him every night. Christ, they slept together – at least I thought they did. So why her going with him to Texas should be any different, I don't know, but it was.

Besides, I wasn't going to get hooked up one hundred percent with anybody. Not after Sheila. I was going to Berkeley when my time was up if my SAT scores were good enough. I didn't want to be tied up in College. But, until then I might as well be in love, or whatever.

March 14, 1962: 118 Days

The big problem was with the MG. It was just too cramped. We had to twist every which way just to be together. So I thought about getting another car one that two people could stretch out in, side-by-side.

I saw an ad on television in the Day Room for a place called Ford City in LA.. Tom said it was a big used car place. Takes up the whole block, he said. He said I could drive the MG there and trade it in for a bigger car. No sweat, he said. I'll go with you. We can stay at my folks' place.

Early on Saturday we got in the MG and went straight through to Ford City on Crenshaw. We drove into the lot right up next to a red, '56 Mercury. A salesman came right over.

Hey fellas. How's it going?

I said I was looking to trade. He took a good look at the MG. You like the Merc? he said. I told him I did. Well, he said, I think we can work something out.

A mechanic came out to check out the MG. He drove it into the shop. He'll just look it over, the salesman said. About fifteen minutes later the mechanic came out and gave a thumbs-up to the salesman. I signed off on the MG and the salesman gave me the title to the Merc. It was an even trade. The last I saw of the MG was in the rear view as we drove away.

We stayed at Tom's place that night and the next day we drove back to the Base. When we got between Santa Barbara and Lompoc the left rear time of the Merc blew out. I got off the road and onto the shoulder.

Jesus Christ, said Tom. You've had this car – what – twenty- four hours? We took a closer look at the other tires. They were all going bald. There was a spare and a jack in the trunk. I got the Merc jacked up and changed the tire. We got to the Base in time for evening chow.

When I picked Neva up the first time she was shocked.

You traded the MG? Why? That was such a good car.

When we got to The Bends I think she figured it out. The back seat of the Merc was much better than the front seat of the MG. We could get it going pretty good. Of course, it wasn't like a real bed.

I took my last leave in April to go and see Pop. I tossed my bag in the back seat of the Merc and drove across to U.S.99. My plan was to go straight through.

But something happened outside Dunsmuir. There was this big bang from the engine and then a clanging noise. I pulled over. When I looked under the hood except for a little smoke I couldn't see anything wrong. It was lucky because there was a gas station just down the hill. I got the car going with a push and then jumped in and coasted down to the station. A mechanic came out wiping his hands.

Now then son, looks like you are having some trouble.

Yes sir. She gave out a bang up on that hill so I shut her down.

Umm. Let's have a look.

I opened the hood and Jack – that was his name – took a look under the hood. The smoke or whatever it was was gone. There was a bit of oil smeared over the engine.

Yes, you do have a problem. I'd bet my bottom dollar that you've blown a valve. Yep, I'd bet on it.

So, I said, it can't be driven?

Nope. Not on your life.

Can you fix it?

I sure can but not today. There's a job ahead of you. And, I'll have to get parts from the Ford dealer.

So, how long do you figure?

About a week, maybe less.

A week? I can't wait around for a week.

Jack shrugged.

Can I leave it here and pick it up on the way back?

Where do you live?

I told him Vandenburg Air Force Base.

That's a coincidence. My boy is in the Air Force. In Germany. Where are you headin' now?

I told him I was on leave to see my Pop.

Here's what you can do, said Jack. I'll drive you to town where you can catch a Greyhound. You go home, see your folks and call me long distance about the car. Like I said it should be ready inside of a week. You take the bus back down here and she'll be waitin' for you.

There wasn't much else I could do so I gave Jack the keys. He drove me to the bus station in Dunsmuir.

It took almost ten hours to get home on the bus. I called Pop who picked me up at the station in his Chevy.

Well, well, he said, look who's here. Ain't you a sight for sore eyes.

He gave me a big, bear hug and we drove out to his place. Nothing much had changed since I joined up. Looks about the same, I said.

Yep, you're right.

The house looked the same. There's a short driveway to the garage. A line of trees hides the house from the road – not that there's anything to hide or anybody to look. It's pretty deserted out there.

Come on in Son. Pauli is waiting' on us. Pauli is short, maybe five feet even or a little under. Her hair is all grey but her eyes are still blue – come to think of it eye color never does change, does it? She gave me a big hug.

Welcome home Philly. Where's that MG you wrote about? We thought you'd pull up like you were in from Hollywood.

I traded her in. Trouble is the Merc I traded for blew something on the way up here. I had to leave it in Dunsmuir to get fixed. I'll take the bus back down and get it.

Pauli had put together a nice dinner. The house is small: Pop and Pauli's bedroom downstairs, mine and Pat's upstairs. Pat wasn't around. The kitchen is small but there's enough room for a table by the window. Pauli had her best table stuff out. I felt like the President.

At dinner I told them the story of the Atlas blowing up after liftoff. It's as tall as a six story building, I said. I saw it rise up from the launch pad ok but when it was up – I don't know – eight, nine hundred feet it started to turn in the air like a big pinwheel.

Jesus, said Pop, where were you?

I was standing with a bunch from Guidance outside the building. There wasn't any danger – least I don't think there was.

What happened, said Pauli.

It turned around once and then started going higher. The Base is right down on the ocean so when it got high enough and far enough out over the ocean the Blockhouse Commander had it destroyed. It blew to pieces.

That must have been somethin' to see, said Pop.

Yep, it was. But I've seen others almost as bad.

Pauli did her usual good job of cooking. I love her chicken pot pie. It has this light crust on top with bits of chicken and vegetables floating inside in a gravy. She knew it was my favorite.

So how's this stack up to mess hall chow, said Pop.

No contest.

After dinner Pop and me sat in the living room. The Gillette Friday Night Fights were on. Pop made sure we finished dinner before the fights started. He said he once tried to eat while he was watching but the knockout happened while he was scooping up some mashed potatoes so all he got to see was the fighter flat out on the canvas. There wasn't any replay back then.

You're just in time, said Pop. Welterweight title fight. Griffith against Kid Paret. Should be a good one. This is their third time. Griffith won the first and Paret the second.

Between rounds we talked. He said big changes were on the way with Kennedy in there. I don't know if Pop was in favor of the changes or not. He did say that he thought his union would be stronger with Kennedy than Nixon. His job at Alcoa was union all the way.

Jesus, look at that, said Pop. Griffith was taking a pounding: It looked like he was done.

Man-alive, said Pop. This is a real woopin'.

Lucky for Griffith the bell rang and he got back to his corner.

You think he's all done?

I wouldn't bet against him, said Pop. He's a tough customer.

Griffith did go out for the seventh round. It went better for him after that.

Between rounds a woman with long, blond hair wearing shorts walked around the ring holding up a sign with the round-count. The guys at ring-side gave her the once-over.

So, what's next Son after they let you out? Or are you going to re-up? There's a pretty good bonus if you do.

I was thinking of that. They said I could get sent to Germany. I wouldn't mind. I wrote you about the trip to England.

Yah, sounded pretty good. All those museums and such that you visited.

But if I do that what happens after? Make a career of it?

Well, you know you can retire in twenty years. Not bad. I still get a retirement check on top of my machinist's pay. Works out pretty good.

Yah, I know. The only thing is I'm thinking about college. I took some courses on-base at Allan Hancock Junior College: History, Mathematics, Philosophy. I liked it. It made me want to do more. You know, go full time.

That's interesting. When you were in high school you didn't show any signs about College.

I know but in the back of my mind I thought I would go.

Hmm. Well, for sure it's up to you.

The fight was in the tenth round. Both fighters were beating the crap out of each other. Paret's corner had to stop his bleeding between rounds; Griffith looked like he could hardly keep upright.

Wow, did you see that punch? Pop swung his fist through the air. Man, this is some fight.

The bell rang ending the eleventh round.

Do you think this will go fifteen? I said.

Pop shrugged. Where will you go to school? If you go.

U.C. Berkeley, I said. I can go as a California resident.

Expensive?

I'll have to get a part-time job. Maybe I can find some roommates to share the rent.

In the twelfth round Griffith got Paret in a corner. He pounded him and pounded him. Kid Paret couldn't do anything to stop it.

Jesus, said Pop, he's tied up in the ropes. He can't move. God damn ref should stop it.

Finally the ref did stop it. Paret slid to the floor. He didn't look good.

I'm glad we ate dinner before watching that, I said.

Pop agreed.

I called the garage the next day. Jack said he'd have it done in two days. Good as new, he said.

I caught the bus back to Dunsmuir. The Merc was ready. I slept in the car that night and rolled into Vandenberg the next day.

June 15, 1962: 25 Days

On Monday I met up with Neva after work. We drove to The Bends. She was not too happy.

You're getting close to getting out, she said. What are you going to do?

I told her about my plan to go to Berkeley. I'm taking the SATs in Santa Barbara next Saturday. I guess I'll know if I get in or not pretty soon.

Berkeley? That will be exciting for you.

Yah, I guess.

New friends. New … girl friends.

I just nodded. I wanted to get the talking over with. She had to be home in an hour. I put my arm around her shoulder and turned to her but then I saw that there were tears in her eyes.

I'm never going to see you again, am I?

I said I didn't know. I told her my Pop always said there was no way to predict the future. This didn't help but she gave me a kiss. That got things going in the right direction. Exactly why I got the Merc.

My SATs weren't great but I got accepted at Berkeley.

When I told Neva we were standing in the hallway at Hq. She looked like she would start crying right there.

Oh no, she said, oh no.

Look, I said, I know it can't happen but it would be great if … well, if we could spend the night together. I mean: I know you can't.

This seemed to make her feel better.

Maybe, maybe I can. I'll try. But where would we go?

I don't know. Santa Barbara?

Oh, that would be special.

Just about then Sergeant Willis came toward us. I acted like I had just given Neva some papers. She turned back to her office.

Hey Airman. Still trying to win that bet? It's not going to happen, you know.

Oh, I said, you're right. She's not the type.

He agreed with me.

The next time I saw Neva she said she could stay overnight on a Friday night. She said she was going to a meeting in Santa Barbara for the Colonel.

I hadn't really thought that she would be able to do it so I hadn't been thinking about where we could go. In the end I figured we would just go there and look around for some place.

And we did. The Merc was finally driving ok but it wasn't as good as the MG. I was sorry I got rid of the MG.

We got to Santa Barbara about three. There was a motel with a "Vacancy" sign. I was nervous because we had to check in. Maybe they would ask to see a marriage license or something. Neva said we should give our names as Mr. and Mrs.. Wow, that gave me a fright.

The clerk or whatever he was had me sign a book. I put down Mr. and Mrs. Smith. It was the only name I could think of.

We carried our bags up the stairs to 207. I just had my duffel but Neva had a real suitcase with her initials on it in gold. "N.R." is said.

Well, the room was ok. There was a double bed, two chairs and a table. The bathroom had a shower and a hair dryer. There were little, plastic bottles which were marked "shampoo" and "lotion". It was ok.

Neva unpacked putting her things into one of the dresser drawers. I left my duffel as it was.

From the small balcony we could see the ocean. I thought about the time Aunt Betsy and me stayed in Santa Barbara with her friend from New Jersey. I couldn't remember her friend's name.

Neva fixed her hair in the mirror which made me think of Sheila at our place on Boone street in Santa Maria. It was like I had done all of this before. It made me a little dizzy. I sat down on the edge of the bed to clear my head. It was all I could do to stay upright.

Philly, are you ok? You look white as a ghost. Neva came over and put her hand on my forehead. Her hand was cool and soft. I felt better right away.

It's ok, I said. Maybe I need some water.

I'll get you some.

Neva went into the bathroom. Here. Is that better?

I said that it was.

Neva sat down on the bed next to me. I think she thought something should happen but for some reason I didn't feel like it.

What time is it?

She looked at her watch. A little after six. We've got plenty of time.

She put her hand in mine. She was so close I could feel her heat through my shirt. Her perfume smelled like freshly peeled oranges.

Well, I said, we need to figure out where to go for dinner. There's a brochure on the table. I'll check it out.

I set down at the table. The brochure listed a couple of nearby restaurants.

This one says it has top grade beef. I could go for that, I said. There's pasta too. What do you say?

It's ok with me.

Well, let's go. Maybe we can get a beer or a glass of wine, if you want.

We got directions from the clerk. The restaurant was on a pier. We parked on the street and walked down some steps to get to the boardwalk. We held hands. Neva smiled non-stop.

The restaurant was good. We got a table by a window looking over the ocean. The sun was just going down. We couldn't stop looking at it. It turned all gold and purple and then slipped away.

Neva ordered a glass of wine and I had a draft beer.

To us, she said, as we clinked glasses. I didn't say anything. We bumped knees.

After dinner we drove back to the motel. I was nervous as hell. I brushed my teeth and got into bed. Neva was already tucked in. It was quiet except for the sound of cars outside. I don't know why but just then I thought of her husband. It was the first time I had given him any thought. I must have frozen up because Neva raised up to look at me.

Philly, is something wrong?

What could I say? Was I feeling bad about being in bed with his wife?

Maybe this time was more, like, permanent. It was like we had passed some road sign: "Danger, detour ahead, keep right".

What happens is that I do something that seems like it's just for that time but it isn't. Something else happens. I didn't know it but at the time I had been on a hill when I started my slide. A slide I couldn't stop. It had happened with Sheila almost the same way.

But here I was. I couldn't disappoint.

I pulled myself together.

Oh Philly, you feel so good.

Maybe, but I saw tears.

It's nothing. Don't stop. Please.

The next morning I woke early. Neva was still asleep. Her long hair was black against the white pillow. I guess I never noticed before how long her eyelashes were.

Hi. Good morning. I feel great, she said.

I felt good too. It wasn't my fault that her husband was being taken advantage of.

Neva pushed closer. Her body was soft and warm. She kissed me. Oh Phil, she said, oh Phil …

July 9, 1962: 1 Day

I was down to the last day. I had said goodbye to the whole crew. Aunt Betsy had moved to Burlingame. She took a job there. Neva and me parked at The Bends. It was tough getting out of there. I figured she and her husband would get it back together with me out of the picture. I won't forget you, is the last thing she said. Colonel Ev wished me good luck. You'll be the BMOC, he said. I didn't ask about Sheila and he didn't say anything. I told Tom I would drop him a line as soon as I found a place. Yah, he said, maybe I'll come up there one day. He and his old girlfriend had gotten back together so he was talking about getting married again.

I had to go through a bunch of steps at the processing center but in the end I got a check for my sixty days of accrued leave. For sure I would have to get a part time job.

It was strange driving out of the main gate for the last time. I had butterflies in my stomach. To top it off the AP on duty must have thought I was an officer because he snapped to as I went through.

The plan was to drive straight through to Berkeley. The catalogue said there was a housing office on campus for students who needed a place to stay.

The trip was easy. The Merc made it all the way without even a loud burp. I had the Base Garage give it a tune up and I put on four rebuilt tires. I was pretty confident.

I got to the Campus around two and went straight to Sproul Hall. The Housing Office did have a bunch of listings. Luck was with me because the first place I called sounded good. It was on Dwight Way which was easy to find because it was right off Telegraph Avenue. I met the owner Mrs. King who showed me the room. It was bigger than the barracks' room. The bed was comfortable and there was a good desk. The latrine was down the hall but I was used to that. There was a sink in the room and a hot plate. Soup, I figured and tea. I rented the room on a month-to-month basis. I had to pay for the next month by the twentieth.

I brought my duffel in and left the Merc parked on the street. I surely regretted swapping it for the MG.

It was Friday and summer classes would start on Monday. I unpacked the duffel and headed out.

It was a short walk to the Student Union and Sather Gate. I got a hamburger in the Bear's Lair. The student sitting next to me said his name was Pierre and that he was from New Orleans. I guessed he was around eighteen. He said he had an apartment on the North Side. We got to talking and he gave me his address. I said I would look him up.

After the Bear's Lair I walked through the Student Union. There were lots of comfortable chairs with students sprawled out everywhere. (I almost said "Sprouled out": Pop was good at puns). I sat down in one of the chairs. There were a lot of good-looking co-eds – as Colonel Ev called them – in the room. I got the feeling that it was all going to work out. I was smiling for the rest of the day.

After twenty minutes or half-hour, I asked the person sitting next to me where I could find the bookstore. She told me that she was going there and I could follow her.

She said her name was Rose. I asked her what she was studying.

Biology, she said. I'm first year. Probably pre-med. And you?

I said I wasn't sure but maybe Philosophy.

No kidding? Philosophy?

Yah, no kidding.

The bookstore was down a short flight of stairs. Rose headed for the Biology aisle and I went for the French texts. The course was French 1, Summer 1962. I got the book and headed to the cashier's. Rose was already in line. She wanted to see my book.

Oh, French 1. Gee, I should take that too. If you go for a Ph.D. you have to have two languages.

You're going for a Ph.D.?

Don't know. Maybe. I've heard it's really important if you want to teach. But I'll probably pre-med. My Dad is a doctor. Did you just finish high school?

I can't say why but I was embarrassed to tell her I had graduated four years ago or that I was just out of the Air Force.

I ... graduated in 1958.

Four years ago. Did you work after that?

I nodded.

That's cool. I did have a job last summer. My Dad got me a job in his hospital: Lab work mostly. How about you?

Well, I said I worked on missiles at Vandenburg Air Force Base. I said it as if I was one of the civilian contractors. Atlas, Titan, I said.

Wow, that must have been something.

I punched down on my nerve button. How about a coffee? I said.

Sure.

Student Union?

Instead let's go to the Mediterranean. It's just down Telegraph Avenue. The coffee is way better there.

The coffee was definitely different. Kind of bitter, really, but I acted like it was what I was used to.

The café was crowded. Some guys with long hair and beads and girls with bracelets and dangling earrings. We found a table on a second floor up a flight of stairs. Guys were playing chess.

Rose said she was from Daly City. I know, I know, she said: Ticky-tacky all the same. But, really, our house is quite nice even if it looks the same as everybody else's. My father owns two more which he rents out.

She asked about my family.

Well, my Mom is dead. I was nine when she died. I lived with my Dad and Stepmom.

Oh, I'm sorry to hear about your Mom. That must have been hard.

Yah, it was.

I don't know why I decided to tell Rose about her because I never told anybody that didn't already know.

She committed suicide, I said.

Rose looked like somebody had hit her from behind with a baseball bat.

Oh God, she said.

She looked like she was watching a horror movie.

I didn't say anymore: She took my hand.

We said we would meet next week for a study date.

Can you find Tolman Hall? I like the Psych library there the best. It's not so big. See you on Wednesday?

We shook hands. Rose went off to wherever she was going. I wanted to get a couple of things for the apartment.

Just then the thought hit: It would be the first time in my life that I would have my own room. At home I had to share with my half-brother. I thought I could walk on air.

Well, I did walk across the street to a poster shop. I wanted something that I could put on the wall. I liked a poster by someone named Renoir. It was a picture of flowers in a blue vase. It was pretty good.

I bought tea bags, a loaf of bread, butter and jam and walked back to the apartment.

My next door neighbor was in the hall. We said "hello". The poster got pinned up on the wall over the desk. It looked good. I sat down at the desk with the French text book. Might as well get going, I thought.

That night I went to the Rathskeller on Telegraph Avenue for a hamburger and a beer. It felt like I had suddenly grown up like the world was wide open and I was just about to walk through.

The first class went well. The professor was French or, anyway, he sounded French. There were maybe twenty students. I told myself that I had to be out front, that I had to participate. I didn't do too bad for the first day.

I met Rose at the library Wednesday afternoon. She seemed happy to see me. I guess I hadn't noticed that she had a beautiful smile, but she did. We took a break later and sat down on the grass outside. It hit me how beautiful the campus was with the trees and grass. I thought my chest might explode.

Hey, what are you smiling about? Come on, give.

I was just feeling … happy.

Rose gave me an odd look at first but then she said that she got that. She said that she felt pretty much the same.

We studied for another couple of hours and then walked back through Sather Gate past the Student Union. I left Rose at her dormitory and then took my time walking home.

Just inside the front door were mailboxes for the tenants. My name had been added to the box probably by Mrs. King. I didn't expect any mail but I had the key. There was an envelope addressed to me. Nobody, as far as I knew, knew my address. I slitted the envelope open and took out the letter.

Hi. Surprise!

I'm staying at the Campus Motel on Shattuck Avenue, number 24. Come see me.

Neva

I was pretty well floored. What was she doing here? I thought our goodbye was over. And what about her husband?

Actually, I felt a little angry. I'd just got started on something new and now this.

But, as far as I could see, I didn't have a choice. I got in the Merc and drove down Shattuck Avenue until I found the motel. I parked on the street and walked upstairs to number 24. I knocked. And there she was!

She pulled me inside and gave me a big kiss. Her smile – like Pop used to say – went from ear-to-ear. We fell backwards onto the bed. I got up. Neva, I said, what are you doing here?

Her smile seemed to float off.

Aren't you happy to see me? What you said about us in Santa Barbara?

Yah sure, I said. Only, well ... I didn't expect you.

No, I know. I didn't expect it myself only after you left I felt like I was ... hollow, kind of empty. I had to do something.

What about your husband?

He's hurt, of course. I hated to hurt him but it didn't feel like I had much of a choice. I said I needed to get away for awhile, be by myself.

So, this is just ... temporary?

She looked at me as if I was pointing a gun at her.

I guess so. I can see that you don't like it. Maybe I made a mistake.

Jesus, this reminded me of Sheila. I didn't want anything to screw up my plans. But I took the chicken way out – again.

No, no, I'm glad you're here.

I reached over and we kissed. She seemed to melt like a popsicle on a hot day. Pretty soon we were all tangled up on the bed. I admit that I didn't do anything to stop where we were going. Afterward I felt about ten times as bad as I had before.

Not Neva. Jesus, she started making plans. She said that she had called a company in San Francisco that had advertised for a secretary. She said she had an interview the next day.

If I get the job I'll find someplace to live. Don't worry. I won't mess up school for you. You can come to see me when you can. No promises.

That made me feel a little better. Maybe it could work out, is what I thought. But then I thought about Rose. There would be a lot of new things. I wanted it all.

I went back to Dwight Way. I had to do some serious studying for a quiz the next day. Oh my Lord, I thought, oh my Lord. It hit me that I was using Pop's saying.

I did ok in French class. The last class was on August 17 and I got the postcard from the professor on Monday: "B". I felt pretty good about it. In fact, I felt real good. I was hovering around "C" for the first half but I knuckled down and raised it up. I knew now how much studying I was going to have to do if I was going to do well.

From the job listings in Sproul Hall I found a part time job at Interstate Motor Lines in the Oakland Army Terminal. The job was from four to eight in the morning and it paid real well. The shift boss was Mr. Maban. He said a U.C. student ought to be able to handle the billing so he put me in the office filing bills of lading. The time was good because I could get back to campus for an eight-thirty class.

Except that Neva got that job and she found an apartment in San Francisco near Golden Gate Park. I felt like I had to go there on the weekends. She had left her husband. I think she calculated that the two of us could finally get together. I felt squeezed real tight.

Just before the fall semester started I got a knock on the door. There was this young guy in a suit and tie. He said he got my address from those cards at the University. He was pretty apologetic. I hate to tell you, he said, but Beneficial Finance is looking to you to make good on the loan to Sheila. You co-sighed and she's defaulted.

I was stunned. Defaulted?

How much, I said.

$100, he said.

He said he could give me twenty-four hours to think it over. He gave me his address. Don't delay, he said.

I did have $100, barely. But I figured with my paycheck coming I could pay the rent and next semester's tuition. How I would eat I couldn't predict.

And so it went. I saw Rose once or twice. Neva decided that it wasn't going to work out with us. She quit her job and moved away.

The thing is she didn't tell me she was going to do that. As usual I went over to her place after class on Friday. I had a key but when I went in the place was empty. She left a note which I still have which said it was best if she left me to find myself.

I guess that was right.

Printed in the United States
by Baker & Taylor Publisher Services